THE
Merchant's
DAUGHTER

Other Books by Melanie Dickerson

The Healer's Apprentice

THE
Merchant's
DAUGHTER

Melanie Dickerson

ZONDERVAN

ZONDERVAN.com/
AUTHORTRACKER
follow your favorite authors

ZONDERVAN

The Merchant's Daughter
Copyright © 2011 by Melanie Dickerson

This title is also available as a Zondervan ebook.
Visit www.zondervan.com/ebooks.

Requests for information should be addressed to:
Zondervan, *Grand Rapids, Michigan 49530*

ISBN 978-0-310-72761-3

Cover design and photography: Mike Heath
Interior design and composition: Publication Services, Inc. and Greg Johnson/
Textbook Perfect

Printed in the United States of America

11 12 13 14 15 /DCI/ 20 19 18 17 16 15 14 13 12 11 10 9 8 7 6 5 4 3 2 1

To Joe, Grace, and Faith

Chapter
1

August 1352, Glynval, England.

Annabel sat in the kitchen shelling peas into a kettle at her feet. A bead of sweat tickled her hairline while only the barest puff of warm air came through the open door.

"Annabel!"

Her brother called from the main house. As she hurried to finish shelling the pea pod in her hand and see what Edward wanted, the pot over the fire began to boil over. She jumped up, banging her shin on the iron kettle on the floor.

Snatching a cloth from the table, she used it to pull the boiling pot toward her and away from the fire. But as the pot swung forward on its hook, the cloth slipped and her thumb touched the lid. She jerked back. Spying the bucket of water she had used to wash the peas, she plunged her hand into it.

"Annabel!" Edward yelled again.

He thinks he doesn't have to help with the work, but I should abandon my task and come running whenever he calls.

She blew on her burning thumb as she hurried from the kitchen.

Edward stood propped against the wall in the spacious front room of their stone house, scraping under his fingernails with a sharp stick. When he lifted his head, his green eyes fixed her with a hard look. "Mother was summoned this morning to appear before the hallmote."

"I know that." The manorial court, or hallmote, was being held today, and a jury of twelve men from their village of Glynval would decide the penalty for her family's neglect of their duties.

"The new lord is coming to Glynval. Even if the hallmote is lenient, I've heard he is far from forgiving. What will happen to us? To you?" He thrust the stick at her face.

Annabel bit back annoyance at her brother's derisive tone. For the past three years he had stood by, just like the rest of her family, refusing to do any of their required work in the fields, putting them all in this situation.

"I've decided to help with the harvest this year." She crossed her arms as her brother moved closer to her. "We should all help."

"Do you want to end up sleeping in ditches and begging bread? *Help with the harvest?* It's too late to start doing your share now, little sister." He flung the words at her, jabbing his stick in her direction with each phrase. "If you are wise, you will try to think whose bread you need to butter to see that you have a home after today."

Annabel's back stiffened, and she prepared for whatever offensive thing her brother would say next.

"We have to fend for ourselves. You're seventeen years old now and well beyond the age of accountability. Maybe you know of someone who might marry you. Do you?"

"Nay, I do not." She glared back at him, wishing she could think of a scathing retort.

He began rolling the stick between his fingers, smirking at it. "But there is someone. Someone who is prepared to smooth over our trouble with the new lord and pay the fines so we don't have to work in our lord's fields."

Her brother wasn't concerned about her, she knew—he wanted to solve his own troubles by throwing her to the wolves. But which wolf was he planning on throwing her to?

A pleased smile spread over Edward's thin lips. "I am speaking of Bailiff Tom."

Bailiff Tom? "He's as old as Father!" Annabel's face burned at the notion. She tried to think of some dignified reply, but the words tumbled out. "If you think ... for one moment that I—" She clenched her jaw to stop herself.

"He has been widowed these three years. Surely you've seen him look at you with the eye of one who is looking for a wife."

She *had* seen the bailiff once or twice with a lecherous sneer on his pinched face—and been thoroughly disgusted that a friend of her father's would stare at her that way. Marry Bailiff Tom? She would rather sleep in a ditch.

"You will marry him, because there's no other way." Edward leaned over her, his eyes cold and dark. "Besides, where will you get a better offer of marriage than from the bailiff?"

"I won't marry him." Annabel spoke through clenched teeth. "If Father were still alive, he'd never force me to marry Bailiff Tom."

Her brother turned his attention back to cleaning his nails. "I'm afraid you don't have a choice. I've already told the bailiff yes."

Heat climbed up her neck and burned her cheeks. *How dare you?*

"Don't look at me like that, dear sister. I had no choice. The new lord arrived in Glynval last night, and the reeve came this morning when you were out picking peas, summoning Mother to come to the manor house. Something had to be done to help our poor family." He gave her a simpering grin. "Oh, I nearly forgot. Mother wants you to go to the village, to the butcher, and get us a goose for dinner." Her brother raised his brows in challenge.

She glared at him then lifted her nose in the air, as if her life weren't teetering on the edge of a cliff. At least this errand would get her away from Edward and give her time to think. Snatching the piece of delicate white linen from a wooden peg by the door, she wrapped it around her head, securing all loose hair away from her face, and tied it at the nape of her neck. She jerked the door open and flung it closed behind her.

The pain in her thumb drew her notice to the new red blister. She blew on it as she started down the lane toward Glynval and William Wagge's butcher shop.

Spending the last of their money on a goose on the day their fate was being decided by a jury of their fellow villagers. Pathetic.

They would be penniless outcasts tomorrow if Mother couldn't persuade the jury to have mercy on them. But could they truly hope for leniency from a village that resented them for not doing their share of the work?

Her family did not deserve mercy. Father had been a wealthy merchant, fully able to pay the censum so that his wife and children did not have to do the lord's required fieldwork during harvest and at other times of labor shortage. But they were left destitute when his ships were destroyed in a storm, and shortly after that, he died in the pestilence. Even as the family of a freeman, due to their inability to pay the censum, they were now required to perform some of the same duties and work as the villeins. But her mother had insisted her health was poor and she was unable to work, and in her typical manner, she also announced her children should not have to do such menial work as harvesting grain.

For three years her family shirked their duties and went unpunished, kept safe by the old lord's corrupt steward, who managed to postpone their fines.

But with the new lord arriving, Annabel had a feeling her family's comeuppance was due in full. Bailiff Tom's offer was proof enough. The bailiff, an old family friend, was using their lapse to his advantage, holding their predicament over them to force Annabel to marry him.

She shuddered.

The path to Glynval was empty, and Annabel realized most of the adults of the village would be at the hallmote to watch and see how each case played out, who won their complaint against whom, and what the ale brewers' fines would be. She usually stayed away from the proceedings, but today she would go to see how her family fared with the twelve jurors. Whatever the jurors assessed, whatever the fine or punishment, it would be supported and upheld not only by the lord's steward but also by the assembled villagers.

Lost in her thoughts, Annabel was surprised to see a form emerge from the shadow of the trees around the bend in the road. The figure progressed haltingly toward her, his right hip twisting at an abnormal angle with each step he took. Stephen Blundel.

She smiled at her friend. Having grown up with her, Stephen was more like a brother to her than her own blood brothers were. Stephen lifted his hand and waved.

At that moment, seven ragged, barefoot boys crept out from the trees and surrounded him. The malicious looks on their faces made her heart thump in her throat. Stephen neither flinched nor altered his pace, as though he did not see them.

With a flick of his wrist, the tallest boy sent a small stone flying. Then they all hurled rocks at Stephen, shouting ugly names at him. Dragging his foot along the ground and snickering, one of them mimicked Stephen's crooked stride.

Annabel tried to read Stephen's expression, but he stared straight ahead, his jaw set.

Frustration with the morning's events surged through her. "Get away!" she screamed at the boys. She bent and dug her fingers into the dirt as she snatched up some rocks of her own. "You leave him alone or I'll—!" She drew back her fist full of rocks and aimed them at the largest boy, the leader.

The boys scattered and halted a few feet away then formed a circle around her.

Turning on her heel, she tried to face them all at once and pin them down with her glare. They were younger than her, but some of the boys were tall enough to look Annabel in the eyes.

She checked over her shoulder. Stephen's awkward gait had taken him far down the road, but he stopped and turned around. He frowned, probably waiting to see if she would need his help, and perhaps a little embarrassed that she had defended him.

The young ruffians began laughing and sneering at her.

"Trying to hurt someone who'd never hurt you," Annabel accused. "For shame."

The tallest boy crossed his arms, his tattered sleeves flapping. His bare legs were brown with filth. "My mother says you won't be so high and holy, Annabel Chapman, now that our lord is here. Woe to the Chapmans." The rest of the boys took up the chant. "Woe to the Chapmans. Woe to the Chapmans. Woe to the Chapmans."

She stomped through the circle of boys, staring straight ahead as Stephen had done. The boys continued their taunts and insults, but she held her head erect and pretended to ignore them. They drifted down the road, launching a few weak insults at Stephen as they rounded the bend, their gloating laughter disappearing with them.

Stephen was coming toward her. She waited for him to catch up.

"I'll walk with you," Stephen said, giving her a sympathetic lift of his brows. "Are you going to the hallmote?"

Annabel nodded. "I have to go to the butcher's to get a goose for Mother, but I thought I might see how my family fares in the court first." She tried to look unworried, but she couldn't fool her friend. They walked together down the dusty road.

"My mother is waiting for me at home to help her patch a leak in the roof. But I will stay with you at the hallmote if you need me," Stephen offered.

"No, I'd rather you didn't stay." Annabel's cheeks heated at the thought of her friend seeing her family's name scorned and abused in front of nearly everyone they knew. She'd rather bear her shame alone. "I'll be fine."

The two of them passed an old woman bent over the field of beans next to the road. *Let her not notice me*, Annabel prayed as she ducked her head.

The older woman straightened as much as the hump in her back allowed and leveled her narrowed gaze at Annabel. "A Chapman. It will be your turn to tend the fields now that the new master has come, dearie!" She cackled a high-pitched laugh.

Annabel stared at the ground. Today wasn't the first time she'd experienced the villagers' contempt, but she blushed again at what must be going through Stephen's mind.

It seemed to take forever to walk past the woman, for her lingering laughter to fade away. Stephen said softly, "Don't let it bother you."

Annabel tried to smile and say something flippant, but she couldn't think of anything. Dread slowed her feet. Fear crept up her spine and gripped her around the throat as she came closer to the place where her family's fate would be decided. She imagined each person at the hallmote today, derision and glee mingling on their face, as they too anticipated her family's reckoning.

Annabel stopped and faced Stephen. "You better go on back home. Give your mother my love." She gave him a little wave and started to turn away.

"You always have a home with us," Stephen said.

"Thank you." She waved again as she walked toward her fate. His words seemed to emphasize even more the trouble she was in.

She would refuse to marry Bailiff Tom, of course, and under church law no one could force her to marry. But by doing so her family would lose the only offer of help they were likely to receive—Tom's offer to pay the lord for the work the Chapmans had not done. The lord *would* get what was owed him, one way or another. Would the jury order that their home be seized and given to the lord? Or would they devise some other punishment? The old lord had lived far away and never came to Glynval, choosing to send his steward instead, a man who accepted bribes. But the new lord, it was rumored, had come to Glynval to build a proper house and live here. His new steward would make sure he received all that was owed to him.

Annabel shivered at the thought of the new lord, Lord le Wyse. He was getting harder to force from her mind.

The hairs on the back of her neck prickled as she remembered the things she'd heard about him. Exaggerations, surely. He couldn't be as frightening as people said. But they would all soon find out.

As she rounded another curve in the road, the houses and shops of Glynval came into view. Each wattle-and-daub structure was made of white plaster and a thatched roof. Chicken coops, looking just like the houses, only smaller, crowded in the backyards along with slick, muddy pigsties full of snorting swine. The animals filled the air with their pungent stench. Annabel wrinkled her nose and hurried on, forcing herself to go to the manorial court meeting first before going on to the butcher's to get the goose. *Besides, the butcher is probably at the hallmote with everyone else.*

She passed quickly through the main road of the village, which was also nearly deserted. She turned down the lane that led to the manor house, a structure more like a hall than a house. The upper floor was one big room where the hallmote was held in bad weather. But today, as the weather was fine, though a bit hot and cloudy, the court would be held outside in the courtyard.

She walked up to the outskirts of the crowd unnoticed and pushed through to see the jurors standing or squatting in a group off to the left. Only two men were sitting—the clerk, who was busy writing on a long strip of parchment, and another man Annabel guessed to be the lord's new steward, who was in charge of the meeting. The steward and clerk would probably only stay long enough to conduct the hallmote and then leave in the morning, off to see to Lord le Wyse's other holdings.

When the clerk had finished writing, he stood up and proclaimed, "John Maynard complains of John, son of Robert Smith." Then he sat down.

John Maynard came forward and described, in great detail, an argument he had with John, son of Robert Smith, which resulted from a missing chicken he claimed John stole from him, killed, and ate. John Maynard also brought five men with him who swore on the holy relics either that they knew what he was saying was true or that he was a trustworthy man. John, son of Robert Smith, had failed to bring his own "oath helpers."

While the case was being decided, a man near Annabel kept looking at her out of the corner of his eye and then nudging his neighbor with his elbow and motioning at Annabel with his head.

Had her family's case already been decided? She looked around but didn't see any friendly face she could ask.

Finally, the case of the missing chicken was decided in favor of the complainant, John Maynard. The jury fined John, the son of Robert Smith, four pence for stealing and consuming the chicken. Four pence was a heavy fine, but chickens were valuable.

The clerk announced the next case. "The steward of Lord Ranulf le Wyse accuses Roberta Chapman and her three grown children, Edward, Durand, and Annabel Chapman, of shirking all their required fieldwork, harvest work, and boon work for the three years past, as of this Michaelmas."

Annabel felt her face grow hot as she kept her eyes focused on the jury members and the steward. She felt as if everyone was staring at her, but she didn't want to look around to confirm her suspicions.

Mother came forward and stood in front of the entire assemblage of villagers. She looked tense, her lips bloodless and pursed, but defiant. *Oh, Mother, please don't make it worse.*

The steward called the reeve forward to attest that this accusation was true.

Annabel was surprised Bailiff Tom wasn't there also, either to confirm or deny that her family had not done the work required of them.

The reeve confirmed the accusation, and her mother refused to deny it. The jury conferred for only a few moments, then the foreman turned to the steward and his clerk and said, "The jurors find that the Chapmans are all equally guilty and therefore must pay sixty pence per person, totaling two hundred forty pence, or twenty shillings."

The entire assembly gasped.

Annabel felt sick. She had never heard of a fine anywhere near that amount. It was impossible. Her mother's defiant expression, however, never wavered.

"Roberta Chapman, are you or your children able to pay this fine?"

"No, sir steward."

"Jury, the Chapmans are not able to pay their fine. What will be their alternative penalty?"

The jury huddled together. Annabel watched them, unable to walk away until she learned her family's fate. She should have gone straight to the butcher shop instead. More people were staring at her, and she took a step back, partially hiding behind the miller's overfed son.

Finally the jury foreman broke away from the other eleven and stepped forward. "Sir steward, the jury says that Roberta Chapman, who is not able to pay the fine of two hundred forty pence, will send one of her grown children to work as Lord le Wyse's servant for the next three years, doing whatever tasks his lord deems fitting, to pay for the three years the family did not do their work. If they are unwilling, they will forfeit their home and property immediately to Lord le Wyse."

Annabel backed away as murmurs of approval rose from the circle of villagers. Soon she was on the lane, heading back toward Glynval.

Her face still burned from her family's public humiliation, and she kept her gaze on the ground as she reentered the village, drawing her head covering closer around her face. A few more steps and she'd be inside the butcher's shop and away from prying eyes.

"Annabel? Is that you?"

She recognized Margery's voice and groaned. It would be impolite to ignore her, so she tried to smile. "Good morning, Margery."

Both girls had blue eyes, blonde hair, and evenly proportioned features, so people occasionally remarked that the two of them could be sisters, but Annabel hoped the resemblance was only physical. She always dreaded Margery's embarrassing questions. Lately she was even harder to take, bragging and smirking at having married the wealthiest man in Glynval and remarking on the fact that Annabel was still unwed. But Annabel couldn't imagine marrying such an old man. Or any man, truth be told.

Margery caught Annabel by the arm and leaned close. Annabel leaned back to get away from the smell of garlic emanating from her.

"Have you heard the news?" The girl placed a hand on her slightly protruding belly. "I'll be a mother before spring plowing!" She giggled then stopped abruptly. She clamped her free hand over her mouth while her eyes widened and her face turned gray.

"Are you unwell?" Annabel grasped the girl's elbow and took a step away, afraid Margery would heave her breakfast on Annabel's only pair of shoes.

Margery took a deep, slow breath, then another, and lowered her hand from her mouth. "That was nearly the third time today." She smiled in spite of her pallor.

"I've heard that dry bread eaten in the morning before you rise is helpful for the sickness."

"All is well with me, but I'm distressed for you." Margery's brows drew together.

"Oh, I'm well. I'm on my way to the butcher's and must hurry—"

"All the people say your mother and brothers have played our lord very false. Some say you'll all be turned out of your home, your mother put in the stocks—or worse. Where will you go? Do you have any other family who could take you in?" She put one hand on her hip and pointed her finger at Annabel's nose. "You should marry. I hear Bailiff Tom is looking for a wife." Her eyes grew wide with excitement at her brilliant new idea.

Annabel's family deserved to be turned out of their house, as they'd not served their lord according to the law—and now that would indeed be their fate, as decreed by the hallmote, unless she or one of her brothers became Lord le Wyse's servant. But Annabel had to feign confidence or risk Margery going on about Tom.

"When everyone sees how willing we are to begin doing our share of the work, I'm sure everything will be well. In fact, the jury only moments ago decided our punishment. One of my family will work for the lord in his manor."

A visible shudder went through Margery. She whispered, "I've heard the new lord is a beast."

"Nonsense." Annabel fixed her eyes on Margery, anxious to know if she had actually seen him.

"He has a beard and one of his arms is afflicted. He holds his arm up like this—" Margery demonstrated by crooking her arm across her midsection. She drew nearer, until her lips were almost touching Annabel's ear. "And he has only one eye."

"One eye?"

"He wears a black patch of leather over his missing eye, and a scar runs through his beard all the way to his chin."

"You saw him?"

"I heard it from Butcher Wagge's wife, who heard it from Joan Smith, and she heard it direct from Maud atte Water, who's to be one of the dairy maids in the new lord's buttery."

"You mustn't believe everything you hear." She could not let Margery's description frighten her. Maybe the new lord was only very ugly, and that was why people made up such horrific stories about his appearance.

"I must go now," Annabel said quickly, trying to walk away. "May God favor your child and bless you. Good day."

"I'm sorry you're in haste. You didn't tell me what you're going to do when they turn you out—"

"We won't be turned out. Good day." Determined to get away from Margery, Annabel headed straight for the butcher's shop. As she hurried inside, she immediately collided with a man, her sundrenched eyes almost blinded inside the dark shop.

"So glad you could come."

Annabel blinked as the man's face came into focus. It was Bailiff Tom.

The bailiff wrapped his hands around her upper arms.

She looked up into his small-eyed, sharp-nosed face, and

then down to the hands that were holding her arms unnecessarily. Even though he wasn't a large man, he still loomed over her.

Bailiff Tom's greeting was odd, as if he had been expecting her. He must have arranged with Edward to send her to the butcher shop, where he'd be waiting for her. The realization made her feel sick.

She straightened her shoulders and tried to free herself from his grip by taking a step back, but he did not let go. "Pray excuse me. I was looking for the butcher."

"Are you sure?" He chuckled in a way that made her stomach clench. His dark, oily hair hung below his ears. He leaned over her, and she smelled his sweaty odor. When had he last taken a bath? It was summer, after all. He couldn't use the excuse that the water was too cold.

"The butcher's not here, but I would be right pleased" — he paused as though to emphasize the last word, reaching his rusty-looking hand toward her face — "to help you."

She jerked back to avoid his touch.

He took a step toward her. She dodged away from him, but as he was still holding her arm, she couldn't get away. He leaned so close she could smell his breath, see a black spot on a side tooth and black hairs protruding from his nose.

"Has your brother told you about my generous offer?" His smile grew wide.

Imaginary bugs crawled over her. "Get your hand off me." She jerked out of his grasp and turned to leave.

The bailiff leapt around her, pushing her back and blocking her way. He hovered over her with menacing eyes.

"I shall help you, help your whole family. Your brothers will be very disappointed in you if you say no to me."

"My mother is handling the situation, and I will not accept your offer."

She tried to dodge around the man, but he moved another step and covered the doorway with his body.

"Let me pass."

His leer made her clench her teeth.

"Tarry awhile. No need for haste." He grabbed her hand. "I think of you, Annabel. With your mother about to get you all turned out of your house, you should marry me. I could take care of you, could keep your family from trouble with the new lord."

Her eyes darted to the door.

He grasped her arms again, and suddenly his lips were coming toward her mouth. Annabel turned her head, and his slobbery lips landed on her cheek. She struggled to break free, but he tightened his grip on her arms until pain shot up to her shoulders.

The bailiff growled and tried to kiss her again, muttering his vile intentions, what he planned to do to her. She couldn't move her arms, so she stomped down on his foot as hard as she could. He oomphed, then shook her until her teeth rattled.

Her heart beat so hard it vibrated from within, but she refused to let him know she was afraid. "Get out of my way. Let go of me or I'll raise the hue and cry. I'll scream until every person in the village—"

He dug a finger into the underside of her wrist, sending shards of pain up her arm. "You think you're too good for me, but who's going to help you now? Do you think the new lord will not punish you, will not throw you out of your fine stone house? Eh?"

Anger surged through her. She gave a sudden tug at her arm and, managing to maneuver around Tom, she stood in the doorway. He let go with a shove, sending Annabel falling backward through the door. She struggled to right herself as she fell, and landed on her hip in the dusty street.

Hooves pounded toward her, and a horse's high-pitched whinny sounded above her head. Annabel raised her arm to protect herself.

Just inches away, the horse danced to a halt, snorting and throwing dirt into her face. The animal's hot breath ruffled her hair. Dust clogged her nose and throat and made her cough.

The rider dismounted. "What are you doing?"

The man's voice and accent were unfamiliar. Her hair had fallen in front of her eyes, making it difficult to see the hands that slipped under her arms and hauled her to her feet. She pulled away, looking around on the ground for her headscarf. Darting a glance at the butcher shop doorway, she saw Bailiff Tom lurking in the shadows. She wiped his vile saliva from her face with her sleeve.

"Throwing yourself in front of a galloping horse?" The stranger's voice reminded her of a snarling animal in its pitch and intensity. "We could have both been killed."

Shiny black boots waited beside her. Even the stranger's stance showed his irritation.

Finally seeing her scarf, she bent and snatched it from the dirt.

Her eyes traveled from his expensive leather boots to his broad chest. He wore the most elegant clothing she'd seen since the last time she visited London with her father — a red velvet doublet and gold-embroidered shirtsleeves — a vast departure from the dull gray and brown of the villagers' coarse woolens.

She beat the dust from her skirt as anger boiled up inside her. It wasn't her fault she'd fallen in front of his horse. Did he think she had tossed herself into the street? First that disgusting lecher Bailiff Tom, and now this stranger . . . Her gaze finally met his face and she stifled a gasp.

A black patch covered his left eye, and a scar cut a pale line down his cheek, through his thick brown beard, all the way to his chin.

The back of her neck tingled. His expression demanded an answer as he glared at her from one brown eye.

Her surprise at his formidable appearance quickly turned to anger. She was determined to let him know she wasn't a lack-wit and didn't relish being treated like one.

"My lord." Her voice was surprisingly steady. "My name is Annabel Chapman, and I am not in the habit of throwing myself in front of galloping horses. I was pushed." She had to bite her tongue to keep from adding, *And perhaps you shouldn't gallop your horse through the village as though you're the only person on the street.*

She leaned down to continue beating the dust from her clothes.

"Who pushed you?" He shouted the question so thunderously, she forgot about her dusty clothes and stared up at him. "Where is the man who would push a woman into the street?"

Her gaze involuntarily shifted to the butcher shop's doorway, where Bailiff Tom stood just inside. He immediately stepped back into the shadows.

The lord followed her gaze and then looked back at Annabel. "Wait here."

His expression became even fiercer just before he turned from her and strode into the shop.

"Bailiff Tom? How dare you shove that maiden?" His booming voice easily carried into the street.

He reappeared in the doorway, clutching Bailiff Tom by the back of his neck.

Pushing Tom toward her, the stranger jerked him to a halt only an arm's length away.

"My bailiff wishes to ask forgiveness for his behavior."

Tom didn't look her in the eye but said in a strained voice, "Forgive me."

She nodded, aware of the small group of wide-eyed villagers gathering to watch.

The man let go of Bailiff Tom's neck. After straightening his elegant waistcoat, the lord stood tall, his back straight and his broad shoulders looming over the small group of villeins that now surrounded him. He held one arm tight against his midsection as he spoke. "I am Ranulf le Wyse, the lord of this village."

The people immediately sank to one knee and bowed their heads before him.

"I will not tolerate loutish behavior from the men of my demesne." The people lifted their heads. Lord le Wyse's commanding tone riveted every eye. "And I warn you not to hope for preferential treatment. My father's steward may have taken bribes, but I'm the lord now, and," he fairly growled, "it isn't in my nature."

He turned in one swift motion, mounted his black horse, and galloped away.

Annabel watched him disappear down the road, then she turned to go home, moving quickly to get away from all the people staring at her. What kind of man was this new lord? He'd assured them that he didn't tolerate bribes or lawlessness. Her mother had been guilty of both.

What would her family's future be at the mercy of Lord Ranulf le Wyse?

Chapter 2

Instead of going inside when she reached home, Annabel ran around to the back of the house, unable to stop her mind from reliving the confrontation with Bailiff Tom—and with their formidable new lord. Her hands were shaking as she stared down at the ugly bruise that had formed on the underside of her wrist.

She found Dilly nibbling the grass in her pen and sank down on her knees beside the goat. Dilly grunted and nudged Annabel with her soft head. She stroked the animal's furry sides and her hands gradually stopped shaking.

She let her fingers find the scar on Dilly's leg. Just after Father died, she had discovered the goat in a muddy ditch. A bloody wound oozed from the animal's foreleg, and she had bleated so piteously Annabel climbed down and rescued her. The leg soon healed, leaving a scar. It reminded Annabel of the new lord's scar that ran down one side of his face, cutting a line through his beard. What had happened to cause Lord le Wyse's scar and the loss of his eye? A fight? Some kind of accident?

She moved away from the goat's leg and rubbed her ears. Thankfully, no one had yet claimed the lost goat. It was a serious offense to steal another person's animal. But Dilly's milk supplied a valuable part of the family's daily sustenance. If anyone told their new lord that she'd found the animal, he might take Dilly away, claiming the goat belonged to him. She probably did, as did almost everything in Glynval.

In addition to having to live off the milk from a lost goat, many things had changed when her father died, including Annabel's future. While her family and the villagers expected her to marry, Annabel's dearest wish was to enter a convent, to read the Holy Writ, to know all that God had spoken. But without money from her father's ships, it was impossible. Convents were a haven for the daughters of wealthy families.

A familiar donkey's bray sounded from the lane. Annabel stood and peeked around the corner of their house. She leaned against it, the sharp stones' edges digging into her hip, reminding her that the rest of the villagers lived in wattle-and-daub structures with dirt floors. The stone house had never seemed so dear.

Roberta Chapman came into view, sitting astride their donkey. Annabel shrank back from running out to greet her. Mother's shoulders slumped as she slowly dismounted, her eyes weary as she went inside. Annabel said a quick prayer, squeezing her eyes tight, then opened the back door from the kitchen.

"What news?" Her brothers stood facing their mother.

Annabel leaned against the doorway between the kitchen and the main room of the house and watched, unseen, as Mother took off her wimple, her face drawn and pale. Mother sank onto a stool, which creaked beneath her weight, and laid her hands, palms up, on her knees.

"Tell us," Edward demanded.

"It is a very hard ruling." She shook her head and sighed. "The jury said we must begin immediately to do our share, as free landholders, of the demesne fieldwork."

Annabel huffed. Leave it to her mother to moan about the easiest part of the ruling. What was so bad about that? At least no one could accuse them of shirking their responsibilities any longer. And as free landholders they wouldn't have to work as many days as those of villein status.

"Surely you can pay the censum so we don't have to work." Durand, who was two years older than Annabel, looked ready to cry. He had always claimed he was too sickly to work. He wrung his hands as he awaited his mother's answer.

Edward stood with his head high, looking down his prominent nose at their mother. He—and their mother—thought it beneath their dignity to work in the lord's fields. But what good had pride done them? And if they were this upset by having to simply do their share, what would their reaction be to the jury's actual punishment?

"We're still in debt because of your father's lost ships. There is no money. But that isn't the worst of it." Their mother hung her head.

After a few moments of silence, with Edward clenching his fists by his sides, Mother told them of the jury's demand that one of her children serve the lord for three years, keeping her eyes on the floor the entire time she spoke. "The worst is that our lord will seize our house if we don't comply."

Silence fell over them. When their mother spoke again, her voice was flat. "In the morning, the reeve will come to fetch ... one of you."

Durand gasped. "An indentured servant? Mother, not I. You know I'm sick. I get fevers, chills. I can't do it. I wouldn't last a week. That kind of hard labor would kill me." He sniffled and wiped his nose with his hand.

"Well, I don't think we have to worry about it." Edward casually glanced down at his hands and then brushed off his sleeve, as though ridding himself of a speck of dirt.

Mother and Durand stared at him with open mouths.

"It will all be taken care of. Bailiff Tom will speak to our lord today and pay our censum for us."

"Why would he do that?" Durand asked.

"Because Tom wants Annabel, and I've given him permission to marry her."

Annabel watched her mother's face, waiting for her to protest and say that such a thing could never be. But she didn't say a word.

"Will Annabel marry the bailiff?" Durand looked not doubtful but hopeful. It seemed he wanted to sell her to the bailiff as much as Edward did. *Mother, please say no. Say you won't let them do this.* Besides, Edward didn't realize the enormous fine the jury had set against the family. The bailiff could never pay such a fine. In fact, Tom must have known the fine would be extreme and lied to Edward so the family would force Annabel to marry him.

"What choice does she have?" Edward's voice was hard and forceful. "She has to marry the bailiff, or one of us will be forced to indenture ourselves to the new lord."

Mother returned her sons' gazes and sighed. "If Annabel will marry him, it will smooth things over, if not solve our problem, and raise our status with the villagers. But she may refuse."

A stabbing pain went through Annabel's stomach. She only half listened to the rest of their conversation. *Oh, God, I wish Father were here.* She thought about what her father would say and how he would protect her.

Other things were said before Edward gestured with his arms, angrily slashing the air. "Don't look at me. Can you see me as a servant? Preposterous! Doesn't everyone know our father's family was nobility, that our grandfather was a knight? I won't do it."

"Nay, son, of course not," Mother muttered.

Mother couldn't defy their lord. They would be thrown out of their house, and who would give their mother shelter?

But Annabel realized the jury had given her a way out, another choice besides marrying Bailiff Tom. She could go to Lord le Wyse and offer herself as an indentured servant. Her brothers would still have to do the boon work and the other days' work required of them, but they could go home every night, and most of their days would be their own. Annabel would be bound as a servant to the manor house and to Lord le Wyse's household, sleeping at the manor, eating at the manor, working alongside his other servants without pay.

As much as she dreaded serving under the fierce new lord who had accused her of throwing herself in front of his horse, it was preferable to marrying Bailiff Tom. If she hadn't fought back and gotten away from him at the butcher's shop, he might have succeeded in ... She didn't want to think about what.

The villagers resented the Chapmans as idlers, too proud to work, but Annabel would prove that she was not, and she would prevent her mother's home from being taken from her. She tried to imagine Mother sleeping outdoors, with no food and nothing to protect her from the rain or cold or wild animals. What a sin it would be if she and her brothers allowed that to happen to their mother.

But her brothers would run off, abandon their demesne village to join a band of outlaws before they would become indentured servants forced to do the most menial tasks, carting dung and herding sheep and geese at the lord's manor house.

Edward was the oldest at twenty-two, and so should be the one to go. However, besides keeping his personal appearance tidy — his black hair cut and combed, his face shaved and clean — all he did was sit around all day and drink ale with the miller's sons. Now that a crisis had come their way, could Edward not play the part of a man this once?

She looked again through the crack in the door. Durand clutched the back of his neck, emitting a sound somewhere between a groan and a whimper. He was always fancying himself ill and expecting to be waited upon. Father had not become a wealthy merchant by refusing to work, but her brothers couldn't seem to grasp that. They'd expected to have wealth dropped into their laps and could not accept that their father's riches had disappeared forever the moment his ships were destroyed.

"I'm afraid Annabel won't marry the bailiff," Durand said, sinking down in a chair and covering his eyes. Then he suddenly lifted his head, almost smiling. "Perhaps she would agree to become the lord's servant for three years."

Edward snorted. "Even if she did, we'd still have to work in the harvest fields."

Durand's bottom lip poked out like a petulant child. "You're all healthy and strong, not like me."

"Oh, for pity's sake, Durand!" Edward took a menacing step toward his brother. "Do you expect us to feel sorry for you when we're all in the same predicament?"

Durand cringed, as though afraid Edward would strike him.

Edward walked away from his brother and stared out a window. "We'll just have to convince Annabel to marry Tom. It's the only way."

Annabel backed away from the door, already planning what to do. She would leave early in the morning before anyone else woke up. And that vile Bailiff Tom would never touch her again.

For the rest of the day her brothers tried coercion, coaxing, and manipulation to convince her to accept Bailiff Tom's offer, and even her mother tried to tell her all the reasons marrying the bailiff would benefit her. Annabel said very little, allowing them to think she was wavering. But secretly she was vowing she would never marry the vile bailiff.

When her family wasn't badgering her, Annabel's mind churned, skittering back and forth between thoughts of her family, the villagers, Bailiff Tom, and Lord le Wyse. Evening encroached, and Annabel collected her belongings—a few books her father had bought for her long ago, clothing, a comb, and a coif and veil to wear to church—and stuffed them into a bag.

The thought of leaving home and living at the manor house, being at Lord le Wyse's mercy, tied her stomach in knots, but she had little choice. He was as scarred and disfigured as everyone had said he was, but it was his ferocious manner that made her nervous.

She would have to avoid him and not make him angry. But would that be possible? She had seen his outrage at his own bailiff for pushing her. The episode in the village had shown that Lord le Wyse had an ill temper—though it could also show his desire to protect women. But he hadn't seemed very chivalrous when he accused her of throwing herself in front of his horse. Perhaps he was simply ... fierce.

She'd heard the rumors about a nearby lord, young like Lord le Wyse, who regularly took advantage of the young maidens of his village and then bestowed a "dowry" on them, which amounted to paying someone to marry them. Was Lord le Wyse capable of doing something so vile?

She pictured him again, forcing Bailiff Tom to apologize to her. The eye patch gave him a sinister look, and while his fine clothing made him look sophisticated, the beard was strangely out of place. Nearly all the men of the village were clean shaven. He had looked like a bear of a man while holding Tom.

Tom.

Her hand stopped in the middle of placing a dress in her bag. Since Bailiff Tom was Lord le Wyse's bailiff and worked directly for him, he would be at the manor house—with her— skulking about every day. He would look at her, speak to her, could manage to get her alone . . .

The noise of a thousand bees filled her ears. *Dear God, how can I do this?* How could she work so closely with the bailiff? See him every day?

She couldn't do it.

But what choice did she have? If she didn't become the lord's servant, Tom would still remain a problem. Even if she told her brothers that she was afraid of Bailiff Tom, even if she told them exactly why, it wouldn't be enough for them. She imagined Edward, his face twisted in that intense way of his when he was agitated. She knew what he would say: "And what did the bailiff do to you?" If she told him the whole story, how the bailiff had grabbed her, what he intended to do to her, her brother would shrug and say, "Well, I did tell him he could marry you."

He would see the issue as resolved. And Durand would say the same thing, that she should simply marry the bailiff. He would think her objection nothing compared to his sickliness.

As always, her brothers would fail her.

She had no choice. She had to go—but she also had to find a way to protect herself.

⁂

Annabel got up early after sleeping very little. The black of night still cloaked her window, but rather than lighting a candle, she groped until she found her second-best dress and slipped it over her head. Her heart pounding, she grasped her cloth bag and tiptoed down the hall into the kitchen. A sliver of gray light was now illuminating the room enough that she was able to see, on the table, their sharpest cutting knife. Her hand closed around the smooth handle. She took a piece of leather and wrapped it around the blade, then slipped the knife into her skirt pocket.

Her hand lingered over the knife, pressing it against her thigh. The bailiff would surely see her at the manor, would quickly learn of her servant status. Would he be able to catch her alone, away from the other servants? Would he finish what he had started yesterday? The thought of him touching her again almost made her heave.

Could she truly use the knife to do harm to Bailiff Tom?

Yes. She could. She would.

Clutching her bag, she went out the back door and stepped into the goat pen. Dawn gave a glow to the sky and revealed a foggy morning. The little garden seemed fresh and waiting, shimmering with droplets of dew. *I hope someone will remember to pick the peas.* What would her family eat if they didn't tend the garden?

She couldn't worry about that now.

She rubbed the goat's head. "Farewell, Dilly."

I shouldn't feel so sad. I'll be coming back in three years. But a feeling of finality came over her, a sense that she would never live in her family's home again.

❦

The gray manor house, a plain, rectangular building, emerged out of the mist, its large yard empty of all the people who had witnessed her family's reckoning yesterday. A rooster crowed, and a boy appeared from behind the dovecote, herding a flock of geese. He yawned so big she wondered if his jaw would come unhinged. The fog that obscured the sun and surrounded the manor and its grounds lent the scene before her a dreamlike quality. The dewy grass had soaked her feet, and her worn-thin shoes squeaked with each step.

Annabel fought to gain control of her thoughts before she reached the manor. *I am no longer a merchant's daughter. I must accept my plight and forget the hopes and dreams I once cherished.* The other servants would hate her if they thought she expected any sort of preferential treatment. She must show that she was strong and capable, not a girl mourning the loss of home, comfort, and security.

There was another reason she couldn't allow herself to appear weak. Bailiff Tom would no doubt be nearby and would sense her fear and be emboldened toward her.

She straightened her back and shoulders, determined to face whatever dangers or indignities awaited her. Anything was better than marrying Bailiff Tom.

Annabel climbed the stone steps to the upper hall and took deep breaths to calm her racing heart, praying with all her might that the bailiff wasn't in the upper hall with Lord le Wyse. Of course, the bailiff didn't know she was coming to offer her services to the lord. No one knew.

She reached the top and knocked on the tall, rounded door. It opened and a hefty older woman stood with a broom in her hand. "Yes?"

"Good morning. I'm Annabel Chapman." *How to explain?* "My lord, Lord le Wyse, is expecting me—that is, I'm to serve..."

"Come in. Annabel, is it? Call me Mistress Eustacia. I'll tell Lord Ranulf you're here."

Mistress Eustacia stepped back, and Annabel entered the dim room. As her eyes adjusted, she noticed a few people engaged in various tasks around the large hall, a single room encompassing the entire upper floor of the manor house. A dairy was set up at one end of the room, where two young women were churning butter. Some people she recognized, including the bailiff's daughter, Maud, who was stirring up the fire in the fireplace and adding more wood. Another maiden was sweeping cobwebs from the walls, as the building hadn't been occupied for as long as Annabel could remember, except for occasional visits by the old lord's steward.

By the confident way she handed her broom to a passing maid, Eustacia must have been the head servant. She shuffled to the back of the chamber, where a large tapestry screen hid a portion of the room. "My lord? Someone is here to see you."

"Who is it?" The voice on the other side of the screen boomed louder than necessary, probably cross at being disturbed so early in the morning. *Help me, God.*

The stranger who almost ran her over with his horse the day before appeared around the side of the partition, fully dressed. Just as Margery had reported, and as he had done when he addressed the villagers in the street, he held his left arm crooked at the elbow and resting against his midsection. If she read his stance and the tilt of his head correctly, he was vexed.

Mistress Eustacia continued. "Begging your pardon, my lord, but a maiden is here saying you were expecting her. Annabel Chapman."

"A maiden?" He sounded even angrier. "Chapman? Come here." He beckoned Annabel with his good hand.

Annabel's knees turned to mush as she stepped forward.

Recognition flickered across his brow. "So you're Roberta Chapman's eldest?"

"Nay, my lord. Her youngest."

"I'd expected her to send her eldest." He stared hard at her with his one brown eye.

Annabel didn't know what to say.

"So you have brothers and sisters?"

"Two brothers, my lord."

"Are your brothers married, then?"

"Nay, my lord, they are not." He no doubt would have preferred Edward or Durand and wondered why she had come instead of one of them. She fervently prayed he wouldn't question her as to why she offered herself, why one of her older brothers had not come in her place.

Several moments went by while he frowned at her. "So you are prepared to serve here, to stay at the manor house, for three years in payment for the three years of work your family shirked?"

"Yes, my lord, I am." She looked him in the eye, highly aware that the other workers in the room had grown quiet.

"Very well, then. Eustacia has much need of you in the kitchen, with all the extra workers here. But today we begin the harvest. You will join the rest of the villagers in the barley fields."

"My lord, begging your pardon." Eustacia lowered her voice to a whisper. "Perhaps she should stay with me today and work in the kitchen instead of the fields. She doesn't look strong. Too skinny."

"Doesn't look strong?" The question was a shout that echoed through the hall.

All activity ceased. Annabel felt everyone's eyes on her, but the most intimidating one was Lord le Wyse's. She could feel the contempt in his stare. As the silence lengthened, the others in the room began whispering, probably reminding each other who she was. A Chapman, synonymous with lazy. She felt her cheeks begin to burn, but she continued to stare him in the eye.

Lord le Wyse growled, "Are you strong?"

"Yes, my lord."

"Good." He strode past her, thus ending the conversation.

"My lord."

The voice echoed through the room. Annabel turned to see Bailiff Tom with his hands on his hips, facing Lord le Wyse.

"This maiden is intended to be my bride. Her brother has arranged for her to marry me in exchange for paying her censum."

She'd been right: he might pay *her* censum and *her* fine, but he wouldn't help the rest of her family, and either Edward or Durand would end up indentured to Lord le Wyse.

Lord le Wyse turned on her, his lips a dangerous, thin line. "Is this true? Did you promise yourself to this man?"

"Nay, my lord, I never did." Her face heated again as she realized all the people who were listening to this exchange. But at least she would have witnesses to her refusal.

The bailiff stared at her with murder in his eyes.

"Are you willing to marry him?" Lord le Wyse's voice was hard, and he squinted his eye at her, as if she was suddenly even more distasteful to him.

"I am not, my lord. I want to be your servant, to pay for my family's neglect." She made sure everyone could hear her, even as her hands shook.

He turned back to Bailiff Tom. "She will not have you, apparently."

A low titter of amusement erupted around the room. As Lord le Wyse resumed walking toward the door, he muttered gruffly to the bailiff, "Count yourself fortunate."

His words felt like a slap. A couple of gasps went around the room at the insult as Lord le Wyse exited and Bailiff Tom followed him out.

As the rest of the workers went back to their tasks, Eustacia frowned but didn't seem surprised by the lord's rude behavior. "Pay no heed to the master. He's grumpy this morning." Her focused gaze started at Annabel's feet and slowly took her in, all the way to the top of her head. "You don't want to go to the fields in that dress, that's certain. It'll be mussed from here to Lincoln. Put on your worst clothing and tie up your hair. Come."

Eustacia took Annabel's bag and walked to the far corner of the large, open chamber to a much smaller partition than the one around which Lord le Wyse had appeared. "You can change behind here." Eustacia smiled, revealing a broken front tooth.

Annabel ducked behind the screen with her bag while the mistress spoke to her on the other side.

"Not much privacy here now, which makes the master a bit quarrelsome, but once he gets his new castle built, that will change."

Annabel took off her dress. When she pulled her oldest and worst-looking kirtle over her head, she remembered to retrieve her knife from her other dress and slip it into her pocket. It reminded her that she might see Bailiff Tom again at any moment.

She imagined his mocking smile when he saw her working in the fields or found her in the kitchen cooking and cleaning for Lord le Wyse.

Holding her hand over the knife, she clenched her teeth so hard her jaw ached. *Bailiff Tom will never touch me again. Never.*

Chapter 3

The house servants, all except Eustacia, quit their various tasks that morning to join the villagers, including children, in the demesne fields. The barley was ripe and needed to be gathered quickly, and no one, except the very old or very sick, was exempt from working the harvest fields.

A foreman, a stranger like Eustacia who had accompanied Lord le Wyse from Lincolnshire to Glynval, handed Annabel and three other women scythes so they could start mowing the stalks of barley. A thin-shouldered man with a weather-worn face, his hose rolled down below his knobby knees, was assigned to follow behind them to gather the stalks and bind them into sheaves.

The three women, one old enough to have grandchildren and the other two a bit younger, bent forward at the waist and began to slice the barley stalks close to the ground. Annabel drew back the unwieldy instrument, her arms feeling weak. Why hadn't she eaten breakfast? That might have helped.

She tried to imitate the women's motions, but the blade of the scythe bent the lithe stalks instead of cutting them. Hoping no one had noticed her blunder, she hurried to pull the scythe back and try again. This time she managed to cut through a few stalks but left others standing. The other three continued slicing ahead, making a flat swath through the sea of grain.

Annabel gritted her teeth and focused. She watched, trying to mimic the other women's body posture and grip on the wooden handles of their scythes. She drew back and swung, flattening the stalks, but they sprang up again to bob their heads at her, taunting her for her futile efforts.

She exhaled in frustration. Soon she would attract everyone's attention. Already the binder had passed her as he gathered the barley the other women cut and tied it into bundles. He glared back at her over his shoulder, shaking his head and muttering.

"Well, Annabel Chapman. Having some trouble?"

Her blood went cold as she turned. Bailiff Tom atte Water stood by her side.

"Let me show you how to do that." His hands reached toward her. Annabel shrank away from him and clamped one hand over the knife in her pocket.

Bailiff Tom grabbed the scythe and she let go.

His small black eyes narrowed and his lip curled. "You've never done this before, so I will teach you. You hold the handle like this."

He reached out and clasped her hand, but she snatched it away from him and took a step back.

"I'm trying to help you. Are you too good to accept my help? Too high and lofty?" He stepped toward her, and as he leaned forward, Annabel could see the blackness in his eyes. "You're no better than the rest of us, as it turns out. Now take this scythe and I'll show you how it's done."

Taking the tool from his hands would only allow him to touch her, to get close enough for him to whisper in her ear. She couldn't let him get that close. *God, help me.*

"Bailiff Tom."

At the sound of the lord's stern voice, a scowl darkened the bailiff's features. When he realized who addressed him, he plastered on a smile that did nothing to hide the black look in his eyes.

"Bailiff, I need you to go to the barley field behind the grove of chestnut trees and make sure everything is progressing with the harvest there."

"Yes, my lord." Tom turned to Annabel, but she kept her

eyes focused on Lord le Wyse. Tom thrust the scythe at her and stalked away.

Her knees went weak with relief, but also with trepidation. What would her lord say? Had he noticed her lack of usefulness with the scythe?

With his mutilated hand, the patch over his eye, and his scarred face, he was probably accustomed to inspiring fear, even repulsion, in people. She tried not to show anything but respect for him and turned her gaze to the ground.

"Forgive me, my lord. I'm afraid I don't know how to use a scythe." She shook her head apologetically.

He reached out and took the scythe from her. Once empty, her hand trembled violently. She quickly hid it in the folds of her faded blue dress.

He cleared his throat. "It takes practice to master the proper technique. Since we need every pair of hands to get in the harvest, you will work with the binders tying up the sheaves."

"Yes, my lord."

She was so grateful to him that the corners of her mouth went up in a relieved smile. His expression immediately changed to an angry scowl.

"Come." His voice sounded like it had when he spoke to Tom. Of course he would misinterpret her smiling at him. She must force herself to behave like a servant. *Servants don't smile at their masters*, she scolded herself. Though it seemed the lord despised her before she'd even arrived. But why? The fact that her family hadn't done their required labor didn't seem like reason enough.

She kept a safe distance behind him as he led her to a section of the field where three young girls were slicing the barley stalks at a slower pace than the older women. He gave her a roll of twine, then he bent and gathered an armful of the cut grain. He used his mangled left hand to hold the stalks against his chest while he gathered with his right. His dark brown hair and beard glowed in the sun as he wrapped the twine tightly around the stalks and tied it, leaving the sheaf standing in the field to dry.

He met her eyes, scowled, and seemed to be waiting for a response.

She gave him a curt nod and started gathering the spears of grain awkwardly in the crook of her arm, trying to mimic his movements.

As she finished tying her first sheaf, she glanced up and saw that he was striding away. She sighed in relief, glad he wasn't watching her.

She continued gathering the barley, still tasting her fear like copper in the back of her throat, and still hearing the threat in the bailiff's voice. *Thank you, God, that Lord le Wyse came when he did.* It was almost as if he realized Bailiff Tom was threatening her. God had sent an angry lord to protect her from a lecherous bailiff. But she was grateful.

Thankful to have a task she could do, she worked steadily. It didn't take long for her shoulders to grow hot under the relentless heat of the sun, which had burned off the fog of early morning. Her back and shoulders ached from bending over, and her arms felt like two boulders as she lifted and tied, lifted and tied. Her hands burned from the rough twine and prickly stalks. She paused in her work to wipe the sweat from her brow with the back of her hand, watching the girls ahead of her mow the barley with expert strokes. They often flicked their gazes around to make sure they weren't being observed before stopping to whisper to each other and giggle. Annabel was thankful for the girls' lack of enthusiasm for their work, since it prevented her from getting too far behind them, and she even allowed herself to hope that the girls might one day accept her as a friend. She couldn't remember the last time she'd whispered and giggled with a girlfriend. Perhaps now that she was working as a servant, the rest of the village girls would accept her.

Glancing up, she saw a familiar form bending over the barley stalks. Edward was working not far away, also gathering and binding sheaves. He straightened, stopping his work to press a hand to his lower back. Annabel quickly looked down, hoping her brother didn't see her.

"You just couldn't go along with my plan, could you?" Edward hissed the words at her, coming to stand beside her.

Annabel pretended to ignore him.

"You couldn't do this one thing for your family, could you?" He sounded angry, and the ridiculousness of his attitude hit her.

"You're the one who tried to force your only sister to marry an appalling man she had no wish to marry. I *am* helping the family by serving Lord le Wyse." She continued with her work while she spoke, not even looking up, too aware that Lord le Wyse might be nearby watching them. "And even if I had married Bailiff Tom, he wouldn't have saved you from your share of the work. He wasn't planning to pay your censum at all. He would have let you be indentured to Lord le Wyse."

"That's a lie!"

"If I were you, I'd lower my voice and get back to work. Lord le Wyse doesn't tolerate people who won't do their share."

Edward huffed and stomped away from her. Annabel couldn't help but chuckle inwardly at her brother's discomfiture. At the same time, her heart ached to think that her own brother didn't care about her. Father would never have let him treat her this way.

Annabel again focused on the stalks, though her stomach growled intermittently all morning. Soon her head ached from the sun's heat, and her mouth was so dry it was as if she'd been chewing a ball of wax.

She tied off yet another bundle of barley. When she looked up, a young boy with green eyes and a dirt-streaked face stood beside her with a bucket and a ladle.

"Water?"

"Thank you." Annabel took the proffered ladle and drank. As she handed it back to him, she noticed a cut on the boy's upper arm, oozing fresh blood. "What happened to your arm?" She bent lower to get a better look.

"Got too close to a scythe." He stared at her with big eyes.

"You must have a bandage for that. Here, sit down." Annabel's dress was old and threadbare, and so she hoped would

41

tear easily. She took hold of the hem, giving it a good yank until she felt it rip. Tearing off a long strip of material, she knelt beside the boy, who sat obediently on the ground. Carefully, she wrapped the cloth around the wound and tied it in place.

She gazed into his complacent eyes, and compassion welled up in her. "What's your name?"

"Adam."

"How old are you, Adam?"

"Eight years."

"You be wary of flying scythes." She pointed a finger at him but smiled to soften her words. "You wouldn't want to lose an arm."

He grinned and his eyes twinkled. He pointed behind her. "Over there's my father. His name's Gilbert Carpenter."

She turned and spied a man who was talking to Lord le Wyse several feet away. Lord le Wyse was frowning at her but quickly turned away.

So he was watching her. She'd better get back to work. She bent to gather more barley stalks and the boy came closer.

"My father and I came here from Lincoln, to help the lord build his castle."

"That's a long way. Did your mother come too?"

"Nay. My mother's dead. But my father says he's looking for my new mother. You could be my mother."

Annabel's eyebrows went up in alarm, but her heart expanded at the hope in his eyes. Poor fellow. Every child needed a mother.

He flashed her another grin as he picked up his bucket. "I'll bring my father to meet you."

She scrambled for a suitable way to answer him. "But I'm too young to be your mother." His face fell, his eyes wide with hurt. A pang of guilt assaulted her. "But I'm just right to be your sister, eh?"

His face brightened a little. "You'll like my father. He's the master mason."

"Let's get our work done first, and later we can talk."

Adam moved on to take the water bucket to other laborers.

What would the boy say to his father? She imagined him declaring that he'd found a mother. She cringed. Her first day and already she'd gotten herself into an awkward predicament. More than one.

As the day wore on, a constant stream of sweat slipped from her hairline down her cheek. The thin shift underneath her dress plastered itself to her body. The work seemed endless, as the ripe barley stretched on and on across field after field. Over and over she bent to gather the stalks in the crook of her arm. Her elbow ached and her back felt as if it would break in two. Her hands were covered in dust and her shoes were filthy. She wondered if later in the evening there would be a safe, private place for her to bathe.

Annabel tried to keep her eyes down, for whenever she met the gaze of one of the other women she saw either hostility or amused curiosity. At least she'd seen no more of Bailiff Tom.

By the time the sun was no longer directly overhead, weariness snaked up her legs and into her arms. When were they supposed to take a rest? She longed to ask one of her fellow workers, but they were all keeping a distance of several feet. Her head felt light, and each time she raised herself from her stooping position, the world swayed and her eyes clouded. To faint now would show the villeins she was as useless as they imagined. They might even think she was pretending to faint to avoid doing her work.

They worked their way to the edge of the field, near the bank of the river. She gathered another armload of barley stalks and began tying the twine. The stalks in the middle slipped through the sheaf, and then the whole bundle slid limply to the ground. Annabel bit her lip. Tears of pure exhaustion sprang to her eyes.

She took a deep breath, willing the tears away. She bent and started gathering the stalks again. When she stepped forward to reach the last ones, her toe struck a rock and she stumbled. Her legs gave way and she fell forward, landing on her hands and knees in the clump of weeds that grew beside the barley stalks at the edge of the field.

An intense stinging seized her hands and lower legs. She pushed herself up, but before she could stand, someone caught her under her arms and helped her up. When the person let go, Annabel swayed precariously and her eyes refused to focus.

When her surroundings gradually lost their blur, a young woman about her age stood beside her.

"That's stinging nettle you just sat in. Don't you know to stay away from that?" Wisps of light brown hair swayed against the girl's cheeks.

Annabel wanted to say that she hadn't sat in it, she fell, and no, she didn't know. But the painful stinging made her suck in an agonized breath through her clenched teeth. Her skirt must have flipped up just enough to expose her bare legs to the plant. Millions of tiny, likely poisonous needles seemed to have invaded her skin, but staring at her hands, Annabel could only see a few barely visible, hairlike thorns. She yanked a few of them out as the horrible stinging made its way up her legs and spread over her arms, into her cheeks, and along her scalp until her whole body tingled in misery. She closed her eyes, thinking death would be pleasant.

"You don't look well. Are you apt to topple over again?"

"Nay, I am well." Annabel opened her eyes, but her surroundings looked blurry again. She put out her hand to try to steady herself.

"Sit down before you fall again." The young maiden's voice seemed slightly amused as she grabbed Annabel's arm. Annabel sank heavily to the ground.

She leaned away from the stinging nettle plant, wanting to get as far away from it as possible. Her head spun faster now, so she closed her eyes and tucked her chin to her chest. *Breathe in. Breathe out. O God, don't let me faint.*

A child's voice broke through her daze. "Miss Annabel?"

She looked up. Adam stood in front of her, this time holding a brown jug and a sack.

"Some bread and ale for Beatrice and Annabel."

He handed the heavy jug to the maiden, whose name was

Beatrice, apparently, then dug his hand into the sack and pulled out a small loaf of bread for each of them.

Annabel stared at the bread, and her trembling fingers slipped around it. Never had she been so grateful for bread. She carefully pinched off a small bite and put it in her mouth, hoping it would cure the weakness in her limbs and the rolling of her stomach. She chewed slowly, struggling to control a shudder.

Beatrice took a long drink of ale and smacked her lips. She wiped her sleeve across her mouth then handed the jug to Annabel.

She dropped the small loaf into her lap and grasped the ale jug with both hands. As with the bread, the sour beverage never tasted so good. After several swallows, she handed the jug back to Beatrice.

Adam moved away to deliver bread and ale to other workers, and Annabel and Beatrice ate in silence.

The agony in Annabel's body never lessened as the prickly sensation swept over her arms and down her spine. She shivered. The bread had calmed her stomach, but the rest of her body felt as weak as a newborn lamb. She imagined herself pitching face forward again.

But everyone else was working and so would she. Falling into the harmless-looking nettle plant was no excuse to stop, no matter how bad the stinging that enveloped her whole body. The barley had to be harvested or the entire village would suffer lack this winter.

She placed one hand on the ground and the other on her knee and pushed herself up. With effort she bent over, picked up her ball of twine, and took a step toward the piles of barley on the ground. Though she swayed and her head began to spin, Annabel focused her eyes on a spot on the ground, willing herself to stay upright.

"Annabel? Beatrice?" Adam's voice sounded near.

Carefully, Annabel turned to look at him.

"Lord le Wyse wants you to go back to the manor house and help Mistress Eustacia."

Behind Adam, Lord le Wyse was scowling at her. No doubt he thought his new servant miserably lacking.

She thanked God anyway for her reprieve. A sigh of despair threatened to escape, however, when she turned toward the manor house and realized how far she would have to walk to get to it. The linden trees hid the building from view, and the field's furrows stretched out long before her, littered with the dull shades of brown, white, and gray of the villagers' clothing, the barley, and the dirt.

At least she saw no fiendish green nettle plants.

"Saints have mercy, how pale you look." Mistress Eustacia stared at Annabel. "I told him you were none too sturdy, and he sending you out in the fields." She clucked her tongue.

Beatrice offered, "It might be because she fell into a patch of stinging nettles."

"Stinging nettles! Why, child, don't you know to stay away from those? You'll be stinging for hours, you will. Come, sit." Eustacia pulled out a stool then addressed Beatrice. "Did you rub some fern on it? The underside of a fern leaf does some good, it does."

"I didn't see any." Beatrice shrugged then walked toward the window and the basin of water at the end of the upper hall. "I'll start on the churning." She proceeded to scrub her hands and wrists with the water.

A fine red rash covered Annabel's hands, and a chill crept over her face and along her arms.

Eustacia's brows creased, her fists planted on her hips. "No more," she said with a firm set of her ample jaw.

Annabel stared at her.

"I don't care what the master says, you're not working in the fields anymore. I have need of you here in the kitchen." She bent over and yanked up Annabel's skirts.

Annabel gasped, scrambling to push her skirt back down. The same angry red rash covered her legs.

Eustacia scrunched her face disapprovingly and turned in Beatrice's direction. "That butter can wait. Take Annabel down to the river to wash, then put some mud on this rash." Facing Annabel again, she said, "Lots of mud. Smear it on these legs and hands and sit on the bank until it dries. But before you go ..." Eustacia pulled out a small table from the wall, laid out with a chunk of cheese, some bread, and two pitchers. "Eat."

Both girls sat and Beatrice quickly sliced the cheese. More tears pricked Annabel's eyes. This time they were tears of gratitude.

After a cooling dip in the river, Annabel's legs and hands still stung, but the discomfort ebbed after she washed off the mud. Another relief came as the villagers went home at midafternoon, finished with their fieldwork for the day. Work at the manor fell into a rhythm as Beatrice began her duties in the dairy while Annabel helped Eustacia prepare supper for the servants and the workers building Ranulf le Wyse's new home.

Though careful to stay out of her lord's way, she glimpsed the plans for the new house as she brought the food into the upper hall. The plans were laid out on the trestle table while Lord le Wyse discussed them with his master mason.

House was not a strong enough word for what the lord had planned. It was to be a castle with many rooms and three towers, one rising up a full two stories higher than the rest of the building. Annabel was one of the few villagers who had traveled outside the demesne, and the only place she had ever seen anything as grand as this was in London.

The grand house was at least two years from completion, although she overheard that a portion of it would be livable in several weeks.

To prepare for the meal, the servants set up trestle tables end to end down the middle of the upper hall floor to accommodate all the servants now living at the manor. Despite the crowd, Tom atte Water managed to sit across the table from her.

She stared down at her plate, the table, anywhere but at him, knowing he was probably leering at her. When he spoke to her, she pretended not to hear.

After long, uncomfortable minutes of trying to ignore him, she heard him scrape his chair back to leave. She breathed a sigh of relief to see him leave with the rest of the men after the meal and leapt to help the other maidservants clean up, clearing tables and tossing the excess food into the slop bucket.

By the time the room was back in order, her legs trembled with fatigue. All the maids began to scatter and she wondered where she would sleep. Annabel looked for Beatrice, hoping the girl could provide answers, but she realized the dairymaid had been strangely absent since dinner ended.

Eustacia was busy giving instructions to a serving girl about what to purchase at the market the next day, so Annabel retrieved her bag from behind the small screen and stood nearby. She prayed Mistress Eustacia would notice her soon and tell her where she might sleep. She hoped she didn't look as exhausted as she felt, not wanting to draw attention to the fact that she wasn't accustomed to such hard work.

Feeling nearly invisible in her shadowed corner, Annabel watched Lord le Wyse cross the room and address Gilbert Carpenter, the master mason and foreman over the skilled craftsmen working on the castle.

Lord le Wyse was almost a head taller than his foreman. In the dim twilight of the upper hall, he looked darker than he had in the fields. His hair lay in a heavy swath across his forehead, grazing his black eyebrows. His shoulders were massive next to the much-smaller Gilbert. But while comparing him to Lord le Wyse, she realized Gilbert's features were perfect and symmetrical. He had a well-formed nose, light-colored eyes, and light brown hair. He looked to be no more than thirty years old and was quite handsome.

Lord le Wyse's looks were harder to sort out. One side of his face, the side with the leather patch, was thrown into shadow, giving a soft glow to his good eye and strong, prominent cheekbone. He would have been considered handsome before his face had been scarred and he'd lost his eye. Annabel watched as he gestured with his right hand while keeping his left arm tucked against his midsection. She'd heard someone say he was only five and twenty years old. It was hard to tell, as his face was obscured by the patch and the beard. He held his head and shoulders at a commanding angle, the posture of a powerful man.

She had every intention of avoiding him as much as possible. She was his servant and as such was at the mercy of his harshness. But she felt oddly mesmerized by his scar, eye patch, and maimed hand.

"Miss Annabel," called an insistent voice.

"Hello, Adam." She forced her face into a smile. "How is your arm?"

"'Tis well."

She saw that the bandage was still there, though quite covered in dirt.

"Miss Annabel, you didn't meet my father."

"Oh, Adam, I don't think now is the best time." Annabel glanced desperately at Eustacia, but she was still talking with the same young woman.

Adam's smile disappeared. "Oh. My father wants to meet you. I told him you would make a fine mother." The timid smile returned.

She swallowed and felt a ridiculous urge to run from the room and go home. She could not face the inevitable meeting, not tonight. "Thank you, Adam, but I'm very tired. I promise you'll see me again tomorrow. Now it is time for you to go to bed. And besides, we can't disturb your father while he's speaking with Lord le Wyse. Tomorrow. I promise."

Adam cocked his head to one side. Finally, he nodded then wandered away.

Her head ached with the weight of fatigue, and she prayed she hadn't hurt the little fellow's feelings.

Mistress Eustacia talked on with the maidservant, gesturing with one hand while her other rested on her hip. Annabel again looked around for someone to ask about sleeping arrangements, but the other maids and workers had already slipped out the door of the upper hall, leaving her to stand conspicuously still while everyone else had somewhere to go. She thought of her little bed in her father's house. If only she could crawl under the familiar sheet and lay her head on her own pillow.

Desperate now, she moved toward Mistress Eustacia. *Oh, thank you, God*, the maid was walking away. "Mistress Eustacia." Annabel bit her lip at the tremor in her voice.

The woman turned, and her eyes grew big at the sight of Annabel. "Oh, my dear, what is it?" Eustacia's eyes flicked down to Annabel's bag. "Ah, you haven't found your bed. I'll take you there, I will. Come." She huffed a tired breath, grabbed a candle, and turned toward the door at one end of the now almost-empty hall. "It's the best time of day, when a body can fall into bed after its labors."

Annabel followed her. When she turned to close the door, Lord le Wyse's eye met hers. She turned away quickly.

"All the women servants, except me, sleep down here in the undercroft," Mistress Eustacia said between huffs, making her way down the stone steps. "The men are bedded down in the barn and the sleeping shed. I'm in the upper hall with the master, in case he needs anything. I've been with his family since before he was born, and a gentler boy you never saw." Her voice lilted and ended with a sigh, as though the memories were dear. "'Tis only too sad that he's had such pain in his life, it is." She shook her head.

She must mean whatever destroyed his eye and mangled his hand.

Her mistress clicked her tongue. "The attack was the beginning of his sorrows. But the other, well, I shouldn't even speak of—I, who know more than anyone." They had made it to the bottom of the steps and stopped at the door to the undercroft. She stared at Annabel in the moonlight and a slight smile crossed her lips. Lifting her hand to Annabel's cheek, Eustacia caressed it for a moment, then let her hand fall. "You're a kind, gentle lass.

50

I see it in your eyes. He should have married someone like you instead of—" She shook her head again and turned away. "But there's no wisdom in speaking of that."

Annabel's tired mind registered surprise at her mistress's implication.

Eustacia pushed the door open and entered the barely lit undercroft, a large room the size of the upper hall but with stone arches undulating the ceiling and columns interrupting the open space here and there.

Women lay or sat on at least a dozen cots. Mistress Eustacia found one in the center of the room and pointed. "Here. This one's unclaimed as yet. Do ye have need of anything? I was young once, so there's naught you can't confide in me."

"Nay, Mistress Eustacia, thank you." Annabel dropped her bag onto the thin straw mattress.

"I'll talk to Lord Ranulf tonight. I need your help in the kitchen tomorrow. There's to be no more fieldwork for you. The lord listens to me, he does." She stared into Annabel's eyes, holding the candle up, as though to better inspect her features. She seemed about to say something then smiled wistfully and squeezed Annabel's shoulder before quitting the room.

Chapter
4

Annabel opened her bag and pulled out her nightgown. She changed her clothes quickly, not even looking to see if anyone was watching. She crawled onto the bed and wrapped the sheet around herself. There was no pillow, so she rested her head on the crook of her arm.

"You there. New girl. It's Annabel, isn't it?"

Ruefully, Annabel turned her head toward the voice coming from the cot to her right, her hopes of sinking into sleep crushed.

Beatrice leaned toward her, resting her elbows on her knees. "I came from Lincolnshire with Lord le Wyse, along with most of us here. My mother was a milk maid and my father's dead. What about you? I heard you tell Lord le Wyse that you didn't want to marry that ugly bailiff."

Annabel sat up, trying to sound friendly instead of exhausted and lonely. "My father's dead too, I'm afraid. As for the bailiff, that was simply a ... misunderstanding." She hoped the girl wouldn't press her further.

Beatrice eyed her with a shrewd expression. "You have a very pretty face, although you're a little skinny. Why haven't you married yet?"

Annabel swallowed. "I ..." She probably shouldn't say that she had yet to meet someone she would want to marry, so she shrugged.

Someone called out from the corner behind Annabel, "She thinks she's too good for Glynval men, that's why!"

Her face burned as a few snorts erupted around the room.

A slow smile spread over Beatrice's face. "Perhaps she is too good for Glynval men. But maybe one of the Lincolnshire men has caught her eye." A few protests rang out from the Glynval maidens.

Annabel shook her head. *Just smile*, she told herself.

"No? Why not? We have handsome men. More than one, I'd say."

Maud came through the door and slipped over to the bed on the other side of Beatrice. Annabel realized she hadn't seen either of them after supper, and fleetingly wondered where they could have been.

"Eh, Maud, you met the new girl?" Beatrice flicked her head around to Annabel again, her pale brown hair clinging to her neck. "What was your name again?"

"Annabel."

"Of course I know her." Maud's voice sounded harsh and cross. "She's from my village, isn't she? Are you addled, or just simple?"

A couple of guffaws were joined by *oooh*s from several points in the large room.

Beatrice stared back at Maud. "So you're the smart one? I suppose you already know her life's story, then."

"Of course." Aiming her eyes at the ceiling, Maud went on. "Her father died three years ago of the pestilence. He was once a rich merchant, but he lost all his money and ships. She and her two precious brothers were never made to do their share of the boon works or harvest work, so when Lord le Wyse came, the jury told her mother she had to send one of her children to work for him. Since Annabel's two brothers are too lazy to soil their soft, white hands, Annabel had to do it. What of it?" Maud threw herself onto her bed and turned her back on Beatrice.

"Well, if I ever need information, I'll certainly know who's full of it." Beatrice casually strode over to the candle nearest her and blew it out. On the way back, Beatrice whispered to Annabel, "So you're the one whose ma got you sent away from kith and kin."

"I suppose you could say that," Annabel whispered back. She squeezed her eyes shut, hoping the other girls were ready to go to sleep. She tried to pray, but tears came before any thoughts were able to congeal into words. She kept her eyes closed, hoping anyone who looked at her would think she was asleep. Someone blew out the rest of the candles and the lamp and plunged the room into darkness.

God, why have you put me here? Do you truly care? If only she had a Bible, she would be able to find guidance. She had dreamed of becoming a nun because as a nun she believed she would be allowed access to a Bible. Not only that, but in a nunnery she wouldn't have to be around Bailiff Tom ever again. But unless God gave her a miracle, she'd never be a nun.

She reached down from her low bed and fumbled in her bag. She fished out her prayer beads and small cross, clasped them to her chest, and felt a measure of peace. Praying for sleep, she closed her eyes and blocked out the shadowy figures of the other maidservants.

The maid in the bed beside her, a villein's daughter from Glynval, whispered loudly, "So what happened to our lord to cause him to be maimed?"

An unfamiliar voice answered, "I know that story well. When he was sixteen he came to the aid of a servant girl who was being attacked by a wolf."

"A servant girl? Truly?"

"He fought off the animal. Mistress Eustacia's husband shot the wolf through the neck with an arrow, but not before it had clawed out the lord's eye and mangled his hand."

Annabel's chest ached at her lord's fate.

"Some say he's part wolf now, that he prowls the woods at night."

Several low hoots and a couple of gasps went round.

"Some say they've seen him."

"Could be," a voice chimed in.

More offensive comments, punctuated by laughs, swept through the sleeping quarters.

"But what of his scars?" Beatrice's shrill voice rose about the laughter. "Aren't you curious to see how extensive" — she lingered over the word *extensive* — "they are?"

Laughter echoed throughout the large room, and Annabel pressed her hands over her ears to keep out their banter as they discussed the possibilities.

How could they speak so of their lord, and he only one floor above them?

She could take no more of their talk. And besides that, she didn't think she could fall asleep until she visited the privy. Annabel quietly slipped from her bed, and after putting her dress back on, hurried across the room and out the door. She shut it behind her with a sigh of relief at escaping the group's notice.

The dark silhouette of trees surrounded her, alongside the manor house and a few outbuildings illuminated by the moon. Standing still to listen, she heard only the faintest rustling sounds around her. She slipped her hand into her pocket and felt her knife.

She turned and rushed through the trees, down the newly worn path to the women's privy. Holding her breath as she hurried, almost running, her gaze darted around in search of any perceptible movement. She made it to the small wooden building and shut herself inside.

When she came out of the privy, she looked around again. Nothing moved and there were no ominous sounds, only a frog croaking in the distance. She began walking back along the path, wrapping her arms around herself, feeling the cool night air on her face.

Annabel dreaded going back into the undercroft with the other maids. But not wanting to be caught outside alone by anyone — especially the bailiff — she walked steadily toward the manor house.

She then noticed someone coming through the trees — not along the path toward her, but far to her right. She froze. The form was too tall to be any woman she knew. Had he seen her? Annabel ducked behind a large oak and watched.

The figure wandered among the trees, veering away from her into the thick of the forest. She was fairly certain now that the figure was Lord le Wyse, based on his height and his build. She started to sidle quietly away, hoping he wouldn't hear or see her. Then he fell to his knees on the ground.

Is he hurt? Does he need help? Perhaps she should go get Mistress Eustacia.

Before she could rush away, he bent forward and moaned as though from deep inside. The sound grew, raw and wrenching, until it became a howl. Then he bowed lower and was still.

Was he sick? Somehow she sensed his pain was not physical. She watched and listened, but he didn't move.

The silence seemed to weigh on her shoulders. She wanted to get away before her lord saw her, as he clearly wished to be alone, but she was afraid of making a noise and drawing his attention.

Her legs were beginning to cramp with fatigue, impelling her to take a step toward the manor house. Her foot landed on a twig and it snapped with a loud crack.

She stopped and held her breath, watching Lord le Wyse's bent body. After several frozen minutes, she tried again. When she stepped back onto the path, this time her footfall made no sound. She walked carefully until she reached the clearing and the manor house. Darting inside the undercroft, she hurried to her bed.

The room was quiet except for the heavy breathing of sleep. Annabel got undressed and crawled under her sheets. But when she closed her eyes, Lord le Wyse's anguished body posture and groans haunted her. *What caused him such pain?*

As she pondered her lord's actions, a loneliness settled over her as a burden in her chest. Even though she was in a room full of people, an occurrence she had rarely ever experienced before, she had never felt so alone. She tried not to think about how hurt she felt by her mother's and brothers' treatment of her. She pushed the thoughts away, but they stubbornly returned, until the tears streamed from her eyes and she was hard-pressed to keep silent.

The next morning the clouds hung low, threatening rain, as Annabel carried a bucket of water into the kitchen, setting it down beside the stone hearth. Mistress Eustacia gave her a sharp look.

"Are you well? Your eyes are puffed up as though bees have stung you."

"I am well, Mistress." Annabel shook her head and turned her face away, not wishing to confess the true cause of her puffy eyes.

After last night, she was startled to see Lord le Wyse at the head of the table, his usual place. He seemed in a wretched temper throughout the morning meal, however, grunting or snapping at anyone who spoke to him. His hair was brushed back off his forehead and he looked haggard, his pallor heightened by the dark circles under his eyes.

Terrified of drawing his wrath, she filled his cup, her hand trembling lest she should spill anything upon him. Mercifully, he ignored her, and she accomplished the task and moved on. Throughout the meal, however, she found herself glancing in his direction, but he showed no sign that he had seen her the night before.

After the maidservants, carpenters, and stone masons had broken their fast, they all dispersed to their various tasks. Annabel headed toward her mistress.

The older woman sighed heavily and wiped her face with her apron. "I'm off to the kitchen to prepare the midday victuals. Annabel, I need you to set to rights the upper hall. Sweep and strew new rushes and straw—that's a good lass."

The upper hall was now completely deserted. Annabel went to work ridding the room of the old rushes that had lost their freshness, as well as the dirt tracked in by all the workers coming in for their meals. She cleaned the entire room except for the screened-off section where Lord le Wyse slept.

She hesitated. Should she find Mistress Eustacia and ask if she was allowed to clean behind his screen, in her lord's sleeping quarters? She would waste time going out to the kitchen to speak with her, and it seemed too trivial for that. Besides, she wanted to show Eustacia she was competent and eager to do a thorough job. Lord le Wyse was outside supervising the building work; he could be gone for hours, or he could come back at any time. What would he say if he caught her in his private area? Annabel glanced at the door and shook her head. Surely she would hear the door open and could scurry away before he saw her.

Resolute, Annabel rounded the corner of the screen. She swept around the bed and tried not to look at anything. She intended to simply finish her sweeping and move on, but her gaze was arrested by three painted pictures that were propped against the wall. They were similar enough that she guessed they were all created by the same artist. She continued with her sweeping and tried to stare down at the floor, but her eyes kept flitting to the paintings. Finally she stopped her work and bent to examine them.

The first illumination depicted a dead woman lying on a wooden bier. Around her stood many people, but they were all looking away from her, at a baby lying on a similar, smaller bier. The child was swaddled and its eyes were closed, its tiny fists resting against its chest.

The next one portrayed a group of skeletons smiling maniacally, holding up tankards as if in a toast. Behind the skeletons stood several people bent over and weeping into their hands.

Annabel ached for the person who had painted such a scene. The artist's hurt and sorrow showed in each character, each color choice, each line. The pain-filled paintings brought to mind what she had seen last night in the forest—Lord le Wyse bent over, moaning in anguish. Perhaps these paintings held the answer to the mystery of why he was in so much agony.

The third picture was a wolf snarling at a young woman who, from her plain, ragged dress, was a poor villager or servant.

A young, dark-haired man stood between her and the wolf with an upraised arm, bracing for the wolf's attack.

Annabel leaned closer. This last image was somehow familiar, and she gasped as she remembered the story the maidens from Lincoln had told the night before about the wolf attack causing Lord le Wyse's scars.

The sound of footsteps made her realize someone else had entered the room and was walking toward her. She'd been so engrossed in the paintings, she'd barely noticed.

"What are you doing here?" a voice rasped behind her.

Annabel spun around. Her heart leapt into her throat at the fierceness of Lord le Wyse's tone. His eye was rimmed in red and his jaw muscles twitched as he clenched his teeth. Would he strike her? She shrank back.

"Answer me!" he commanded. "What are you doing?" His dark eye flashed as his words rumbled from deep in his chest. "No one is allowed behind this screen. *No one.* Do you understand?"

She opened her mouth to answer him, but no sound came out. "Go."

"Forgive me, I didn't know," she mumbled as she stumbled away from him and out of his reach, the broom still clutched in her hand.

As she darted past, she glanced up at his face. A flicker of some inscrutable but intense emotion passed over his features.

She hurried to the corner of the room where she'd left her basket of fresh rushes. Should she leave? Lord le Wyse's presence in the room was so unnerving, she could hardly breathe.

She snatched up the basket. What else could she do but go on with her work? She grabbed a handful of straw and dried lilac and clumsily strewed the prickly stalks on the flagstones.

Footfalls echoed in the sparsely furnished room. She glanced over her shoulder as Lord le Wyse's broad back disappeared through the entry and he shut the door behind him.

Annabel leaned against the cold stone wall. She should never have gone into his sleeping area, should never have had the audacity to examine his private things, those paintings. The memory of his angry face looming over her felt forever embedded in her mind. His lip curled and she saw the flash of white teeth and the rage in his eye.

Would she be punished? She'd wanted only to do her duty and avoid Lord le Wyse. Instead she'd enraged him, the last thing she ever wanted to do.

Chapter
5

Annabel retreated to the hot kitchen as the rain sprinkled her head. Sitting as far as she could from the huge fireplace and the pungent smell of two pigs roasting on a spit, she and Mistress Eustacia chopped beans and leeks and cabbage. Eustacia commented on how much nicer things would be once the lord's new home was finished. Annabel murmured a reply, then listened to the rain pattering on the roof and against the shuttered windows.

Lord le Wyse burst through the door.

A puddle formed around his feet, his beard dripped, and his dark hair was plastered to his forehead and temples. His fine linen shirt, alarmingly transparent, clung to his shoulders and arms, revealing muscular upper arms and shoulders.

His eye locked with Annabel's and she glanced away, uncomfortable with seeing him again, especially in such a disheveled state. She looked down at the cabbage then chanced another glimpse.

He was still looking at her. Her heart thumped painfully against her chest as his eyebrows drew together and his lips parted. What would he say? Would he tell Mistress Eustacia that she'd snooped in his sleeping area when she was supposed to be cleaning? Would her mistress regret making Annabel her helper, thinking her too nosy to be trusted?

But by the look on his face, she actually wondered if he would tell her he was sorry for yelling at her earlier. That was foolish thinking, of course. Lords didn't apologize to servants.

She ducked her head, trying to concentrate on the cabbage, thankful for the dim light in her corner of the room.

"My lord!" Mistress Eustacia fussed anxiously. "You must get out of those wet things at once. You'll be sick, perhaps with some deadly fever, and then what will become of the rest of us, says I?"

"Dry clothes ... Precisely why I'm here."

"In your trunk—oh, nay, saints have mercy, your shirts are all here." Eustacia jumped up, spilling beans and leeks onto the floor. Annabel immediately dropped to her knees to pick them up.

"I shall iron one this minute, this minute, I shall." Mistress Eustacia went to the basket of clothing she had taken in off the line the day before.

As soon as Eustacia turned, Lord le Wyse backed out the door and was gone.

Eustacia snatched a cloth and used it to take the heavy iron from where it was warming in front of the fire. She ironed furiously, and in a few moments was done. She held up the shirt. "Go take this to Lord le Wyse."

"Me?" Annabel croaked.

"Of course. I'll wrap it in this sheet so it won't get wet. But be careful you hold it gently. No wrinkles. He's particular about his clothes, he is."

Annabel stared at the shirt Eustacia was holding out to her. How would Lord le Wyse react when she brought it to him? Would he be angry, thinking she was trying to invade his privacy again? Worse yet, would he be undressed?

Mistress Eustacia said, "Don't worry. He frightens most people, but the master would never harm you." She reached out and patted Annabel's cheek with her work-roughened fingertips.

Hating that her fear must have shown on her face, and not wanting Mistress Eustacia to think she was like "most people," she took the piece of clothing and hurried out into the rain.

She ran across the yard and up the slippery steps of the manor house, holding the shirt close to keep it from getting wet.

She knocked on the door then opened it, trying to steady her breathing. "My lord?"

Annabel closed the door behind her. Her eyes adapted slowly to the dim light.

"I am here." His muffled voice came from behind the screen.

Detecting no anger in his voice, she pressed on. "Mistress Eustacia sent me with your shirt. Where would you prefer me to put it?" She panted, feeling breathless after stringing so many words together in his presence.

"Bring it to me." He thrust out his hand around the side of the screen.

Annabel crossed the room, unwrapping the garment as she went. Standing as far away from the screen as possible, she stretched her arm out and placed the shirt in his open hand. It disappeared behind the screen.

Instead of leaving, she decided this was her opportunity to apologize for being in his screened-off quarters. She began to speak before she could change her mind.

"Lord le Wyse, please forgive me for this morning. I would never invade your privacy. I know I did just that, and I'm very sorry I did. I didn't know I wasn't supposed to clean behind your screen. No one told me." She felt like someone running down a steep hill, unable to stop or slow down. "I tried not to look at your illuminations, I truly did, but they were so fascinating. I didn't intend to invade your privacy, and I'm sorry, and I will never do it again. Please forgive me."

She felt a small measure of relief that she'd explained her actions and asked forgiveness. She turned and started to walk back across the room.

"Annabel."

His commanding tone made her heart skip a beat. She turned to face him as he stepped from behind the screen. He was fully dressed, *praise God*, his hair still wet and clinging to his temples.

"You should not have gone behind my screen. I forbid it."

"Of course, my lord." She bowed her head, hoping to appear meek.

"I suppose you think my behavior this morning to be …
beastly." He glared at her, as if daring her to smile.

"Nay, of course not, my lord."

"You will mention my paintings to no one." His voice was
flat, quiet.

"As you wish, my lord."

"They belong to me, and they are no one's concern but my own."

"Of course, my lord. I never meant to pry. I am most
sincerely sorry, and I shall not tell anyone of your paintings."
Feeling a bit mischievous, and on a whim, she couldn't help adding, "Even though they are very well done. They must have taken
you a long time to paint."

His one eye narrowed at her and his jaw twitched, as though
he was grinding his teeth. He opened his mouth to speak, but
at that moment two maidens burst through the door, squealing
about being wet and muddy.

An angry scowl further darkened his face as he focused on
the two maidens. "You aren't supposed to be here now. Get out."
His voice boomed across the spacious hall.

The young women's eyes grew wide, and they bumped into
each other, stumbling on each other's hems in their scramble to
get back out the door.

Annabel hurried across the room and followed them out.

❦

Ranulf shook his head like a dog shaking rain from his fur.

The girl thought she was clever, no doubt, but he felt almost
as if she had peered into the deep, ugly corners of his soul. Those
paintings weren't meant for anyone's eyes but his own. In fact, he
often toyed with the idea of burning them.

Women. They were all false. Disloyal to the core. And the
beautiful ones were the worst. This one—Annabel—was from
a family that had refused to do their share of the harvest work for
years, and still clung to their vanity and pride though they had
nothing but a stone house. He didn't trust the girl for a moment.
The fact that her eyes were a vivid blue, her lips perfectly formed,

and her features feminine and alluring, made him trust her even less. And now Eustacia had elevated her to a kitchen assistant, her right-hand girl.

He snorted in disgust. He had come here to forget; to forget women, to forget his past, and to enjoy the quiet, soothing life of the country. But there was no joy for him, a wounded beast of a man. He'd dreamed of *her* again last night, almost as soon as he fell asleep, the wife who had betrayed him. Every time he dreamed of her he ended up wandering through the woods, trying to outpace his mind and find peace. He was haunted, without hope of breaking free from his torturous memories.

No matter how far he ran.

"My father is here!" Adam grabbed Annabel's hand, pulling her toward the sheepish Gilbert Carpenter. "He wants to meet you."

Stifling a groan, she allowed Adam to pull her to the other side of the upper hall, where his master-mason father stood watching them with a shy half smile. *O God, save me from this!* Determined not to get anyone's hopes up, Annabel set her jaw. She would be honest and firm and set the man straight right off.

But she had to do it without hurting Adam's feelings.

Whatever could she say?

Gilbert Carpenter nodded. "Good evening, miss." The master mason stood smiling at her, a faint blush creeping into his cheeks as he crushed a piece of cloth in his hands, working it over as if he were wringing laundry.

"Father, this is Annabel. She's very pretty, isn't she?"

The man cleared his throat, his ears taking on the same crimson glow. "Yes, Adam. Miss Annabel, I wonder if you would take a walk with me—only in the courtyard."

"Um, well, I—" She cast about in her mind for a good excuse to say no.

"I promise I won't bite." His smile was genuine, and his stance and voice were so nonthreatening that she found herself smiling back.

"I cannot be away from my work very long."

"We won't be gone long," he assured her. "I asked Lord le Wyse for his permission to take a walk with you."

Annabel's smile wavered, and she saw Lord le Wyse's glare as he watched them from where he stood against the wall. What was he thinking when he looked at her that way? She felt sick.

"Shall we go?" Gilbert looked down at her, his smile making him look a bit foolish.

Annabel hurried out. She made it to the bottom of the manor house steps and began walking around the perimeter of the court-yard, forcing Mr. Carpenter to hurry and catch up with her.

They talked about the lack of rain, the heat, and the bugs that were eating the wheat, before he abruptly changed the topic.

"You like children, do you?" He chanced a quick glance at her.

"Well ... yes." *Will he now tell me that he's searching for a mother for Adam? Will he be that blunt?* Surely he wouldn't hint that he wants more children.

"I hoped I would have many children, six or seven at least, but my wife was rather sickly, and then she died three years ago of the pestilence."

Yes he would. God, save me. "That is very sad."

Their conversation moved to the progress of the lord's new house and the journey from Lincoln to Glynval before Annabel told him how she'd come to be at the manor house in Lord le Wyse's service. She was embarrassed to admit the reason but wanted him to know the truth, since someone was sure to tell him eventually. As they talked, she caught several people staring at them, making her feel even more uncomfortable.

After a few minutes, Gilbert turned to her, his neck and ears glowing red. "I know you don't know me at all, Miss Annabel, but Adam likes you, so you must be a kind person. Therefore I'd be pleased if you would begin to consider me as a possible husband."

He stood waiting for her answer. Annabel felt her own cheeks glowing. *Could I imagine myself married to this man?* She did her best to picture it in her mind. All she could think was that his nails were dirty and his clothes were baggy, although she knew those things didn't matter. What mattered was his character, whether he was kind and would be a good husband to her.

"I-I'm very flattered and honored," she began, then realized she wasn't sure if that was the truth. "I—" She looked up at him and shrugged apologetically. "I don't know."

He nodded. "That's fair enough. Perhaps we can talk more another day."

Adam came running toward them and grabbed Annabel's hand. "My father knows how to sing five songs. He learned me all of them when I was only six years old. Do you want to hear them?"

She laughed and squeezed his hand. Her laugh sounded nervous and high-pitched.

"Another time, Adam," his father said, grabbing him affectionately by the neck. "Miss Annabel has work to do inside the manor house now."

"Thank you." She smiled, bobbed a quick curtsy, and fled from them, her face tingling with a self-conscious blush.

Like a bird escaping its cage, she flew up the manor house steps into the upper room and over to Mistress Eustacia's side, and began helping her set the trenchers on the table for the evening meal.

She'd heard the other maids talking about Gilbert Carpenter and supposed they were right—he was handsome, in a boyish sort of way. But the thought of him holding her hand, or hugging or kissing her, just made her feel ill.

❦

The next day Annabel dreaded the evening meal. Mealtimes were always torture because of having to see Bailiff Tom. Every time she encountered him, her mind would go back to his slobbering lips sliding over her face and the disgusting things he'd said he was going to do. She hated being afraid of him, but she couldn't seem to stop. The knife in her pocket contributed very little to her peace of mind.

She had been able to force down only a few bites at the midday meal, and though she was hungry, her stomach churned dangerously at the thought of being at the table with the rest of the manor house workers and builders. It was awkward enough seeing Adam and his father again. Thank goodness Gilbert had been too busy to approach her, although she couldn't believe Adam would give up so easily.

But most of all, she dreaded seeing the bailiff, his horrible, leering face with his disgusting, pointy nose and stubby chin. Thankfully, the bailiff's duties kept him out of doors and away from the manor house, supervising the fieldwork and making sure the crops were properly harvested and stored and that the manor was stocked with all the supplies it needed.

She clenched her teeth just thinking about him, wishing she could frighten him the way he frightened her. May God forgive her, but she hated the man, hated the power he held over her through her own fear.

She consciously strove to never be alone, to stay with Mistress Eustacia or one of the other maids, but she was too embarrassed to ask someone to go with her to the privy, and occasionally Eustacia left her alone in the kitchen or the upper floor of the manor house.

But what good was it doing her to cower in Bailiff Tom's presence? It only increased her anger and dread of him and apparently did naught to deter his interest in her. She'd even been plagued with him lingering outside the kitchen—thus far she had been able to find ways to busy herself until he left, or have Eustacia speak to him so she could avoid his lecherous gaze. What right did he have to sneer at her?

She would try a new tactic. She would show him what a contemptible creature she thought him to be, and then maybe he would stop leering at her in front of everyone. He would see, reflected in her face, what she thought of him.

While she set the trenchers on the table and filled the goblets with ale, the laborers and servants began to filter into the room. Instead of ignoring Bailiff Tom as she normally would—

afraid of making eye contact with him—Annabel raised her head and purposely searched for him. She quickly caught him staring at her from across the room, a bold look in his tiny, black, ratlike eyes.

She set her jaw and glared back, giving him her coldest, most contemptuous look. She converted every ounce of fear within her into anger and hatred, fervently hoping he could read her thoughts as she pronounced him the most repulsive creature on two legs.

The bailiff stared back for a moment. His thin lips spread with a slow grin, as though pleased she was looking at him.

Was he blind? He wasn't supposed to be pleased. She curled her lip and narrowed her eyes, willing him to read derision and hatred in her eyes. Finally, a befuddled look came over his features, and he looked away.

Annabel's chest swelled with triumph. She'd forced him to look away! But she prepared herself to repeat her projected daggers of contempt several times, if necessary, during the evening meal.

A small prickling of guilt niggled at her conscience. Of course, she'd heard the priest say many times that hatred was of the devil, but what else could she do? Perhaps if she were able to read the Bible, the book would provide a better way to deal with the prurient bailiff.

Her desire for a Bible welled up inside her as she continued filling the goblets with ale. Was it wrong to want to read the Holy Writ? Many people would probably frown upon her desire. A woman wasn't expected to have ambitions about increasing her knowledge. And wasn't she supposed to submit herself to the priest's instruction? Only priests and monks and others who had taken holy vows were encouraged to read the Bible.

She pushed the frustrating questions away. She had to gather her defenses and be prepared to deal with the bailiff whenever she caught him staring.

As soon as Annabel and the other maids finished serving the food, Lord le Wyse strode in. Everyone else stood behind the benches and waited for him to seat himself at the head of the table before they took their own seats. She ended up beside Beatrice. This time, instead of planting himself directly opposite her, the bailiff sat a few spaces away. Ready with her glare, she caught him staring at her and pretended her eyes were an invisible dagger. Fervently she ran him through, making him look away again.

Annabel ate heartily of the roast goose and pudding on her stale trencher, smiling inwardly at her victory. She had wiped the smug leer from her enemy's face without having to speak a single empty threat.

An elbow in her ribs caused her to jump and turn to Beatrice.

"What do you think of Gilbert Carpenter?" Beatrice whispered. "Handsome, is he not?"

Annabel hesitated to say. "Do you think he is?"

"I would marry him." Beatrice pursed her lips in what was almost a smile.

"Forget him," Maud said from the other side of Beatrice. "His little boy is set on him marrying Annabel. Looks like you should have spent a little time with the son instead of chasing the father."

"Who says I've been chasing the father?" Beatrice straightened her shoulders and glared at her fellow dairymaid. Then she smiled a slow, sneaky grin. "Besides, he isn't the most handsome man in the room."

Maud squinted. "Who is, then?"

Beatrice glanced sideways at Annabel and winked. "I'll tell you tonight when we all retire to bed."

Annabel stared at the two girls. Beatrice actually wanted to confide in her? She only hoped they didn't ask her who she thought was handsomest. The sermons of Sir Matefrid, the village priest, were another reason she had never been interested in attracting men or pursuing marriage. He made it sound as if women were fiends of hell, luring men into adultery. Annabel couldn't imagine doing such a thing, yet Bailiff Tom persisted in leering at her every chance he got. With no father to protect her, staying indifferent to men seemed safer, even if the priest's reasoning seemed askew. Why did God make men thus, preying on women to satisfy their lusts? Perhaps the answer even to that could be found in the Holy Writ.

⁕

That night, as Annabel followed the rest of the maids down the steps to their sleeping quarters in the undercroft, she saw Lord le Wyse talking in the yard with someone.

"Stephen!" How good it was to see his friendly face! Though in truth, it was too dark to see his features. It was his form she recognized.

He shifted in her direction and raised his hand in greeting, then turned back to Lord le Wyse. Annabel lingered outside the undercroft door, hoping to speak with him, her only true friend.

When they finished their conversation, Lord le Wyse strode away. Stephen began, in his twisting gait, to walk toward her.

"How are you?" Annabel reached out to clasp his hand.

He took her hand in his and gave her a smile, faint in the waning light. "I am well, as ever." He lowered his voice. "I heard about you having to come here, of your mother's indenturing you to Lord le Wyse."

"Oh, it isn't like that exactly." *Of course it is.* "I-I offered to come, to help Mother. How are my mother and brothers? Did they ... did they ask you to come inquire about me?" She bit her lip, wishing she hadn't asked the question but holding her breath for his answer.

"Nay." He winced as if he knew it hurt her.

"No matter." She smiled broadly, and her voice went up in volume and pitch in her attempt to appear cheerful. "It's good to see you, Stephen."

"Lord le Wyse commissioned me to build some furniture for him, as well as to do some carving for his new home. I'll be in charge of the woodwork — the doors and shutters, a stair railing, things like that."

Annabel felt genuine joy at the look of pride on his face.

"Oh, that's wonderful, Stephen. Your furniture is very fine, and your carving is the best I've seen." His legs' lack of strength didn't hinder his immense talent at all kinds of woodworking.

"I brought you something." He swung the cloth bag off his shoulder, reached inside, and pulled out a small bundle. "Mother sends you this — her fried pasty that you liked so much as a child."

She took the food, wrapped in a square of cloth, and tears burned her eyes. "Dear Alice." Their former servant, Stephen's mother, thought enough to send her a small message of kindness. She bit back the tears and nodded, unable to look him in the eye. After a deep breath, she was able to say, "Please tell her thank you. It was very kind of her."

"I brought you something else." He reached in again and pulled out a small wooden box. "I thought you might want someplace to put things. See? It has a lock." He took a key from his pocket and turned it in the tiny keyhole. The lid opened to reveal a space about the size of a large fist, rectangular, suitable for storing coins or other small items.

"How clever you are, Stephen. There isn't another man in Glynval with such skill. Thank you." She embraced him then stared down at the beautiful wooden box. Stephen was truly more like a brother than a friend, more her sibling than Edward and Durand.

"I'll be going now, Annabel. But I'll be nearby every day. If you need anything, you'll let me know, won't you?"

She nodded and gave him another quick hug. He turned and began to walk away.

She watched him for a moment, a thickness in her throat, then turned to join the rest of the maids and find her bed.

⁓

"Gilbert Carpenter is handsome." Beatrice made this declaration, drawing giggles and exclamations from several other maidens in the undercroft who seemed much more intent on the conversation than on getting ready for their night's repose.

Annabel tried to look as inconspicuous as possible as she quickly shed her clothes and donned her nightgown. She kept her head down and pretended not to listen.

"He's skinny enough," a buxom, rather large redhead asserted. "I could pick him up and carry him." She raised her eyebrows and smiled suggestively, causing the other maidens to hoot in glee.

Annabel hurried to crawl under the covers of her bed, praying no one would ask her what she thought.

"I would have him," Beatrice declared.

Though the other maidens laughed, no one seemed surprised by her statement.

"But his boy, Adam, has his heart set on Annabel for his ma."

All eyes turned to Annabel amid *oh*s and *ah-ha*s.

She froze, her hands clutching the sheet to her chin. She tried to sound careless. "Don't be silly. I'm not interested in Gilbert Carpenter."

"Why not?" Beatrice asked, a surprised and almost angry look on her face. "He's an eligible, free man, and he could get you out of here, let you be a free woman again—and your future children too. You'd be sleeping in your own bed, keeping your man warm every night."

A few hoots went round.

Of course, it must seem to everyone that the master mason would be an excellent catch for an indentured servant like Annabel. But how could she explain that their crude idea of love didn't seem satisfying, and a good-looking husband wasn't all she wanted in life?

Annabel shrugged and tried to look apologetic. *Please let them forget about me and change the subject of conversation.*

Maud prodded, "Someone else catch your fancy, then?"

She'd been accused of thinking she was too good for Glynval men. She was tired of their teasing, but she didn't want to lie. "Not exactly."

Maud stared hard at her, almost squinting. "Surely not that cripple I saw you talking to."

Annabel sat up, glaring back at Maud's long face. She was about to retort that he was a furniture maker, not a cripple. But Beatrice broke in, "You have something against cripples?" She seemed half in jest and half cross.

"Why? Are you partial to cripples?" Maud challenged.

"Perhaps." Beatrice smiled broadly. "Consider Lord le Wyse. He's the man I think is the handsomest of all."

This brought loud exclamations from the other girls. Some thought she was crazy, others agreed.

"But the lord's not a cripple," a Lincoln girl put in stoutly. "His hand is a bit maimed, but there's nothing wrong with his legs."

"How do you know?" Beatrice asked suggestively, making the girls laugh. "If I could have any man I wanted, I'd choose Lord le Wyse. Who's afraid of a little eye patch, a lame hand, and a few scars? He's rich as the king of England and twice as tall." Her voice turned smooth and silky. "We'd have beautiful, rich children." Beatrice ended with a high-pitched cackle.

The room erupted into a bedlam of squeals, taunts, and laughter.

Annabel sank down into the straw mattress as anger welled up inside her. Lord le Wyse was rude, had a bad temper, and seemed to especially dislike her. Still, she didn't like the way they were disrespecting their lord. If Lord le Wyse heard them talking so, what would he do? His anger would stop their laughter and send them running for cover.

"Lord le Wyse wouldn't let you anywhere near him, you freckle-faced goat of a girl."

The tone of disdain in Maud's voice made Annabel cringe. Several *Ooohs* and *oh*s went through the crowd. She scrunched down even lower, wondering if Beatrice would laugh about the insult or get angry. Her answer came when Beatrice leaned forward, clenching her fists. "I'd rather be a goat than a donkey's behind. Why are you wearing your tail on your head?"

Maud's limp brown hair did somewhat resemble a tail, and the way her eyelids drooped over wide-set eyes in her long face did even more to evoke the face of a donkey.

Both girls stepped forward, quickly closing the gap between them. A few girls screamed and scrambled away, while others yelled, "Hit her!" "Fight!" and "Don't let her talk to you like that!"

A whistle cut through the chaos, so loud and shrill it made Annabel cover her ears.

All voices ceased. Every eye faced the door where Mistress Eustacia stood with her hands on her hips, her face flushed and her jaw set.

She glared for a long moment at Maud and Beatrice then allowed her fierce gaze to rove around the room. "Fighting is reason enough for dismissal or punishment."

Dismissal for paid workers, some form of punishment for indentured servants like Annabel.

Mistress Eustacia went on in a hoarse voice that, though quiet, reverberated off the stone walls. "Shocked at your behavior, I am. You sound like a bunch of half-drunk men with your talk. Have you no shame, speaking of your lord that way?"

Maud looked down at her hands, but Beatrice narrowed her eyes and turned her head to the side, staring defiantly at the wall.

"Some one of you, a few minutes ago, when your lord and master was getting ready for bed, shamelessly came and tried to tempt him."

Annabel closed her eyes, her stomach sinking.

"Who did this? Who knows?"

Silence.

"Tell me now or tell me later, but when I find out who it was, that maid will be punished."

A few murmurs of "Yes, Mistress" came from the girls.

"Now every last one of you, to bed. Take a strap to all of you, I will." Mistress Eustacia's face glowed red and her large bosom heaved, as though from physical exertion. "It would serve you all a good lesson if the master turns you out and hires from the village girls of Glynval. And tomorrow I will expect you all to work two extra hours" — a few soft groans echoed around the room — "for this misbehavior and disrespect for your own lord. For shame." She leaned over and blew out the small torch in the iron sconce nearest the door. The maids blew out the remaining candles while Mistress Eustacia watched, hands on her hips. "To bed." She turned and walked out, slamming the door behind her.

After a few moments of silence, Annabel heard soft weeping. "What are you crying for?" a voice whispered loudly.

From the direction of the crying came, "What if she tells Lord le Wyse what we were saying? Aren't you afraid of what he'll do to us?"

Instead of reassurances, there was an uneasy silence. Several moments passed and the crying started up again. This time, no one said a thing.

⸎

Ranulf walked into the manor house and saw that it was empty.

No, not empty. A woman stood in the corner, her back to him. She wore a beautiful silk dress of deep red, her hair covered by a gold-embroidered coif.

His feet moved slowly, as if weighed down, as he was compelled to go to her.

She turned and Ranulf saw her face. "Guinevere."

A baby rested in her arms, and her lips were set in that familiar, cold smile. She held the baby out toward him, but he realized the infant was strangely pale, even gray. Dead.

Guinevere began to laugh, a sinister sound that sent a chill down his back. She laughed as though mocking him, a noise he'd heard often. She threw the baby at him. He tried to catch the child, but his arms wouldn't move fast enough. But instead of falling to the ground, the baby disintegrated into dust and blew out the open window.

His wife continued to laugh at him. Then she sneered. "No one could ever love you. Look at you. You're *hideous*." She lunged toward him, her silk dress glimmering in the sunlight that streamed through the window. Her hands wrapped around his neck and she began choking him, pressing hard against his throat. He couldn't breathe, and he couldn't seem to lift his hands to fight her. He was suffocating, hurting, dying.

Ranulf opened his eyes and gasped. His own hand was at his throat, and he realized he'd been dreaming.

He swallowed, his throat sore, as if Guinevere had truly been choking him. He could see his wife's eyes as she attacked him, bloody and animallike, and he shuddered.

Will I ever be free from this nightmare? Free from the hold she has over me? Tears squeezed from the corners of his eyes. He flung them away angrily. Even in death, she had the power to make him feel like he was repulsive.

Chapter 6

When Sunday came, Annabel put on her best dress and tied her white-linen covering around her hair. With the rest of the servants, she headed down the lane toward the square tower of the old stone church, just visible over the trees. Each member of the lord's household was required to attend Mass every Sunday, unless they could prove, or successfully feign, sickness.

The small parish church was the most noteworthy building in Glynval, but was naught in comparison to the abbey churches and cathedrals in and around London. Nevertheless, the maidens all grew quiet as they entered the high-ceilinged nave, genuflected, and crossed themselves. Then they each found a spot to kneel.

As Annabel knelt to pray, she pictured herself in St. Paul's Cathedral, with its beautiful stained glass windows depicting various biblical stories. She almost believed she was there—until she opened her eyes and beheld the stark gray walls and the one murky mural over the chancel arch, featuring the devil and his demons casting people into hellfire.

The bells began to ring and Annabel bowed her head and prayed silently, thanking God for the day's respite from work, for Mistress Eustacia's kindness to her, and for Lord le Wyse not punishing her for breaching his privacy. She hoped from now on she could keep her distance from him and remain unnoticed in the large crowd of servants.

The parish priest, Sir Matefrid, plodded down the aisle, a crucifix in one hand, his censer in the other. He wore a long velvet robe, the same one he wore every Sunday, with a chain around his neck that hung so low the attached crucifix rested on his protruding belly. His face bore no wrinkles and very little gray sprinkled his brown hair, but the way he stooped gave him the appearance of a much older man.

Annabel's heart beat faster as she watched him, thinking of the question she would to put to him after Mass. *O Father God, please let him say yes.*

Sir Matefrid had barely reached the front of the sanctuary when Lord le Wyse strode in, bowed toward the altar, and, without looking up, took his place with the rest of the kneelers just to Annabel's left. Unable to curb her curiosity, her eyes devoured his richly embroidered waistcoat, trimmed in crimson velvet, and his crisp white sleeves. The ornate clothing did not surprise her, but his behavior once he was kneeling did. He clasped his hands, his eyes shut, his lips moving silently in prayer. His brow furrowed in concentration as he leaned forward, looking truly humble.

Glancing around, Annabel saw nearly everyone she knew, including Stephen, who knelt beside his mother. Adam stood, fidgeting restlessly beside his father, while Gilbert talked with one of the masonry workers. Margery knelt nearby, but her much-older husband, the miller, was not beside her, as he rarely ever graced the small church with his presence. Margery was whispering intently with two other maidens. Annabel watched them for a moment as they hid a laugh behind a hand or yawned and looked around.

Hardly anyone, besides Lord le Wyse, even pretended to pray.

The priest took his place before the altar and the boys of the choir began to sing a plainsong hymn in Latin. Thanks to her father's teaching, she was able to translate the words in her head, in spite of the choirboys' bad pronunciation.

> O come, O come, Emmanuel,
> And ransom captive Israel,

That mourns in lonely exile here
Until the Son of God appear.

Rejoice! Rejoice! Emmanuel
Shall come to thee, O Israel.

Annabel thought the chorus rather ironic, since no one looked the least like they were actually rejoicing. Some appeared solemn, including Lord le Wyse, who stared straight ahead.

O come, thou rod of Jesse, free
Thine own from Satan's tyranny;
From depths of hell Thy people save
And give them victory o'er the grave.

Rejoice! Rejoice! Emmanuel
Shall come to thee, O Israel.

"Rejoice," the song instructed. How would everyone react if she suddenly burst into an exclamation of joy? She imagined the rest of the crowd gasping in astonishment and Sir Matefrid's face turning red with outrage, that purplish vein in his neck bulging.

But the song commanded it. Did God want her to rejoice? Was that in the Holy Scriptures? *O Father God, give me a Bible. Please let Sir Matefrid say yes.*

As the boys' choir ended their singing, the paunchy, middle-aged priest began to speak. They all stood. Rather than becoming respectfully silent, however, the crowd of a hundred or so began chatting among themselves. A baby cried lustily, drowning out the priest's words for several moments. A brother and sister a few feet in front of Annabel began to fight, punctuating the sermon with squeals of anger before the mother clouted them both, her blows echoing through the high-arcing nave.

Sir Matefrid didn't seem to notice these distractions. He began in the usual way, making the point that women were evil, enticing men to sin with their wily feminine ways. It was the same way he began all of his sermons.

Annabel kept her eyes on the floor so no one would see the anger and contempt that coursed through her and probably showed in her eyes. Was this how the Bible read? Surely not. Surely it did not revile and condemn in such a manner. She wanted to know. She *had* to know.

He went on, as always, to denounce unmarried men — forgetting that he was one himself? — speaking of their passions and lusts, of how they only sought to satisfy their flesh.

She was glad when he finished his sermon and began the Eucharist. He spoke in Latin, which Annabel understood easily, but she knew the rest of the congregation did not know what the priest was saying. Glancing around, she noticed that the few people who were not talking to their neighbor had a glazed look in their eyes.

She chided herself for her own wandering mind and closed her eyes to better concentrate, to imagine the Christ on the cross, dying for her sins.

After Holy Communion, Lord le Wyse turned and strode out the door as quickly as he'd entered. The rest of the parishioners began to file out in a more leisurely manner, continuing the same conversations they'd engaged in throughout the service. She stood still, hoping no one would notice her in the shadows about the wall. She watched the priest as he puttered around, putting away the elements of the Eucharist and speaking with the boys of the choir and altar.

Finally, after everyone else had exited the building, she scurried forward to catch Sir Matefrid before he quitted the sanctuary.

"Yes?" He stared at her, a frown pulling down the corners of his mouth.

Her heart fluttered up to her throat and her face flushed hot, but her intense desire overrode her nervousness. She curtsied as her mother had taught her to do before a man of rank, and when she glanced up at him was careful not to look him in the eye, since she knew he found this disrespectful. "Sir Matefrid, sir, I wish to know what God has said in the Holy Writ. If you would but loan me your Bible, I will swear an oath not to harm it and to return it as soon as you wish. Will you allow me to borrow this book?" She lowered her head, awaiting his reply.

"Young woman."

She glanced up again. He raised his eyebrows, but her momentary hope was crushed as he brought them down in a harsh glower.

"I cannot imagine where you picked up such a fanciful notion. That I should turn over a precious Bible to *you*." He snorted and shook his head.

"But please, you don't understand." She felt panic rise inside her. She clasped her hands and leaned toward him. "I promise my motives are pure. I only want to read it. Surely there can be naught wrong with that."

He backed away a step, his face beginning to turn red.

She realized she was staring and cast her eyes down at the stone floor.

"I am not at all sure your motives are pure. A *woman* reading the Word of God? Are you able to interpret the Scriptures? You aren't even dedicated to God. Never said your vows. Nay. You are to rely upon your priest to give you the interpretation of God's Word. I will tell you what you need to know." He gruffly cleared his throat.

What? That men and women are disgusting in their lusts and care for no one but themselves? "I wish to read it. Please." Her voice began to tremble. "Will you not allow me to come to the church, to read it here on Sundays after Mass?"

"Girl, you are impudent. Remember your place."

Annabel realized she'd balled up her fists. She should leave before this priest insulted her further and she lost her tenuous control over her frustration. But before she turned away, something prompted her to ask, "Do you have a copy of the Holy Writ?"

"Nay, as a matter of fact, I don't." He spat the words at her. "So you see, I cannot satisfy your silly whim even if I were so inclined, which I am not. You must say ten Ave's to absolve yourself of your insolence today. May your penitence be swift and sincere, or I cannot say what shall come of such ... such wicked boldness." He turned and stalked away.

Annabel felt heat creep up from deep inside. *I am not wicked.* She turned and stalked down the aisle of the church.

She should have known! A man who preached the kind of sermons he did could not even know what God's Word said. *He doesn't have a Bible.* The unfathomable words went through her mind over and over.

The man who proposed to teach her God's will did not even have a Bible.

She stopped at the door, feeling that anyone could take one look at her face and see how angry and upset she felt. She stood unmoving, her hand on her chest as she waited to get her breathing under control.

Finally, taking one last steadying breath, she pulled her white headscarf closer about her face and stepped out.

She immediately saw Lord le Wyse astride his horse several feet away, as though he was waiting for her, and looked down so as not to meet his eye. *He probably wants to make sure I stay where I belong.* She walked briskly, hoping to catch up with the rest of the servants and workers.

Then she spotted Bailiff Tom twenty feet ahead of her, standing by the side of the road with another man, watching her. He reminded her of a fox with its tongue hanging out, staring at the henhouse. Out of the corner of her eye, as she pretended to look down at the ground, Tom elbowed the man beside him and nodded at Annabel.

She moved over as she passed the two men, angry that he had the power to make her afraid.

Continuing to walk as fast as she could, she could hear Tom and his friend walking not far behind her, muttering. What were the two of them planning? She heard only snatches of their conversation: "high and haughty," "too good," "get her alone," "nothing but a—"

Horse's hooves clopped at a trot not far behind. Annabel glanced over her shoulder. Lord le Wyse was getting closer. Would he ride on ahead? If he did, she would be left behind with these two men following her.

Her heart pounded hard and fast in her throat. Lord le Wyse

closed the distance, but instead of riding ahead, he placed himself between Bailiff Tom and Annabel.

She glanced back at Lord le Wyse. When he ignored her, she turned around and continued walking.

◦⌒◦⌒◦

After escorting Annabel and the other servants home after Mass, Ranulf urged his horse into a run as he took a small path across a meadow and over a hill toward the river. Finally, he slowed the horse to a trot and patted Shadow's neck. He surveyed the undulating countryside, green and lush along the river bank, despite the lack of summer rain. The river shimmered and tripped over short, rocky falls and wound around bends and through bogs where bluebells bloomed on the banks. He couldn't have chosen a more picturesque village for his new home.

Guinevere would have hated it.

Just thinking her name sent a painful, sick feeling through his gut. But he'd learned to live with the pain, to think of it as a helpful reminder to him to never be so foolish again.

It was good to be away from the too-familiar paths and discover a new, as yet unspoiled place. If such a place existed.

Glynval was the location he had run to, an area where he intended to live at low ebb, flow with the simple rhythm of village life, breathe fresh air, and keep aloof. His peace would come from the natural beauty of the countryside, from his own independence and freedom. There would be nothing and no one to stir strong feelings of any kind.

His plan wasn't working so well.

His mind went back to the girl, the merchant's daughter—he refused to think her name—who had been forced, by him and by her lazy family, into his service. She couldn't even walk home from Sunday Mass without attracting the wrong kind of attention—but perhaps that had been her intention. Perhaps she'd allowed herself to fall behind the rest of the maids for some perverse reason.

That thought made a growl rise up in Ranulf's throat.

Even his master mason, Gilbert, was smitten with her. The bailiff certainly had an unhealthy interest.

But the girl seemed afraid of the bailiff. He would have to have a talk with Bailiff Tom and warn him to leave her alone and stop following her around, now that she had made it clear she had no wish to marry him.

Ranulf hated to think it, but the maiden haunted him too, and he of all people should know better. Her perfect features, her beautiful blue eyes, and her blonde hair waving about her shoulders ... but it was her kindness to others, her quiet nature and the way she performed her duties with meekness and without ceremony that had caught his attention.

He scowled at his foolish idiocy, noticing a woman's beauty, especially a servant's.

He remembered his anger when he'd caught her looking at his paintings behind his privacy screen. Recalled her impertinence.

But intelligence sparkled in her expression, and she was too well spoken to have been born to servanthood. Rather, she'd been born a freeman's daughter and probably had been trained to marry a free burgher or even a landed knight. Her mother was the daughter of a knight, and her father was a wealthy merchant, until fate had turned against him.

How well Ranulf knew about heartless twists of fate.

But she was indeed a servant, and he wasn't the type of lord to dwell on a servant's fairness of face and graceful movements. He resolved to cast her from his mind. Of course, he could also leave this place and find a new village. He'd already made good progress on building his new home, and people would say he'd lost his mind, but why should he care?

Ranulf didn't want to leave, but he also didn't want to let the young woman haunt him. He was haunted enough as it was. His wife, dead these three years, had also been beautiful. And she'd used her beauty like a dagger.

Beautiful women weren't to be trusted or allowed into a man's heart when that man was less than perfect. He'd learned that lesson well.

Annabel was readying the upper hall for supper when Lord le Wyse entered. He seemed to be in his usual grim mood. With the door open behind him, she once again caught sight of the sky, which had bruised blue and purple with clouds and threatened rain. The lord instructed Mistress Eustacia not to prepare anything special for him. He would eat the same simple fare as everyone else.

As the storm approached, Mistress Eustacia brought in torches and set them in the wall sconces so that they could see to eat. The final sconce was lit as the servants trickled in for their meal of bread and cheese. Annabel felt Lord le Wyse's gaze on her as she seated herself near the other end of the table. Bailiff Tom kept looking at her, and Gilbert Carpenter did as well, but she pretended not to notice them. Why did she always have to eat her food with an audience of men staring at her? It was beyond irritating.

Lord le Wyse's mood seemed to grow blacker during the meal, and he growled at a serving girl who spilled ale on the table and didn't wipe it up quickly enough.

Annabel helped Mistress Eustacia clear away the leftovers while most of the other servants remained in the hall, including Bailiff Tom and Gilbert Carpenter, who talked quietly near a corner of the room.

To keep her mind from the two men's conversation, Annabel began to speculate on what Lord le Wyse thought of the day's sermon. Was he accustomed to more uplifting messages? Did his priest back in Lincoln give more intellectual sermons?

While the servants and workers talked or went about their duties, Lord le Wyse suddenly cleared his throat, jarring Annabel from her thoughts.

Everyone became quiet as all eyes focused on him, waiting for what he would say. He looked around the room, scowling darkly—his usual expression.

"I desire reading," he declared in a loud voice. "Does anyone here know how to read?"

They all continued staring at him, not saying anything. His scowl deepened. Annabel's tongue stuck to the roof of her mouth. She would have to speak up if no one else did.

Given his wealth and station, it was almost certain Lord le Wyse knew how to read himself, but perhaps at night, in dim light, it would be difficult with only one eye.

Everyone seemed to be holding their breath. *Hadn't Lord le Wyse considered whether any of the servants he'd brought to Glynval with him knew how to read? Surely there is someone.*

Her heart beat faster as she hesitated.

His gaze came to rest on Annabel. He would find out eventually, and she didn't want to anger him. She took in a quick breath. "I can read."

Everyone turned to stare at her.

"Can you read Latin?"

"Yes, my lord." She met his eye briefly.

"Come, then," he ordered.

She walked toward him, realizing that she had just ruined her plan to keep her distance from him. He stood scowling at her until she had crossed the room and stood in front of him. Then he turned away. He dragged his own high-backed, cushioned chair nearer the fire, pulling a small table up beside it.

"Sit here."

He motioned to Mistress Eustacia. "Bring more candles." He hastened behind the screen, and amid the flurry of activity, most of the other servants hurried out the door.

She sat enveloped in his chair, clasping her hands in her lap to keep them from fidgeting. A creaking sound came from behind the lord's screen, and when he reappeared from behind it, he carried a huge tome. Her breaths became shorter as she watched him come closer, her gaze fastened on the book in his hands.

Reverently, he laid the huge book in her lap.

Her hands trembled as she stared at it. One hand fluttered down and gingerly touched the cover. She began to breathe so fast she feared she would faint.

A Holy Bible.

Tears blurred her vision as she looked up at him. "Thank you, my lord. I—" Her voice cracked and a tear slid down both cheeks. Mortified, she wiped the tears away with the corner of her apron as quickly as she could. "I'm so sorry. Forgive me."

Lord le Wyse actually owned a Bible and was allowing her to read it! She took deep breaths, working to calm herself and force back the tears. What must Lord le Wyse think of her? That she had lost her mind? Besides, she couldn't risk getting tears on the precious book.

Feeling as though she had successfully forced back the tears, she nodded her head. "I am ready now."

When he didn't say anything, she glanced up at him again. She was startled by the expression on his face. He almost looked like a different person. Gone was the scowl, and he stared back as though he were trying to see into her mind.

They were now alone in the large room, except for Mistress Eustacia, who was sitting in the corner by the window, sewing.

Finally, Lord le Wyse asked in a surprisingly quiet tone, "Why did you cry?"

She stared back at him, wondering at the change in his tone. "I have wanted to read the Bible for many years. My father promised to try to get one for me, but then he lost all his ships and his money." She added quietly, "And then he died. Just today I asked the priest if I might borrow his Bible. I begged him, in fact."

She blinked rapidly as she stared down into her lap. *Don't cry, don't cry, don't cry . . .*

"What did the priest say?"

"He said that even if he had one, he wouldn't let me read it. So you see, I cried because I am very happy." She could feel herself blushing, embarrassed at revealing so much about herself to this man who obviously didn't hold her in very high esteem.

He continued to stare, but now he was scowling at her again. She felt almost relieved that he had reverted to himself.

She didn't know how to react to the kind look that had been on his face.

"Please allow me to read for you. Where shall I begin?" She placed her hands reverently on the Holy Writ and prepared to open it.

"Anyplace, I don't care."

"Oh! I want to read it all." She clasped her hands to her chest, a giggle threatening to bubble over.

At her outburst, Lord le Wyse looked at her suspiciously, narrowing his eye. But his tone sounded almost—dare she believe it?—*gentle*, as he said, "Genesis speaks of God creating the world. Or, one may want to begin with the birth of the Christ child and his life on Earth."

"Let us begin there, with Jesus. May I?"

He leaned over her and turned the pages until he found the Gospel According to St. Luke. He sat back and she began to read aloud.

Chapter 7

She wanted to savor every sentence.

She read of Zechariah not believing God's angel and being struck dumb. *I must never doubt what God says.*

She read of Mary's conception, announced to her by the angel Gabriel, showing nothing is impossible with God. *Having this book before me is proof.*

Later, Mary proclaimed, "My spirit rejoices in God." *There's that word,* rejoice.

Annabel read about the Caesar whose proclamation sent Joseph and Mary to Bethlehem during Mary's time of child-birth. *How interesting that God should announce the birth to lowly shepherds instead of rich people or kings.*

Oh, she wanted to read it all! There must be so much she'd never heard, so many stories revealing God's nature and expectations.

Lord le Wyse didn't stop her, so she read on.

She relished Jesus's words, "The Spirit of the Lord is on me, because he has anointed me to proclaim good news to the poor. He has sent me to proclaim freedom for the prisoners and recovery of sight for the blind, to set the oppressed free."

She stopped and silently pored over the words again, trying to memorize each verse. There was something so comforting about the passage. But she mustn't stop; Lord le Wyse would be waiting for her to go on.

She raised her knees to bring the words closer, cradling the heavy book in her arms.

Annabel read about Jesus teaching in the synagogue. When the people in the synagogue, being filled with wrath at his words, tried to throw him off a cliff, she gasped. She looked up at Lord le Wyse. He had a strange expression on his face, but he nodded at her to keep reading.

She smiled at the way Jesus spoke to the Pharisees who didn't want him to heal on the Sabbath day. Then she came to a long discourse in which Jesus said people were blessed when they were poor, hungry, or hated, because God would reward those who belonged to him. *Love your enemies, bless those who curse you, offer to let someone hit you or take your coat.* Most of this she had heard before, but she couldn't recall actually seeing anyone do such things. And she hadn't either, as she certainly didn't love or bless Bailiff Tom. She would have to think about that.

Her eyes burned from reading so long in the dim light, as well as from the candle smoke.

"Perhaps you should stop now." Lord le Wyse's voice sounded hoarse. "You look tired."

Only six chapters. She wanted to go on, but it must be late. She couldn't resist rubbing her eyes with the backs of her hands.

She closed the book. "Thank you." She was amazed that her lord, the brooding and intimidating Lord le Wyse, would be the means of obtaining her dearest wish.

He nodded curtly, taking the heavy book from her.

She curtsied in response and followed Mistress Eustacia out the door.

❧

Eustacia had picked a red rose and placed it in a small pottery flask of water, setting it on the gray stone mantle over the fireplace. Ranulf studied it, admiring the shape, the color, the delicate beauty of the petals. The servants were engaged in their early morning chores, leaving him alone in the upper hall, so he set up his easel and parchment next to the east-facing window. Placing the rose on a table beside him, he took out his materials and began to paint.

It had been a long time since he had wanted to paint. Perhaps the country and this village were good for him after all. He stroked the brush across the parchment until the rose emerged, full and lush, but something else was emerging as well. The real subject was not the rose but the person holding it: a girl with blonde hair—he decided to let it flow loosely about her shoulders—with full lips and a feminine chin and wide blue eyes—

He suddenly realized who was emerging on his canvas, and it made him growl irritably. But he'd already started the painting. It would be a shame not to finish it.

Then he'd hide it in the wooden chest.

He added a slight blush to her cheeks and a wisp of hair touching her jawline, the way she had looked when his horse nearly trampled her. He took particular care in forming her nose and eyebrows, trying to get them exactly right—if he was going to paint her, he might as well do it to the best of his ability. He pulled the parchment closer to the window, since the sun was nearly overhead and not streaming in as brightly as before. When he did, he caught sight of movement next to the manor house. The subject of his painting—the girl, Annabel—sat washing laundry with Beatrice. But sneaking up behind her was Bailiff Tom.

Annabel worked opposite Beatrice on the tub of dirty laundry. She let her mind wander over the passages she'd read the night before, and she marveled again at how God had given her exactly what she'd longed for. Through the person of Lord le Wyse, God literally laid it in her lap. Perhaps God had heard her prayers and he wanted her to read His Word.

While scrubbing a sheet from one of the servants' beds, she marveled at how the rude and scowling Lord le Wyse had seemed almost kind and ... human, at least for a few minutes. He was formidable to look at, but he seemed to be bringing stability to their village. He'd made sure all the grain was harvested, and he seemed to be successful in keeping the miller from stealing a good portion of it, as had happened before in all the years Annabel could remember.

She supposed it was proof that God could use anyone to accomplish His will.

Yes, God was blessing Glynval after the tragedy of the Great Pestilence, and in spite of the recent drought. God did love them, even if most of Glynval chose not to believe it.

"Annabel. You look as if you're solving the world's problems, you do." Mistress Eustacia stood beside her, holding a bundle of laundry that overflowed her arms.

"Forgive me. I was thinking." She took the bundle from the mistress's arms and plunged the load into the warm tub of water.

"There's naught to forgive, my dear. You girls have washed much in a short time." She picked up the basket of clean linens that Annabel and Beatrice had finished wringing out, groaning as she lifted the wet laundry and carried it toward the clothesline.

Annabel glanced up at Beatrice then stared as the servant girl held one of Lord le Wyse's unwashed shirts against her cheek and closed her eyes. She seemed to be inhaling the scent of it, an intense, almost pained look on her face.

Beatrice's eyelids flickered open and she caught Annabel gaping. Beatrice scowled and pushed the shirt down into the water, applying soap and roughly scrubbing the material between her hands.

Annabel wondered how Beatrice could have such strong feelings for Lord le Wyse. She herself had never felt such attraction for any man, and couldn't imagine men having such appeal that she would sniff their dirty shirts!

Beatrice clearly had what the priest called "natural lusts and desires," and therefore Annabel must be "unnatural," since she felt no such lust. But if it was natural, why did God condemn it? It was all so confusing.

Though she'd learned much from the six chapters she'd read last night, Annabel still wondered about many things contained in the Holy Writ. Perhaps she could pose a few questions to Lord le Wyse—when he was in a good mood.

It could be a long wait.

Beatrice finished wringing out Lord le Wyse's shirt and laid it in the basket. Annabel concentrated on her own scrubbing, though her thoughts wandered again to Beatrice's infatuation. Why did Lord le Wyse appeal to Beatrice? She'd probably discovered, as Annabel had, how quickly one grew accustomed to the lord's mangled hand and the patch over his eye and ceased to take note of them. The confident way he held himself, as well as his impeccable clothing and cleanliness, gave him such a presence that, now that she thought about it, she could indeed imagine how Beatrice would consider him superior to every other man living at the manor or in Glynval.

Ah well, it was none of her business, after all. She wasn't in love with him, and people's love affairs could hardly concern her. Though if Lord le Wyse married, his wife might not allow her to read his Bible. The thought gave her a sickening pang. *But*, she soothed herself, *he isn't courting anyone — there isn't anyone here in Glynval for him to court — and he isn't likely to marry Beatrice.* Besides the obvious ways they seemed unsuited for each other, Lord le Wyse was powerful and quite wealthy, and he'd certainly never marry a servant. He'd probably marry only a noblewoman.

Beatrice's plight reminded Annabel of her brother Edward hoping to use his family's tenuous claims to nobility to help him make his fortune. And she wondered for the hundredth time how her family was getting along without her. Who was doing the cooking? Did they get enough to eat? Were they milking Dilly every day? Now that the barley harvest was over, they'd have more time on their hands. Perhaps Edward was no longer in Glynval and had gone to London, as he had planned. In her mind's eye she saw Durand lying abed all day, fancying himself sickly, while their mother coddled him. Was Mother able to cope with Durand and all the chores Annabel had once taken charge of?

With a start, Annabel realized she had been scrubbing a shirt more vigorously than intended. Eyebrows raised, Beatrice announced that she was going to get the rest of the dirty laundry then got up and walked to the undercroft.

Someone was walking toward her, but Annabel didn't pay attention, thinking it was a servant. When she looked up, Bailiff Tom was striding toward her with an ugly leer.

"Have you had enough of all this hard work?" He leaned over her, blowing his breath in her face. "Not used to working from sunup to sundown, are you?"

"I rather enjoy it," Annabel said, going back to washing the clothes before her and pretending to ignore him. Surely Beatrice would come back soon. *Hurry, Beatrice.*

He snorted. "If you change your mind, I believe the lord will let you out of your forced servitude and allow you to marry me. Three years is a long time for such hard labor, especially for a delicate maiden like you."

He began to run his hand down her arm. She jerked away from him and leapt to her feet. "Don't touch me." Her hand went into her pocket and closed around the handle of her knife. "I told you, I will not marry you."

"What were you doing with the master last night, eh? The two of you alone for so long."

"We weren't alone. Mistress Eustacia was with us, and it's none of your business."

"Mistress Eustacia." With a hand on her shoulder, he shoved her back down on her stool. He leaned down, and stroking her arm again. "Come with me to the woods tonight, and I'll show you what a real man is like."

"Get away from me!" Annabel raised her voice, desperately hoping someone would come and help her. Surely someone was in hearing distance.

"Bailiff." Lord le Wyse's voice cracked like a whip behind her.

The bailiff let go. Annabel stood and stepped away from him, her knees suddenly weak.

"What are you doing?"

"Merely speaking with the girl about her work. She's a known slacker, shiftless and slow and — I wouldn't trust her, my lord. Don't allow yourself to be alone with this one, as you never know what she might do. Her family, the lot of them —"

"Come with me." Lord le Wyse took a few steps toward the manor house, then stopped and waited for Tom to march ahead of him. The two walked away.

Annabel bit her lip against the anger, relief, and shame waging war inside. She shuddered at the way the bailiff had held her down. And what about the things he said about her? The lord already had a low opinion of her. Would he let her continue to read to him after the bailiff said she was not to be trusted? *Please, God, don't let the bailiff turn him against me.*

※

"Bailiff Tom, I don't like the way you are harassing my servant." Ranulf gave Tom his most serious glare. "You are never to touch her again. Is that understood?"

"Yes, my lord. But her family—"

"I am well aware of what they did. She has accepted the punishment for her entire family, and I don't wish you to harass her about it."

"Her brother promised her to me. If she were the submissive sister she ought to be—"

"Not only do I never want to see you touching my servant again, I don't want you to go near her, and I had better not catch you trying to intimidate her. Have I made myself clear?"

"Perfectly, my lord. Forgive my weakness for the girl. I swear it will never be a problem again." The bailiff's gaze turned to the floor, but Ranulf caught the defiance in Tom's eyes.

"You may go, unless you have aught else to say to me." Ranulf fought the urge to dismiss him outright. The sight of him touching Annabel, and her cringing, was still branded on his mind.

"No, my lord." He bowed, replaced his hat on his head, and left.

Ranulf reflected over what the bailiff had said about the girl, that she was not to be trusted. He realized his bailiff was a louse. But that wasn't the only reason he didn't believe what the bailiff said. After seeing her eagerness to read the Bible, her confession that she had actually desired to read it for many years, and the sincerity in her face, Ranulf couldn't help but think he had misjudged her.

He groaned. The last thing he wanted to do was think well of this girl, but she seemed ever before him. It seemed to be his lot in life to see her, hear her—and save her—everywhere he went. She was on his mind much more than was wise or comfortable.

But eventually this maiden would show her share of faults—maybe more than her share. Then he would cease to think of her at all.

❧

Lord le Wyse seemed his usual morose self during the evening meal, scowling as much as usual. Some Bible reading would surely soothe him. Annabel fervently hoped he would suggest it. *Please, God.*

Beatrice was serving the ale tonight, and she was extremely attentive to Lord le Wyse. She refilled his tankard so many times that he finally looked up at her and said, "Thank you, but that is enough." Annabel would have trembled at the look he gave Beatrice, but she seemed rather encouraged than discouraged by it and smiled down at him as if he had just bestowed a great compliment.

"Yes, my lord. Is there anything I can do for you? Can I get you anything, anything at all? It would be my pleasure." She continued beaming at him, but he didn't even glance her way.

"No, thank you. You may sit down." Without looking at her, he waved his hand to shoo her.

Poor Beatrice.

Bailiff Tom glanced at Annabel a few times throughout the meal, an angry look pursing his thin lips, but at least he didn't stare at her. She could only imagine what Lord le Wyse had said to him. That thought and the bailiff's final glance caused her to check the position of her knife.

After the servants began to leave the table and she and

Eustacia began setting the hall to rights, Lord le Wyse caught Annabel's eye. He motioned with his hand for her to come to him.

She ceased her cleaning and hurried to her lord, dropping a curtsy.

He didn't speak right away. In fact, he looked thoughtful, but Annabel waited, holding her breath to see what he would say. Would he blame her for the bailiff's actions? Did he think what the priest thought, that all women were a snare? Could he believe what Bailiff Tom had said about her, that she was not to be trusted?

Lord le Wyse's face was turned toward the fire, which illuminated his high cheekbones and his brown eye but not his hidden thoughts. His hair fell thick over his forehead, and Annabel couldn't help noticing his beard was neatly trimmed. He looked fiercely masculine, with his firm jaw and chin.

Something about the way he turned and gazed at her made her heart beat faster. Finally, he said, "I desire reading. Will you read to me?"

"Yes, of course, my lord." She tried not to seem too eager, but inside her heart smiled with joy.

His features relaxed in response, but the placid look was gone so quickly, she wondered if she'd imagined it.

Several servants were still milling about the room as she sat beside the fireplace in expectation. She hoped he didn't think she was eager because she wanted to spend time with him. Another man looking at her with romantic intentions—it was the last thing she wanted. She evened out her expression before glancing up at him.

He disappeared behind the screen then returned with the Holy Writ. When she opened it and began reading, a few people stood nearby and listened, but after a few minutes they had all filed out and left. Mistress Eustacia was in the corner with her sewing, as she had been the night before. Annabel assumed she would stay there for propriety's sake, to make sure Lord le Wyse and Annabel weren't left alone together, which would stir up gossip.

Though Bailiff Tom had made it seem as if people already had evil thoughts about her and Lord le Wyse.

Annabel started to read, but she'd only spoken a few words when Gilbert came in and apologized for interrupting. He said he had something to ask Lord le Wyse about the castle's foundation. Lord le Wyse stood and he and Gilbert spoke for several minutes, discussing various aspects of the construction.

Finally, Lord le Wyse came back to where Annabel had been sitting and pondering what they had read the previous night.

"Pray excuse the interruption. You may read now."

Lord le Wyse seemed to be in a kinder mood. *Now might be a good time to pose some questions.*

"May I ask you something, my lord?"

He looked at her suspiciously again.

"Forgive me, my lord. I will read, but I wanted to know if the Bible agrees with what Sir Matefrid, our priest, says. Does the Bible say we are all evil and should go about our lives with solemnity and guilt?"

He seemed to consider her question a moment. "The Bible says we have all sinned. We should all repent. But no, the Bible doesn't constantly tell us we are evil. God says we are righteous because he is able to make us righteous. He says there is no condemnation for those who are in Christ Jesus, and all who call on his name will be saved."

These were comforting words indeed. And how wonderful to know the Bible well enough to speak of it the way Lord le Wyse spoke. He still didn't look angry, so she asked another question.

"When we see God, do you think he will be terrifying? Does the Bible say we'll be afraid of him? Or do you think we will see him and be glad?"

Lord le Wyse's eyebrows drew together. "Certainly God will strike terror into some hearts. But the Bible portrays God as a loving father to his children. It says he is compassionate and slow to anger, and patient with us. I believe we will be happy to see him. The Psalms say of God, 'May all who seek you rejoice and be glad in you.'"

So we are supposed to rejoice! She almost felt as if she were dreaming, it was so good to finally talk with someone about these things. "Are there descriptions of hell in the Bible, like the scene on the wall of the Glynval church?"

"There are some descriptions, but perhaps not as graphic as what I've seen on cathedral walls."

How strange. The priest seemed to want to frighten everyone with condemnation. Every Sunday he accused, he berated, he terrified her into thinking God was harsh and unloving. He seemed to be trying to convince himself, as well as the whole village, that women were evil by nature and not to be trusted. But the Bible taught good news. It wasn't all about condemnation and punishment.

"Not all priests preach like yours here." Lord le Wyse interrupted her thoughts.

"Oh."

"I have heard a great many uplifting and encouraging sermons, but your priest's sermon on Sunday was neither. However, his type of sermonizing is more typical, I'm afraid."

His eyes narrowed as he continued to study her. "You are very intelligent and educated. You surely do not want to stay in Glynval all your life, to be a servant or to marry one of these boorish village men. What is it you want?"

Annabel fidgeted with her apron. It was such a surprising thing for her lord to ask. What could she say? Could she tell him her deepest wish?

While she was still wondering how to reply, he said, "This isn't what you were brought up to do, after all. Are you unhappy?"

"Oh, no." She couldn't let him think that she was ungrateful. "Mistress Eustacia is very kind to me."

Lord le Wyse shifted in his chair. "Do you miss your home, your mother and brothers? Would you go back there if I forgave your family's debt?"

"I—" She felt confused. Why was he asking her this? "I do miss my home, but it is only just and fair that I am here. I want to give what I owe. After all, Jesus says we should do more than our share, not less." He looked at her attentively, and so after a short pause, she went on, choosing her words carefully. "You asked me what I want. What I wanted most was to read the Bible. For the past three years I've wanted to be a nun, to study the Holy Writ and take my vows."

She scrutinized Lord le Wyse's face just as he was studying hers. He might think she was hoping he would take an interest in sending her to an abbey. And perhaps, after her three years of service to him, he *would* consider helping her enter a convent.

It may have been her imagination, but his features seemed to visibly soften after she said she wanted to be a nun. He relaxed against the back of his chair, casting a shadow over his face so that she couldn't read his expression or see if he was still studying her face.

"You want to be a nun," he said softly. "You are aware it costs money to enter a convent. Something your family does not have."

"No, my lord, they do not."

Now he was undoubtedly thinking that she hoped he might send her to an abbey. She waited for him to speak again, but the silence stretched on and grew awkward. Finally Mistress Eustacia came toward them, having packed away her sewing.

"It is late, my dears. Are you ready, Annabel?"

She nodded, but the book in her lap was so heavy she was unable to stand.

He stood and stared down at her, still not saying anything. If only she knew what he was thinking. She suddenly remembered again the night she had seen him bent over in agony and the strange, animallike sounds of anguish that had come from him. *Such an impassioned man.* But at the moment she had the impression that he was forcing a look of indifference.

"Of course." He took the book from her lap. "You may go."

She hurried away from him, and Mistress Eustacia went out with her.

When Annabel got down to the undercroft, all lights were out and she could barely see to get to her cot. As she crawled under the sheet, Beatrice sat up in the bed beside hers.

"Annabel?" she whispered.

"Yes?"

There was silence before Beatrice finally asked, "What are you and Lord le Wyse doing every night?"

"I am reading to him. That is all."

Beatrice sniffed. She sounded like she was crying.

"What's wrong?"

"Nothing."

"Do you miss Lincolnshire, your home?"

"Not much." She sniffed again, loudly. "I only wish I knew how to get Lord le Wyse to notice me."

What could she say to that? "We are only servants, Beatrice. Perhaps it's better not to be noticed."

"Does he ever … you know … say nice things to you, tell you you're pretty, when you're reading together?"

"No, of course not. He summons me only because I understand Latin. I read, then I leave." She didn't want to tell Beatrice that the two of them actually had a conversation tonight. Beatrice wouldn't take that well—or understand it was completely innocent.

"He is a good lord, don't you think?" Beatrice wiped her nose with the back of her hand.

"Yes, I think he is." *Better than most, I suppose.* He seemed much kinder tonight, less judgmental of her. She remembered her profound relief and gratitude at the way he came to her aid, protecting her from the bailiff both in the field a few days ago, and today as she was doing laundry.

She could almost forget he told the bailiff that he was *fortunate* because she wouldn't marry him. Almost.

⸻

Annabel awoke a few hours later to the sound of muffled yells from outside. She sat up in bed. Only a tiny shaft of light came through the shutters. *What could be happening in the middle of the night to cause such a commotion?*

The undercroft door flew open, revealing a man's form, an

eerie orange glow behind him. His shoulders heaved up and down as he gasped for breath.

"Fire! Come and help us!"

Then he disappeared.

Frightened squeals and gasps filled the room as several girls scrambled out of bed. Annabel jumped out of bed as well. She hastily pulled her oldest dress over her nightgown and ran outside with bare feet.

Chaos met her. Bright red-orange sparks shot into the night sky from the barn roof. Men ran back and forth, some bearing buckets, others pointing and shouting. A line began forming between the well and the barn; Annabel ran toward it and filled a space between two men, grabbing the full bucket from her left and heaving it into the hands of the man on her right. Gilbert Carpenter dashed from the front to the end of the line, ferrying empty buckets with a grim determination.

The stone barn was discharging red-hot flames from its huge door and tiny windows, flames so hot she felt as though her face was burning along with it, even from thirty feet away. The group's efforts to put out the flames seemed hopeless. The thatched roof was completely engulfed, and the interior of the barn, along with the barley and oats stored within, were being completely destroyed.

Gilbert Carpenter came to a stop near Annabel and Bailiff Tom, who stood nearby. With labored breath Gilbert announced, "Many of the beams have given way. I don't think we can possibly save anything inside."

"Is everyone out?" Bailiff Tom stared at the burning building. The enormous barn housed not only the sheep and the entire barley harvest, but many of the laborers Lord le Wyse had hired to build his castle, who bedded down at the opposite end from the animals.

"Everyone's accounted for," the man to the left told Bailiff Tom, "except Lord le Wyse. I haven't seen him since I first grabbed a bucket."

Gilbert Carpenter flung his arms out wide and yelled, "Has anyone seen Lord le Wyse?"

"No," one man said.

"Went to save the sheep," another offered. A few men nodded in agreement.

Gilbert's eyes darted to the barn. He ran and soon disappeared around the other side of the structure.

With only a moment's hesitation Annabel left the line of men, who were still passing the buckets from hand to hand, and followed the path Gilbert Carpenter had taken. She ran past a huddle of maidens. Their arms around each other, they watched the fire as though dazed. Some cried and others yelled at her as she passed, but she didn't hear their words. She ran as close to the barn as she dared, certain that the flames were singeing her eyebrows.

She came around the back side of the barn and nearly ran into Lord le Wyse and Gilbert Carpenter. Lord le Wyse's arm was around the master mason's shoulders as he seemed barely able to stay on his feet. Her lord looked alarmed. "Annabel! What are you doing? Where are you going?"

"I was searching for you." Her mouth fell open as she got a better look at him. "My lord! Are you hurt?"

His hair stuck out in all directions, and his forehead and face were streaked with soot and sweat. He looked as though he'd been in the fire itself.

"I am well. The sheep are safe."

Annabel's gaze traveled down from his head and stopped on his arm. His charred sleeve, much of it burned away, hung from his elbow. His left forearm — the one mangled by the wolf years before — was covered with angry blisters. A lump formed in her throat as she imagined the pain he was feeling.

She tried to look into his face, to see his expression. Just then his shoulders swayed, like a hewn tree just before it collapses.

"We must get you back to the manor house and tend your burns at once."

He swayed again as he and Gilbert started forward, walking slowly. They made their way back toward the manor house, neither of them even looking toward the barn or the fire, which roared louder than the worst thunder and hail storm.

Several men hurried toward them, asking questions.

"Leave me be." The lord's harsh tone stopped them cold.

Annabel remembered what her mother had done when Durand had badly burned his hand. "He needs water," she told Gilbert. "Two buckets at least."

"I'll go get the water, as I can carry more than you," Gilbert said. "You help Lord le Wyse to the manor house." He lifted the lord's good arm from around his shoulders and placed it on Annabel's. Then he hurried away toward the well.

Lord le Wyse leaned heavily on Annabel as they walked. Neither of them said a word. She suspected the lord was silent because of the pain, and she was concentrating on getting him safely to the manor. He was quite heavy, and she stumbled a couple of times in the dark, but she was thankful he seemed to grow a bit steadier as they moved along.

When they reached the steps of the manor house, which were too narrow to safely accommodate two people abreast, Lord le Wyse stepped away from her.

"I shall go first," he said gruffly, "unless you're afraid I may fall backward and crush you."

The glow of the fire illuminated his features enough that she could see the corner of his mouth turned up, showing him to be in jest.

"Perhaps I will be able to step aside in time to avoid being crushed." She lifted her eyebrows.

He winced, drawing his injured arm closer to his body. "Shouldn't you rather have said, 'It would be a privilege to break the fall of my lord'?"

A strange time for a sense of humor, but perhaps it took his mind off the pain. "Yes, my lord. Pray, make haste. We must get your arm in some cool water."

"As you wish." He started up the steps.

She followed his slow progress, and in her mind she listed all the things she would need to treat his burn.

"Lord Ranulf!"

Annabel and the lord stopped and looked behind them.

Mistress Eustacia came panting across the yard with a pitcher in her hand.

"Water from the well?" he asked her.

"Yes, my lord."

Annabel hastened down the steps and took the pitcher from Mistress Eustacia, whose eyes were full of tears.

"Gilbert Carpenter is bringing two more buckets. Do you know what to do for a bad burn?" Mistress Eustacia looked at Annabel.

Annabel nodded. "We'll need some clean bandages, a flask of honey, and some comfrey if you have it."

"I shall fetch them right away." Mistress Eustacia's voice cracked, and she hurried away.

Chapter
8

Once inside the upper hall, Ranulf sat in his chair and watched the girl, Annabel, scurry to the corner of the room to fetch an empty bucket, still carrying the pitcher of water.

"Now, hold your arm over the bucket." She set it down in front of him.

I was searching for you, she had said. He couldn't get the look on her face out of his mind. When she almost ran into him, when she saw his burned arm ... He was foolish to think about it.

Now she leaned close, taking his hand in hers, and studied his burn. Her long blonde braid slipped over the shoulder of her shapeless work dress to dangle by his arm. Her eyes were gentle and the touch of her fingers was cool on his burning skin.

"I have to clean the burn so I can see the severity, and the cold water will be good for it." She began, slowly, to pour the water over his arm. It was painful and soothing at the same time. The water ran out just as the door opened and Gilbert Carpenter came in bearing two buckets. Mistress Eustacia trundled in behind him.

"Oh, Lord Ranulf!" Her voice was soft but agitated. She had always grieved over every scrape he got into. He didn't like to remember how she reacted to his wolf attack; the poor woman cried for weeks.

"My good woman, 'tis only a burn." The pain caused his voice to sound more like a snarl. He regretted taking his pain out on her, but she was used to his gruffness.

Gilbert set the buckets of water down beside him.

"Here you are, child." Mistress Eustacia set a flask of honey and strips of clean linen on the table beside her.

Annabel stepped aside.

"You do it, my dear." Eustacia got a stool and set it down in front of him, then motioned for Annabel to sit. "You seem to know how to treat a burn. I will watch you." She wiped her eyes and her nose on a corner of her apron. "I looked in my store of herbs, but I'm afraid I have no comfrey. I shall send someone to pick some as soon as it's daylight."

Ranulf's arm throbbed considerably more now that Annabel had ceased pouring water on it. He was relieved when she dipped the pitcher into the clean bucket of water and began pouring it over his arm again.

"It doesn't appear as bad as I at first feared," Annabel said. Her small nose and full lips made a pleasing silhouette against the low fire that still smoldered in the fireplace. *I should stop staring at her.*

She took hold of his hand—his ugly, mangled hand—and held his arm up to the light.

"Does it hurt much?" Her bright blue eyes filled with compassion as she looked into his face—his scarred cheek, his patched eye, his beard that covered the worst scars.

He grunted, wanting to reject her pity.

Just then, the door burst open and Gilbert's little boy, Adam, came running into the upper hall. "Father! What happened? Did you see the fire?"

Gilbert tried to shush the boy, but Adam came straight up to Annabel and peered down at Ranulf's burned arm.

"Oooh. That is the worst burn I've ever seen!"

Ranulf looked to the boy's father, hoping he would remove the child posthaste.

Before Gilbert could take more than a step, Annabel said very softly, "Adam, I need to bandage my lord's arm, so why don't you go with your father to see if the men need help fighting the fire?"

The boy's eyes grew twice their size, clearly believing Annabel thought him capable of assisting the other men. She smiled at the child, and then he ran out of the room.

Gilbert started after him then turned and asked, "My lord, do you need me? The men may need help—"

"You may go."

As Gilbert left the room, Mistress Eustacia came closer, watching as Annabel continued pouring water over his arm. Then she placed a hand on Annabel's shoulder. "Such a good, gentle lass you are. How did you come to know so much about healing a burn?"

"My brother burned himself very badly a few years ago. I watched how my mother and our servant, Alice, treated it."

She looked a little self-conscious after admitting her family once had a servant. She kept her eyes on his burn and didn't look up at him.

Ranulf couldn't help comparing her circumspect behavior to some other serving girls he'd encountered, including the one who had tried to flirt with him at the evening meal.

"Such a fine lass," Mistress Eustacia murmured, and blew her nose on her apron.

A fine lass. Ranulf stared at her. She was the most beautiful girl he had ever seen, with the most flawless features, and he would have needed to lose both eyes not to notice.

And her outward beauty wasn't even the comeliest part about her.

Mistress Eustacia caught him looking at Annabel and raised her eyebrows at him. Ranulf scowled.

Eustacia turned to Annabel. "How fortunate Lord le Wyse has such a gentle, knowledgeable nurse among his servants."

Instead of blushing and looking embarrassed, or smirking and taking advantage of the situation, as most maidens would have, Annabel frowned and shook her head. "I'm merely fortunate to know a little about caring for burns."

The old woman raised her eyebrows at Ranulf again. He answered with a glare so menacing a growl escaped his throat.

Annabel jerked her hands away. "Did I hurt you?"

He made an effort to compose himself. "Nay. You're as gentle as a kitten." He looked at Mistress Eustacia. "You may go." Though he hadn't intended it, the words came out as a bark.

She smiled at him. "I'll go comfort the servant girls. They looked terrified, they did."

She obviously wasn't afraid of him, more's the pity.

Eustacia quit the chamber, leaving him and Annabel alone.

Annabel held one hand under his arm while she took a cloth, dipped it in the water, and began to dab at the soot around the border of his burn.

"How did you get such a burn, if I may ask?"

"There was a fire . . . in the barn."

She frowned up at him in that clever way of hers. "I know that. But how——?"

"I herded the sheep out the back door. One ewe lamb was frightened, however, and wouldn't come out, and so I went in to get her. Even then she wouldn't let me lead her. I had to pick her up and carry her. On the way out, some burning thatch fell on my arm and burned away my sleeve." He said dryly, "So you see what a hero I am." *For the second time in my life.*

"Hero? I'm not familiar with this word."

"'Tis from the Greek, a word meaning someone with great strength and courage. Someone who protects and defends."

"Oh, yes, indeed." She put the cloth aside and reached for the flask. "Indeed, you are a hero. I like this word *hero.*"

She was so beautiful and seemed so unaware of it. The wisps of blonde hair danced around her pink-tinted cheeks just as he had captured them in his painting. But even more devastating than her physical beauty were the glimpses he had seen of her heart and soul.

God help him.

"So what did you do? How did you put out the fire on your arm?"

He stretched out his right hand, palm up.

She gasped. "Oh, my lord, you should have told me." Before

he knew what she was about to do, she took his unmangled hand and plunged it into the bucket of clean water. She stuck her other hand in and began to rub his palm to clean it, since it was black with soot and ashes. The hand was not badly burned, and he struggled to steel himself against the sensations spreading through him from her massaging fingers.

She pulled his hand out. "No blisters. That is good." Then she began dabbing it dry with a clean cloth.

She turned her attention back to his badly burned arm. She picked up the flask and poured honey over the blisters. The thick, golden liquid felt cool and soothing, sending a chill up his arm and across his shoulders.

"How did the fire start?" she said.

"I don't know, but our entire barley and oat crop is gone, I'm sorry to say. It is a tragedy, especially because of the severity of this drought. By God's grace we still have the wheat supply in the smaller barn." The wheat by rights belonged exclusively to him, but he couldn't let the villagers starve. He resolved to buy enough barley and oats to last the village through the winter.

A worried furrow creased her brow. "Surely no one would have deliberately set the fire." She took his hand and poured honey over his palm, rubbing it in with her finger.

He pulled his hand away. She looked up in surprise.

He shook his head. "That isn't necessary. The hand isn't badly burned."

Annabel stared at him a moment. "I'm sorry. Let me clean it off." She picked up the wet cloth, but he took it from her.

"I can do it."

"Of course."

After he finished, she began loosely wrapping his blistered forearm with a strip of cloth.

The pain seemed to intensify as she did so. "It is a severe burn, my lord. You must allow either me or Mistress Eustacia to inspect it every day and continue applying the honey."

She took another cloth and wet it in the bucket. Then she leaned forward and wiped his forehead.

Surprised by the action, he started back and examined her face. He could see from her expression that wiping his face did not embarrass her.

Because she feels nothing for me, nothing a sister wouldn't feel for a brother, or a servant for her lord. She reached out to wipe his right cheek, but he took the cloth from her and wiped his own face.

For a few moments — when she said she'd been searching for him — he'd wondered if her feelings for him were deeper, more tender than was appropriate. But no. She felt only the natural compassion and concern she would have felt for an animal — the same emotion he'd felt for the sheep in the barn.

"I'll get you something for the pain. I believe I have some chamomile in the bag I brought from home."

"Nay. Pray have someone fetch another bucket of water. That is all I require." Dawn was beginning to show a gray glow at the windows.

She held his gaze for a moment then curtsied. "Yes, my lord."

As he watched her leave, the pain in his arm seemed to spread all through him, giving him a headache. The pain was intense, but as he closed his eyes, he couldn't stop remembering the sweetness of her expression, the kindness of her words and actions ... the gentleness of her touch.

His chest constricted painfully. He was a fool.

⁙

Annabel only managed to take a short nap before she was needed in the kitchen. When she stepped out into the manor courtyard, it seemed the entire village was milling there, staring at the smoking ashes and blackened walls of the barn. A sad sight indeed, weighing her down with a feeling of dread. The tragedy of the fire had ignited emotions, and angry grumblings emerged from the throat of more than one villager. Annabel could understand why. They'd all helped with the harvest, even Annabel's family for once, and every family was to get a share of the harvest. Now all their hard work would yield them nothing.

Stephen broke away from the crowd and came toward Annabel. He said quietly, so no one else could hear, "Bailiff Tom is saying that this is the work of a curse, that someone has brought a scourge to our village."

Stephen's words made the back of her neck prickle. There had been ugly talk when Annabel was a small child about a curse on Glynval, started when frost killed all their spring crops and their grain harvest was ruined by drought. Some had pointed fingers at Stephen, who was barely six years old. Because of his twisted body and the odd way he walked, some people were afraid of him, afraid he was cursed. Even though she had been young, she remembered her terror for her friend.

Annabel felt ill. "I hope nobody is listening to him."

"I hope not, either." Stephen brushed his blond hair out of his eyes.

"Who does he say brought the curse?" she whispered.

"He isn't saying it outright, but I believe he means Lord le Wyse."

Annabel felt her mouth go dry. "That's terrible."

"I know." Stephen stared thoughtfully across the yard of the manor house, his face deceptively calm and peaceful.

"Perhaps I should tell Lord le Wyse, warn him."

"I don't think you should get involved." Stephen's expression changed to concern as he looked at her. "Lord le Wyse can take care of himself. He's wealthy and powerful, and the people he brought with him from Lincoln are very loyal to him. No, you shouldn't say anything. He might blame the messenger."

Perhaps Stephen was right. Lord le Wyse was rather unpredictable. Who knew how he might react to the news?

With a final nod, Stephen walked away to begin his day's work, while Annabel went to help Mistress Eustacia with the morning meal.

As the manor staff and castle builders sat down in the upper hall, a little later than usual, to break their fast, impassioned discussions arose over the cause of the fire. As she listened to the various theories, Annabel hated to think that someone in the demesne, including the workers gathered at this table, would have set the fire deliberately. Surely it had been an accident, as some men suggested. Annabel heard Beatrice spout, "But whether accident or no, whoever did this should be banished from Glynval. We'll have to survive on thin pea gruel this winter, if we survive at all, thanks to the scoundrel who started that fire."

Their situation was dire. Most lords would simply let them starve, but Annabel didn't believe Lord le Wyse would allow that. She hoped he would find a way to get more grain.

If only they could have the kind of faith she had read about in the Bible. Of course they should leave their doubts behind and trust God, but ever since the Great Pestilence had killed a third of the people of Glynval, the ones who were left seemed determined to blame God. She'd heard them speak of it many times. They believed God was a cold, unfeeling Sovereign who inflicted suffering on people arbitrarily. Their distrust and hopelessness did not bode well for her village.

<hr />

Annabel looked over the morning's kitchen duties, hers to tend until Mistress Eustacia returned from settling an argument between two servant girls. From the chastisement coming from outside the door, Annabel realized she could be alone for some time.

Suppressing a sigh, she stirred the frumenty with a wooden paddle then swung the pot back over the fire so it would continue to cook. *There, the worst is done. Now for the sweeping.* She lifted her arm to wipe the sweat that had beaded above her lip and saw that Lord le Wyse stood just inside the door. Her heart fluttered, she supposed from seeing him so unexpectedly.

"Mistress Eustacia sent me to have my bandage changed." He looked disgruntled.

She adjusted the pot so that it wasn't directly over the fire then wiped her hands on her apron.

He sat down impatiently on the bench against the wall.

Annabel rummaged through the shelves until she found a

container of honey and some bandages, smiling to herself at his reluctant compliance. Then she took the cloth bag of comfrey leaves Mistress Eustacia had sent someone to pick.

Lord le Wyse's appearance was as sophisticated and tidy as she'd ever seen. His dark hair and beard were neatly trimmed, any minor singes from the flames gone. Not the smallest smudge of soot could be seen anywhere on his face, and he wore a crisp white shirt and bright blue velvet waistcoat that smelled of fresh air and dried lavender. Her lord was quite proper in his elegance. If only he would shave off his beard, he'd look positively noble.

"One would never guess you were a hero last night."

"What do you mean?" He sounded irritable and his eye was narrowed. But the harshness of his voice no longer intimidated her as much as it once had.

"I only meant that you don't look at all like you did a few hours ago, when you rescued that lamb. You look as if you might be on your way to the king's court in London."

"True. I've seen the king's court, and there are no heroes there."

Her lips twitched with an involuntary smile, but instead of smiling back, Lord le Wyse deepened his frown. Annabel could see his mood was dark, probably because of the pain in his arm, and perhaps worry over the fire.

She stood before him and began to unwrap his bandage carefully. His arm was raw, and blistered over a section a little wider than her hand. She winced. It had oozed watery blood, soaking the bandage in a few spots. She grabbed a pitcher of fresh water and a bucket and slowly poured it over his forearm. He sat unflinching, watching first her hands, then her face from his heavy-lidded eye. She dried his arm and poured more honey over it, placed some crushed comfrey leaves on top, then wrapped it with a clean bandage.

As she worked, a thought occurred to her, and she asked quietly, "Would the king's coroner investigate a fire like ours, to see if he could discover how it was set and if someone did it deliberately?" She knew the coroner was in charge of investigating deaths, though she had heard of him investigating other matters as well.

"The coroner of this shire is a friend of mine. I have sent for him for just that purpose. However," he said, fixing his eye intently on her face, his tone becoming harsher, "I don't wish for the whole village to know of this, so you are not to tell."

"Of course not, my lord. I won't say a word."

As she wrapped the bandage around his arm, his attention suddenly seemed arrested by her hand. He watched her with a new alertness, then grabbed her hand and turned it over to stare at the underside of her wrist.

There on her pale skin was the bruise the bailiff had inflicted on her the day he cornered her inside the butcher shop. The bruise was the size of Bailiff Tom's thumbprint, dark blue, with a slight green tinge in the middle.

"How did you get this?" Lord le Wyse demanded.

Her face went hot. She didn't want to tell him, although she didn't know why she should feel ashamed. It was the bailiff who should feel ashamed.

He tightened his grip on her hand. "Tell me the truth," he growled. "Did someone hurt you?"

She swallowed, trying to gather her courage. "Bailiff Tom did it."

"When?"

"Just before he shoved me into the street the day you almost ran me over with your horse." She bit her lip, hoping he wouldn't take offense.

She became quite aware that he was still holding her hand, and she hadn't finished with his bandage. His hand was warm, his palm slightly rough, his skin dark against her much lighter complexion. A cold fear was beginning in the pit of her stomach when he abruptly let go of her.

She quickly finished wrapping his bandage and tied it securely.

"What else did he do to you that day?" Lord le Wyse rasped in a strangled tone.

"He held me against my will, threatened me, and told me I should marry him."

"Has he hurt you any other time?"

"When I was doing laundry, he held me down, as you saw." She chose not to tell him about the bailiff trying to kiss her in the butcher shop. She couldn't think about it without feeling ill. Would Lord le Wyse blame her for the way the bailiff tried to force himself on her?

"I never did anything to make him think I'd marry him," Annabel said quickly, feeling compelled to explain. "I never thought of him as anything but my father's friend. I never imagined he was having … thoughts about me. Well, after I saw him looking at me a few times, I realized … but never before that, and I never tried to do anything to—"

"I don't approve of the bailiff," he said, interrupting her, "or anyone else, laying hands on you. If it happens again, you are to tell me of it immediately, and I will get rid of him and find a new bailiff. In fact, I'll throw him out now."

"Nay, please don't do that. Everyone would hate me if I caused the bailiff to lose his place." Besides, he'd be so angry, he'd find some way to revenge himself on her, she was sure.

Lord le Wyse had looked pale as she worked on his burn, a sign that he was suffering more than he pretended, but now his face was flushed.

Her heart clenched strangely in her chest at the look on his face. "I will tell you if it happens again. I think he will leave me alone now that you have spoken with him."

"Very well."

Chapter 9

Mistress Eustacia, who was fully capable of changing Lord le Wyse's bandage, asked Annabel to perform the task that night after the evening meal. Annabel was a bit suspicious of Eustacia's intentions, and worse, she was afraid the lord was suspicious too, but she had to obey. She only prayed Lord le Wyse wasn't having thoughts about her like Bailiff Tom, or even Gilbert Carpenter.

The thought was so unnerving that she kept her eyes down and said nothing while she sat on a low stool before him and unwrapped his bandage. She bathed his burns in cold water again, poured more honey over the wound, and began rewrapping his arm, inadvertently brushing his leg with her hand.

"I beg your pardon," she murmured.

"You must be tired. You don't have to read tonight if you don't want to."

"Oh, I want to." She looked up and met his eye, then quickly looked down. "That is, if you wish it."

When she finished re-bandaging his arm, he got up and retrieved the Bible. As he handed it to her, their hands touched. She pretended not to notice, not wanting to react the way Beatrice would have reacted if *her* hand accidentally touched Lord le Wyse's. It was more sad than amusing, the way Beatrice tried so hard to get the lord's attention, as Lord le Wyse obviously didn't seek or enjoy the maid's attempt at flirting. Annabel actually empathized with him.

She began to read and came to the story about the sinful woman who washed Jesus's feet with her tears. At the end of the story, Jesus said, "Your faith has saved you; go in peace."

How wonderful to know that Jesus didn't condemn women like the priest did. Even with a sinful woman, he didn't rant about how evil she was. He forgave her and said kind words to her. If only Sir Matefrid could read this! How different his sermons would be.

※ ⁓ ※

Ranulf was hardly listening as the girl read. He couldn't take his mind off the bruise on her wrist and the way he'd felt when he saw it, thinking about the bailiff hurting her. He didn't want to sympathize with her; he wanted to believe she had encouraged the bailiff's advances. But if he was honest with himself, he couldn't believe that. At the same time, he felt like a fool for thinking well of this servant who was young and beautiful—indeed, for thinking of her all.

He tried to concentrate on her lively voice as she continued with the next parable.

A twinge of conscience hit him when she read Jesus's words, "My mother and brothers are those who hear God's word and put it into practice." He felt another twinge when Jesus asked, "Where is your faith?" after calming the storm. But he refused to think about why.

When she read the account of the demon-possessed man whom Jesus healed, again Jesus's words were like a hot iron on his heart. "Return home and tell how much God has done for you." He was becoming more and more uncomfortable with the girl's lilting voice. What was wrong with him tonight? Usually the Bible made him feel peaceful. Now it seemed to reach right into his soul with one hand and squeeze his throat with the other.

She came to the story where Jesus healed a woman with an issue of blood. Jesus said, "Daughter, your faith has healed you. Go in peace." Peace. Where was his peace? For that matter, where was his healing? Before he could recover, she was reading the account of Jesus accompanying Jairus to his home, where his daughter had just died. Jesus said, *"Don't be afraid; just believe, and she will be healed."*

All at once it was as if a voice was saying to him, *You are afraid. Just believe and I will heal you.*

Ranulf's thoughts stilled as he pondered those words.

Was he afraid? And would God heal his scars? He hated his scars because of what they had cost him—his wife's love. But even if his hand had been whole and his face and body completely unscarred, she still would have rejected him.

Besides, his conscience told him it wasn't a physical healing he needed.

He tried to deny that God was truly speaking to his soul. He was the lord of the manor and wasn't afraid of anything. But his conscience pricked him again. He *was* afraid. Afraid of the agony he had felt from loving Guinevere and then finding she never loved him and never would. He was humiliated and betrayed, both publicly and privately, by the only woman he had ever loved.

It was easier to believe the worst about everyone, especially women. But if he held that attitude toward Annabel, he was no better than the village priest, who repeatedly condemned his flock for being full of depraved lusts, and condemned women as universally wicked. Ranulf didn't want to be bitter and cruel like Sir Matefrid, but if he was honest with himself, that was what he had become.

O God, forgive me. He forced himself not to groan aloud as he closed his eyes and prayed for forgiveness. Even as he did so, however, he wanted to cling to his belief that all women, especially beautiful ones, were duplicitous and evil. If all women were evil, then it wasn't his fault that his wife had not loved him, had been repulsed by him, and had loved another man. If all women were evil, he could hate them all to dull the pain of his wife's betrayal.

He hadn't been listening to Annabel read for some minutes. She'd come to the part where Jesus said, "The Son of Man must suffer many things and be rejected by the elders, chief priests and the teachers of the law, and he must be killed and on the third day be raised to life." Then he said to them all: 'Whoever wants to be my disciple must deny themselves and take up their cross daily and follow me. For whoever wants to save their life will lose it, but whoever loses their life for me will save it. What good is it for someone to gain the whole world, and yet lose or forfeit their very self?'"

He knew if he had it to do over, he wouldn't have allowed the wolf to hurt that servant girl. He shouldn't resent his scars. *Are they not proof, God, that I have lost my life to save it?* But he was sorry his inner scars had caused him to lash out at Annabel.

"Wait," he said, stopping her reading before he should change his mind.

She looked up at him with a curious expression.

"I'm sorry for what I said when the bailiff asked to marry you."

Her cheeks flushed red and she looked down.

"I never should have assumed the worst of you. I was wrong when I said the bailiff should count himself fortunate you refused to marry him."

She shook her head and looked confused, no doubt surprised that someone as bitter and ill-tempered as he would apologize. "I don't know what to say," she whispered.

"Simply say you forgive me, and I am satisfied."

"I forgive you," she said.

There was silence for several long moments, then he said, "When a person has been hurt, they must let God heal them or their pain will drive them into sin. You understand?"

A crease formed between her eyes. "I do." She stared down at the page.

Was she thinking about saying something more? Was she thinking of hurts she had experienced in the past? He waited, realizing he was holding his breath, hoping she would speak.

The door creaked open. Ranulf clenched his jaw in annoyance. He turned and saw one of the maids—Beatrice, he thought her name was—walk hesitantly into the room. Her gaze skimmed from him to Annabel and stopped. The girl pursed her lips. He was about to demand what she was doing there when she smiled broadly at him and hurried to his chair.

"My lord, if it pleases you, I would be happy to bring you something for your arm, for the burn." Beatrice stopped a mere handbreadth away and leaned forward. She went on in a breathy voice, "My mother always was the best at collecting the finest herbs for any sickness or injury, and I know what will do your arm good. Allow me to change your bandage tomorrow and I will show you how to apply—"

"Thank you. I will let you know if I need your assistance. You may go."

"Yes, my lord." As she left she curtsied low and shot another glance at Annabel.

He turned away from the girl and saw Annabel struggling to rise from the chair while holding the heavy book in her arms.

"I should go as well." She looked at him for permission, and her expression had turned to one of worry. He took the book from her, and without meeting his eye, she went out the door behind Beatrice.

He was struck again by the difference between Beatrice's practiced flirting and Annabel's open sincerity. But thinking about that only led to an ache in his chest. At the same time, he realized he felt lighter, as if a weight had lifted from his shoulders. He was looking at things from a different perspective than before, and it was as if he had reached the end of a journey, only to embark on a new one.

⌁

Beatrice caught Annabel's arm when she came into the undercroft. "Why do you always get to change the lord's bandage?" she hissed.

"I don't know. Because Mistress Eustacia asked me to?" *Perhaps she doesn't trust you because you're always flirting with him.*

"You had better tell her to let me bandage the lord's arm

tomorrow. Do you understand, Annabel?" Beatrice poked her finger into Annabel's shoulder.

Annabel slapped her hand away. "I'll do what Mistress Eustacia tells me and so will you."

"You just want Lord le Wyse all to yourself. I don't believe you're reading to him all that time, so what do you do up there? Tell us all about it, Annabel." Beatrice stood a few inches taller than Annabel and glared down at her with her hands on her hips.

Annabel forced a laugh through her tight throat. "I'm sorry to disappoint you, Beatrice, but there's nothing happening except reading." *Perhaps you should stop thinking like our priest.*

"Then let me change his bandage tomorrow."

"If that's what you want, Beatrice, you are welcome to take on as much of my work as you like."

Beatrice leaned even closer, until her nose was almost touching Annabel's.

Annabel laughed again. "You can change his bandage tomorrow, Beatrice. I truly don't care." But she did care—a little bit—if she were honest with herself. Beatrice trying to touch Lord le Wyse, trying to tempt him to think of her as more than just a servant … The thought was so unpleasant Annabel had to turn away from Beatrice to keep the girl from seeing the daggers in her eyes.

Beatrice said a few more things about being allowed to help Lord le Wyse, making vague threats if Annabel got in her way, but Annabel wasn't listening. She was too busy pushing away the image of Beatrice enticing Lord le Wyse.

Annabel went about her duties the next day. This time, when she filled Lord le Wyse's tankard, he said, "Thank you." He was still quiet, but his mood no longer seemed so black. As he ate, he gazed out the window instead of staring down at his drink with a grimace on his face. Perhaps the Bible reading was doing him as much good as it was her. She felt a lightness in her heart that she hadn't felt since her father died.

He had also begun staring at a red rose on the stone mantle above the fireplace. It was a beautiful rose, and had been opening a little bit more every day since Mistress Eustacia picked it and brought it inside. Annabel had never seen a more perfect flower. It seemed to grow fuller and more beautiful every day.

Later, when she was outside helping Mistress Eustacia hang out the washing, she noticed Lord le Wyse walking with Gilbert Carpenter, who held a sheet of parchment they seemed to be perusing and discussing. She watched as they strolled with their backs to her, obviously deep in conversation. Gilbert turned to Lord le Wyse and seemed very animated, moving his arms and hands as he talked. Lord le Wyse looked at the parchment and at him, nodding every so often. Then he reached out and picked a sizable leaf off a tree. He studied the leaf in his hand, and Annabel wondered if he was even listening to the mason.

Lord le Wyse's shoulders were very broad compared to Gilbert's. He was several inches taller too, and his posture was regal, yet relaxed. Gilbert was wiry, while Lord le Wyse was solid.

She shook her head, suddenly realizing how long she'd been staring at the two men, comparing their looks. She went back to hanging the clothes on the line.

She determined to dismiss thoughts of her lord and his master mason and think instead on the tasks Mistress Eustacia had given her to do that day. It was a long list, and Annabel ticked off each task in her head until Lord le Wyse and Gilbert Carpenter disappeared down the path toward the site of her lord's new home.

That night after the evening meal, Eustacia brought the bandages, honey, and clean water to Annabel and nudged her toward where Lord le Wyse sat. She looked up into the mistress's face. Surely the older woman didn't have romantic ideas about Annabel and her lord. *I must be imagining it.*

Beatrice sidled up between Mistress Eustacia and Annabel immediately.

"I can change the lord's bandage tonight, Mistress Eustacia. I have some herbs that are very good for burns."

Mistress Eustacia looked at the girl then shook her head. "Lord Ranulf is used to Annabel dressing his wound, and the lord is very picky, he is. You run along and get yourself to bed."

"Please, Mistress Eustacia." Beatrice had lowered her voice to a whisper so no one else would hear. "I have these special herbs. I told Lord le Wyse about them last night—I think he wants to try them."

Mistress Eustacia didn't say anything for a moment, then said firmly, "If you wish to leave your medicines for him, I will take them, but Annabel will do the dressing."

Beatrice held the bags of herbs away from Eustacia's reaching hand. "I'll give them to him myself." She turned and flounced out of the room.

Annabel looked at her mistress. "Last night she asked if she could bandage his arm. I don't mind."

"Nonsense. I will not have her . . . well, never mind. You do as I tell you and take care of Lord Ranulf's arm. That's a good girl."

Annabel carried the stool toward Lord le Wyse, wondering how much of the exchange he had heard. She set about unwinding his bandage. As soon as she had taken it off, however, Beatrice came back into the room and hurried straight over to Lord le Wyse.

"My lord, I brought my mother's herbs to put on your arm, just as I promised. Move over, Annabel." She pushed Annabel's shoulder, and Annabel stood, allowing Beatrice to plop herself down in her place. Lord le Wyse watched Annabel, a masked expression on his face, as Beatrice handed him a cup. "Drink this, my lord. It is my mother's special drink made from herbs. And I will put this over the burn."

Would Lord le Wyse allow Beatrice this liberty? Annabel watched as he seemed to sigh in resignation and allow Beatrice to lightly press some green leaves onto his arm.

"Here! What are you about?" Mistress Eustacia rushed over to the lord's side. "What is that you're doing?"

"It's comfrey," Beatrice stated stoutly, placing her hands on her hips. "It is good for burns. My mother said so."

"It's all right, Mistress." Annabel intervened before Mistress Eustacia did harm to the girl. "Comfrey is indeed good for burns." *And we've been using it all along.*

"Of course it's good! It will make him well!" Beatrice's cheeks were flushed pink. She plastered on a smile and looked at Lord le Wyse. "You will see, my lord."

"Very well. And I suppose I must drink this?" He picked up the cup of steaming water.

"Yes, my lord."

"All right, that's all good and well, Beatrice." Mistress Eustacia flapped her hands at her as though shooing a chicken. "You may go now. You've done your ministrations for one night."

Beatrice stood, holding her head high in indignation. She turned to go, but then looked back at Lord le Wyse and smiled. "I only want to be of help. Please let me know if it helps, my lord. I will come whenever you need me." She batted her eyes and lingered a moment, smiling down at him, then left, her nose stuck in the air.

Annabel could barely contain the giggle that tickled her throat.

Mistress Eustacia nodded to her. "Go on, lass. You can finish your task now."

Annabel sat back down and proceeded to rewrap the bandage over the comfrey leaves Beatrice had spread over his arm. Out of the corner of her eye she saw Lord le Wyse take a sip from the cup Beatrice had brought him. He scrunched his face as though tasting something bitter then set the cup back on the table beside him.

As expected after she finished, Lord le Wyse asked her if she would read to him.

"Yes, my lord."

"You aren't too tired?"

She shook her head. He was her lord and could order her to do anything, and she was obliged to do it. But he treated her more kindly than her own family. He wasn't trying to force her to marry disgusting old Bailiff Tom and was even willing to protect her from him. She realized it wasn't so bad to be here at the lord's manor. She was working all day to pay her family's debt, yes, but she was also able to read the Bible every night, which was what she wanted more than anything. The other girls, though they hadn't accepted her as one of them, were more lively company than her mother and brothers.

Her servant status could almost be a blessing.

This thought surprised her. She'd felt abandoned by God, but maybe He had actually been taking care of her by sending her here.

She moved to one of the matching chairs before the fireplace and began to read. She read so long, in fact, that she glanced up to make sure Lord le Wyse was still awake. He hadn't moved for quite a long time and his face was completely cast into shadow by the wing of the deep chair where he was reclined.

She thought about asking him a question to see if he was asleep, but she was afraid if she did he would ask her if she was ready to stop reading. And she wasn't ready to stop. *Even if he is asleep, what could it hurt to read further?*

Coming to the end of the book of Saint John, she read, *"I have told you these things, so that in me you may have peace. In this world you will have trouble. But take heart! I have overcome the world."*

God wanted her to have peace. But how exactly would that peace come about?

"What are you thinking?" Lord Le Wyse's gruff voice startled her, coming from the shadowy depths of his chair.

"I was wondering about peace and if our troubles draw us closer to God or push us further away from Him."

Lord le Wyse roused himself to lean forward, gazing at her intently. It made her wonder if he'd been staring at her the entire time she'd been reading and she hadn't been able to tell.

"Have you had many troubles?"

"No more than most."

"Have they brought you closer to God?"

"When my father died, I prayed for hours every day, and it

made me feel closer to God." She waited, hoping he would say something about his own troubles. Though it was presumptuous to ask something personal of her lord, she decided to take the risk. "You have had much pain and sorrow, haven't you, my lord?"

His face was a mask that stared past her. Finally he replied. "Yes. As much as most. My wife died, along with the child she had lately bore, during the outbreak of pestilence three years ago."

"Oh, that is very sad. I'm so sorry."

He didn't look sad, he looked angry, as if he didn't want her pity. "It was God's will."

"Do you think so?" Annabel felt dismayed. "Does God cause bad things to happen? Does the Bible say that?"

The familiar scowl came over his features. "Sometimes God metes out judgment here on earth instead of waiting until the afterlife." A low growl came from his throat. He shook his head. "I don't wish to talk about that."

"Of course not, my lord. Forgive me for my presumption."

He blew out a frustrated breath. "It is my own bitterness ... It isn't your fault. The truth is, the Bible says God 'has compassion on all He has made,' wanting all to come to him and be saved. And you may ask me anything you wish. What was your question? Do troubles bring us closer to God? The answer is yes, they do, but we must choose it. Otherwise, our troubles do just the opposite. They push us away from God. 'Cast all your anxiety on Him because He cares for you.'"

His voice had gradually softened with each word he spoke, until it was deep and rich, like the sound of thunder in the distance.

The words themselves were beautiful. The fact that Lord le Wyse knew those particular passages by heart made her think he had taken comfort from them, that he had allowed his pain and sorrow to draw him closer to God in the past. *Father God, may he be reminded of the times that you comforted him.*

"It is late," he declared. "You should be abed."

Annabel let him take the book from her. Their eyes met for a moment. She bid him good night, and as she went down to the undercroft, she was struck by the thought that, right now, tonight, she did feel at peace.

When Sunday came again, Annabel braced herself for seeing Sir Matefrid. Even so, she walked to the church with a light step, humming a lively tune she'd heard her father sing many times. Sir Matefrid's words of doom and indecency and sin would hold no horrors for her today.

She knew what the Holy Writ said, and it was full of joyful words. While she knelt to pray, she meditated on the passages she and Lord le Wyse had been reading. Some whole sentences came to her, and she couldn't help smiling. When she glanced up, she saw Maud and Beatrice staring at her suspiciously.

Perhaps it was irreverent to smile in church. She wasn't sure, although she had a strong inclination to believe that God wouldn't mind at all. After all, it was rather difficult to rejoice without smiling.

When the singing began, Annabel felt as though she were hearing the songs for the first time, or at least in a whole new way.

> O come, Thou Dayspring, come and cheer
> Our spirits by Thine advent here;
> Disperse the gloomy clouds of night,
> And death's dark shadows put to flight.
> Rejoice! Rejoice! Emmanuel
> Shall come to thee, O Israel.

Her spirit seemed to leap within her, her breath expanding her chest, making her feel as though she could rejoice forever. *Yes, God, I do rejoice.* He had given her so many wondrous gifts. How could she not rejoice? He had given her a Bible. Yes, it belonged to Lord le Wyse, but he allowed her to read it.

If only everyone could know this joy she felt.

Her state of joy and communion with God continued through the Holy Eucharist and Sir Matefrid's sermon, which she hardly seemed to hear and of which she remembered nothing. As the villagers wandered out of the church, Annabel joined them, emerging into the sunshine of late summer.

Maud was straining her neck, staring. "What's the matter with you? Your face is too ... happy. Like a dog with a fresh bone."

"I am happy."

Maud narrowed her eyes as she stared even harder at her. "Why? You have little reason to be happy, let alone smile. You're a servant and your family doesn't care about you."

She tried not to let Maud's words wound her. "It's true that I may seem not to have any reason to be happy, but I've been reading the Holy Scriptures and I've learned much about God's faithfulness." Annabel's breath came fast, even though she and Maud were walking slowly, far behind the other maids. She couldn't contain the smile on her face, even when Maud's scowl deepened, her eyebrows low and threatening.

"Is that what you do in the upper hall for an hour every night, just you and Lord le Wyse? I knew you were different, strange and all that, but you sound mad. What makes you think you can read the Bible? Don't you know you're not supposed to be thinking ... I don't know ... that you know something about God?" She said *God* as though He were a fairy tale or an unwanted relative. "Nobody wants to hear that kind of talk, Annabel Chapman." She stuck her finger into Annabel's chest. "You're just a woman. You're no priest, and you don't know God, so just shut your mouth."

Maud stalked away, leaving Annabel staring after her.

She walked slowly, following far behind Maud's stiff figure. Then she saw Stephen up ahead by the side of the road, apparently waiting for her.

"Hello, Stephen! How are you faring?"

"Lord le Wyse has been very pleased with the furniture I'm working on, and I've already finished the front door."

"That is good news." Should she tell him about reading Lord le Wyse's Bible and of all the wonderful things she was learning? Or would he disapprove just as Maud had?

"Stephen, what would you say if I were reading the Holy Writ?" she asked.

Stephen stopped and smiled. "I'd be very happy for you, Annabel. That was always your dream, to read the Bible."

Excitement bubbled inside her again. "Lord le Wyse has me read it to him. It's wonderful to see the words of God." She paused, thinking of Maud. "I think everybody in this village believes God only wants to punish us with plagues and curses and droughts. Don't you think that's sad?"

Stephen looked over at her. "Perhaps you could read the Scriptures to me sometime? I know it's in Latin, but—"

"But I could interpret it for you! Oh, Stephen, would you want me to?"

"Yes, very much. You know what people will say, though, about a woman reading anything, and especially the Holy Writ."

"Not everyone is so backward, Stephen. Lord le Wyse doesn't mind at all. It's good to read the Scriptures."

Stephen shook his head. "I don't suppose you can get in any trouble for it, as long as Lord le Wyse is asking you to do it."

She wanted to tell him how much she enjoyed the conversations she had with Lord le Wyse when they read together, but she decided it was best not to mention that, even to Stephen.

Later that day Annabel and Mistress Eustacia sat resting with the sheep, who were grazing in the courtyard. Mistress Eustacia had brought a stool to sit on while she did some sewing in the daylight, but Annabel was content to sit on the grass and stare at the courtyard before her and the sky above her, letting her thoughts wander. The sun stayed hidden behind the clouds, but the birds chirped cheerfully and a slight breeze puffed at them occasionally. Annabel stroked one particularly friendly ewe lamb, who sighed as she munched her grass.

Annabel's Sunday was not progressing quite as joyfully as it had begun. Maud's reactions that morning made her feel like a warm fire that someone dumped a bucket of water on. Even Stephen had cautioned her that others might not approve of her reading the Bible.

Though Lord le Wyse obviously approved. And dwelling on his approval restored her warm, happy feeling.

Annabel affectionately rubbed the sheep's head. Was anyone at home taking care of her goat, Dilly? The poor animal could mostly fend for herself, she reasoned, but if her lazy brothers didn't milk Dilly, her supply would run dry. *If my family didn't need the goat so much, I would ask Lord le Wyse if Dilly could stay at the manor.*

Before she could examine the thought further, movement and Beatrice's high-pitched voice drew her attention to the manor steps. Lord le Wyse was a few steps behind Beatrice, who tripped and fell back into him. He caught her and set her up on her feet.

"Oh, my lord!" she said, louder than necessary. "My ankle. I don't think I can walk. I must have injured it."

Even from across the courtyard Annabel could see Beatrice's face scrunched up in pain. Lord le Wyse put his good arm around her and helped her down the steps. Beatrice limped and leaned heavily on him.

Was Beatrice hurt? Or did she only want to be close to Lord le Wyse?

Beatrice was smiling now, looking up into Lord le Wyse's face and thanking him profusely, insisting that she couldn't make it to her bed in the undercroft without his help. Lord le Wyse called out to Gilbert Carpenter as he was passing nearby, and Annabel watched Beatrice's smile shift direction. Lord le Wyse turned the limping girl over to Gilbert and then hurried up the manor steps. Gilbert in turn disappeared into the undercroft with Beatrice hanging on to him.

Whether Beatrice was hurt or not, she'd managed to claim the attention of both Lord le Wyse and Gilbert Carpenter, at least for a few moments. But Annabel was surprised at how much the sight of her in Lord le Wyse's arms, then hanging on to him as he helped her down the steps, had made her want to slap Beatrice silly. The dairymaid was obviously only pretending.

A rustle in the grass near her foot made her look up. Gilbert Carpenter stood gazing down at her. He nodded politely.

"Miss Annabel. Would you take a walk with me?"

He'd certainly rid himself of Beatrice quickly.

Annabel sought an excuse not to go with him, but she could think of nothing. She turned to Mistress Eustacia, but her mistress kept her eyes on her needlework and refused to look up. Finally, she made an effort to keep the reluctance out her voice — without sounding eager, either. "Of course."

She pretended not to see the hand he offered as she got to her feet. She glanced around for Adam. He was nowhere to be seen, and she turned to follow the master mason.

Again she asked herself if she could imagine being married to this man. Would she be able to put aside her squeamishness and let him touch her? Somehow the thought remained repugnant. Perhaps she should tell him she had no interest in him, so he could give up on her and hunt for a wife elsewhere. After all, Adam wasn't around to hear.

Gilbert glanced at her shyly from the corner of his eye. He seemed nice enough, and he was rather handsome, after all. Why couldn't she feel for him what the other girls in the undercroft seemed to think she *should* feel for him? She should be grateful he wanted to marry her and make her a free woman again.

They walked in silence around the outer edge of the courtyard, turning toward the trees that led to the site of Lord le Wyse's new home.

Finally, Gilbert spoke. "So you like animals?"

"Yes."

"I saw you petting that ewe lamb. I like animals too. I generally don't have much time to spend with them, with my work."

"Me, neither."

"If you like animals, I would buy you as many as you want—sheep, goats, chickens, geese ..."

Annabel felt her cheeks heat. How could she tell him she had no interest in what he could give her? It made her feel mean and awkward, but somehow, she had to tell him. "I should tell you that although I love Adam and think you will make someone a good husband, I'm hoping to enter a convent some day." Of course, she had no idea if that would ever happen, but she was still hoping, wasn't she?

"I see."

They entered the cover of the trees, ambling slowly now down the lane to the river.

She wasn't sure how to continue the conversation after she'd so thoroughly sabotaged it. They walked along in silence. Finally, she worked up the courage to say, "I know Adam had a notion that he'd like to see us marry, but there are a lot of young maidens who—"

"I see you don't think of me as a husband, Miss Annabel, but if it's all right with you, I'd still like to try to change your mind." He turned to face her, and before she knew what he was about to do, he took her hand in his and stared into her eyes. "I don't mind waiting until you are ready." He lowered his head and scuffed the ground with his foot. "I promise to try not to make you uncomfortable, but ... I still hope you will change your mind ... about me."

His fingers felt clammy and cool. When he let go, she shuddered in relief. Holding his hand made her feel like running away.

He looked so humble and harmless, she nodded. "Very well."

Gilbert Carpenter wasn't ugly or frightening, and she was fond of Adam. The thought of someone caring for her above all others, bound to protect her and keep her safe and provided for, was not an abhorrent thought. She just couldn't imagine that person being Gilbert Carpenter.

It was almost time for bed, and Annabel stepped carefully in the dark, wishing she'd asked someone to come with her, but at least she still carried her knife. Sometimes she asked Beatrice to go with her to the privy, but Beatrice wasn't being very friendly today. Most of the maids didn't walk all the way down the rustic path, as the privy was deep in the woods, well away from the manor house. Most simply found a thick bush to squat behind. But she preferred to avail herself of the privacy of the little wooden building.

She glanced at the trees that crowded the well-worn path on both sides, knowing the wooden privy stood in a small clearing ahead. Just when she was about to lose what little nerve she'd retained during her walk, her destination appeared in the dappled moonlight that filtered through the leaves.

She reached her hand out to open the door and an owl hooted. She jumped, then frowned. *If a bird of prey wants to sneak up on his food, he shouldn't hoot so loudly.*

She spent as little time as possible inside the small privy. When she pushed open the rough wooden door and stepped outside, Annabel caught sight of movement, someone emerging from around the side of the privy. She tried to make out which maiden it was, as it had to be another woman heading for the privy, since only women were allowed in the vicinity.

But as the figure approached, it was clearly not female.

The man lunged toward her and grabbed her arm in one swift movement. All the air rushed from her chest. She opened her lips to scream, but the man clamped a hand over her mouth and dragged her into the trees.

Chapter
10

Annabel clawed at his arm while trying to draw in a good breath. Finally, she gave up on screaming and struggled to bite him, though the rank odor of his hand, like soured milk, sickened her.

"Don't make a sound," the man rasped in her ear, "or I'll break your little neck."

Annabel recognized Bailiff Tom's voice. Her heart pounded and she struggled to keep breathing. His hand completely covered her mouth and was partially blocking her nose. She managed to open her mouth and promptly bit down as hard as she could, her teeth sinking into soft flesh.

Bailiff Tom cursed under his breath. He pulled his hand away, but before Annabel could even react, he used it to slap her across her cheek.

Bells rang in her ears, and for a moment she lost her bearings. When she was able to focus her eyes again, she tried to run but only took two steps before he jerked her arm so hard she cried out in pain. She wanted to scream for help, but he clamped his hand over her mouth again, crushing her lips and her cheeks even tighter than before. *Please, God . . . don't let me faint.*

"If you scream and raise the hue and cry," he said, his breath in her ear, "I'll tell the whole village that you have been with me *and* Lord le Wyse."

The overpowering smell of ale and his bad breath made her stomach heave. She swallowed to stop herself from vomiting.

"What kind of spell have you put on Lord le Wyse? Your brothers and your mother want you to marry me. Why won't he allow it?" His voice was slurred from too much drink, but as drunk as he was, he was still too strong for her. His fingers were like iron around her arm and her face, cutting into her flesh. "Do you think anyone will believe you over me? Stay quiet, or I'll make you sorry, girl."

The people of Glynval would believe the bailiff's lies and she would be scorned even more than she had been before. But that was better than whatever the bailiff planned to do to her. She would scream and raise the hue and cry as soon as he removed his hand from her mouth, at the first opportunity.

He dragged her farther into the woods, her feet scrabbling to stay under her. "You're an indentured servant. Who else will marry you? You should have realized you could never refuse me." He squeezed her face mercilessly. She flailed at him, hitting the hand that covered her face. She wouldn't let him hurt her. She would kill him first.

He went into a fit of dire threats and curses. "Stop clawing my hand, you little witch." He caught her arm under his and pinned it to her side, gouging her ribs with his bony elbow. His voice sounded like an animal's, growling and spitting.

God, help me. She managed to slip her hand into her dress pocket and pull out her knife.

Her head spun so, she was afraid she would lose consciousness. She gripped the knife, still not sure what to do with it. Should she stab him? Or wait for a better opportunity? Perhaps she could threaten him without having to cut him. He still held her arm, his fingers digging into her flesh and sending an ache all the way to her shoulder.

He sputtered, "If you make trouble for me, I'll make double for you. I'll ruin your reputation. Then who will help you? Not your brothers nor your poor mother. Nay, even Lord le Wyse will want naught to do with ye."

Annabel's heart turned over with fear. Lord le Wyse would believe her—there the bailiff was wrong—but the thought of Tom saying terrible things about her, the kind of things the priest was always saying ... She would be an outcast. Even Lord le Wyse couldn't protect her from what the villagers would say about her once they thought she was a loose maiden.

He increased the pressure on her arm, and in desperation she held up her knife until it caught a moonbeam and glimmered.

He spewed a new string of curses. "Ye're possessed. A lunatic girl, waving a knife at your bailiff."

He let go of her face and grabbed her wrist, giving it a sharp wrench. She tried to scream, but it came out as little more than a squeak, as pain and fear caused her fingers to involuntarily loosen. She watched the knife fall to the dirt. The bailiff let go of her arms and fell to the ground, groping for the weapon.

Finally free, Annabel turned to run. Bailiff Tom ranted behind her, "I'll ruin you. I'll say you enticed me and every man in the village."

She only ran a few steps when her foot struck something and she pitched forward, landing on her hands and knees in the sticks and leaves. Someone grabbed her by her armpits and pulled her up.

"Get away from me." She gasped for breath, pushing at the person's chest with her arms.

"Annabel? Are you well? I was at the men's privy and thought I heard a struggle." It was Stephen's voice. He held her away from him, his face illuminated by the moonlight.

"I have to get away." Her heart beat so hard it shook her. She looked over her shoulder and immediately regretted it. The bailiff staggered to his feet and started toward her, the knife in his hand.

Stephen let her go. Annabel ran two steps and stopped, whispering loudly to Stephen, "Run! If we hurry he won't be able to follow." But Stephen stood still, facing the bailiff.

O God, I want to run. But she had to make sure the bailiff didn't hurt Stephen.

"What are you about, man?" Stephen asked. "Will you kill her with that knife? Kill me?"

Bailiff Tom was breathing hard now. "Get away from here, cripple. No one wants you — the devil's own spawn."

Stephen bent down and picked up the rock she had stumbled over. It was large, as big as a man's head. He held the stone against his stomach. "What were you doing to her?"

Tom cackled like a man possessed. Annabel clutched her throat.

"What do you know of what happened? Now get out of here. This here is Lord le Wyse's land. You think he wants daft, deformed cripples putting curses on his crops?"

The bailiff stepped toward them, the knife high, as though he was preparing to strike. He was only a few steps away and coming closer. In two seconds he would be within reach of Stephen.

Stephen hefted the rock and grunted as he let it fly. Annabel gasped as the rock slammed into Bailiff Tom's head near his right eye. Tom fell to the ground, his body landing with a muffled crash in the twigs and leaves of the forest floor.

Annabel held her breath as she waited to see if the bailiff would move. Relief stole through her. *I can make it back safely now.* But the longer she watched his motionless body, the more fear squeezed her throat.

Stephen broke the stillness. "O God, be merciful." He crossed himself and stepped toward the bailiff. He knelt beside him and held his hand against Tom atte Water's neck. Then he placed his hand over his mouth and nose, waiting.

He looked up at Annabel. "I think he's dead."

Dead. The word echoed in her mind. This must be a bad dream. Surely Stephen was mistaken. What terrible thing would happen to Stephen if the bailiff was dead?

Her stomach churned and her knees wobbled, forcing her to lean against the nearest tree. When that didn't stop the buzzing in her head, she sank to the ground, still staring at the bailiff's body.

I am to blame.

The thought struck her hard, like a stab in the ribs.

Her eyes focused on the knife, still clutched tight in Bailiff Tom's fist. If she hadn't taken that knife to defend herself, hadn't carried it in her pocket everywhere she went … She should have simply raised the hue and cry against the bailiff the moment she was free, should have tried harder to scream. Perhaps more people would have come to her aid, and this wouldn't have happened.

She rubbed her cheeks and the spot between her eyes that burned like a bee sting. She hung her head almost to her knees, waiting for the burning sensation to subside.

Cautiously, she raised her eyes. Stephen's body jerked from side to side as he struggled to get off the ground. "It's done. It's done. God forgive me." He crossed himself. "God forgive me."

"Are you sure he's dead? Check again."

"We have to get out of here."

I'm to blame. Stephen was defending me. But she couldn't help being glad that she was now safe from the bailiff's evil intentions.

Stephen was right. They had to get out of there.

She got to her feet and grabbed Stephen's arm. "Should I take my knife? Perhaps they will find out it's mine and will think that I — " She shivered at the unsaid words.

"Nay. Leave it." Stephen looked pale in the scant light that filtered through the trees.

The hoot of an owl split the silence, making her flinch. She turned and saw the largest bird she'd ever seen perched on a branch at eye level, staring straight at her with huge red-orange eyes. Two tufts rose above his round head on either side. Black markings framed his old man's bushy white eyebrows and mustache.

Annabel tore her eyes from the unearthly looking owl. Her heartbeat thundered in her head as she and Stephen hurried away from the bailiff's body. Stephen didn't go straight toward the manor house but led her deeper into the woods before finally turning back.

Annabel let go of his arm and ran, shuddering again at what had just happened. It still didn't seem real. Just a bad dream.

But no, the bailiff was dead, gone, and it was her fault. She didn't want to believe it. She couldn't think it, or it would overwhelm her. Somehow she had to get to the manor house, to distance herself from the body.

"Annabel," Stephen whispered with a new urgency in his voice. He stopped in the woods and they faced each other, but it was too dark to see his face. "Don't tell anyone what just happened. No one. Give me your solemn oath. It's for your protection as well as mine. We know nothing, and will act as we did before."

Her lips felt numb. She opened her mouth to speak, but nothing came out. After swallowing past the dryness at the back of her throat, she uttered, "I promise." She turned away from him and immediately stumbled over a root in the dark.

The owl hooted again. At least the bailiff was farther behind her now. Her stomach quivered. If they could only get out of this wretched forest.

"Who's there?"

The voice made her jerk herself to a halt. It was Lord le Wyse.

Stephen stopped a few feet behind her.

"Who's there, I say?" Lord le Wyse's voice was a rough snarl. He stepped toward them and reached out a hand. Her throat swelled shut and she couldn't even swallow.

"Annabel, is that you?" Lord le Wyse's unmistakable broad frame loomed in front of her.

"Yes, my lord."

He stepped closer. "I thought I heard someone near the privy. Are you well?"

Stephen pulled on her arm, jerking her away from Lord le Wyse.

"I am well, my lord. I must go." Before she finished speaking, Stephen was all but dragging her through the forest. He moved so quickly she had to battle to find her footing. She looked over her shoulder but couldn't see Lord le Wyse through the darkness and trees.

They rushed through the woods, branches and bushes tearing at her clothes as she stumbled at a pace that must have been as fast as Stephen could go and was much faster than she had ever seen him walk before. Would Lord le Wyse follow them? Or would he go farther and find the body of the dead bailiff?

Perhaps Tom wasn't actually dead. Perhaps his breathing was shallow and Stephen was simply unable to detect it. She had heard of that happening before. After all, how many people had Stephen proclaimed dead? Probably none.

But the sinking feeling inside her that hollowed her out and made her knees weak told her he was dead. *Dead.*

They were taking a roundabout way back to the manor house. She wondered if anyone was following her, but all she could hear was the crunch of dry leaves under their feet and branches that brushed by her ears. She stumbled over a fallen tree branch lying in her path, then her toe hit a root and she fell. She registered skinned knees without feeling any pain as Stephen grabbed her arm and pulled her to her feet again.

"Hold on to me," he said.

Without taking time to brush herself off, she hurried on.

She imagined Lord le Wyse finding the bailiff's body. What would he think? She swallowed the nastiness that rose into her throat. Vomiting would only slow them down.

Would Lord le Wyse think she had killed him? Perhaps he would think it was an accident, that the bailiff fell and hit his head.

Annabel and Stephen came to the edge of the forest at the clearing around the manor house. She searched but didn't see anyone as she tried to catch her breath. A few men could be heard laughing in the vicinity of the wooden building that now served as their sleeping quarters.

Stephen hung back in the shadows of the trees. He whispered, "I beg you, Annabel, don't tell anyone I was out here tonight."

She felt sick at the desperation in his voice. Their eyes met. *Oh, Stephen.*

He turned and hurried toward the road to the village, skirting the edge of the greenway to avoid being seen.

Another loud *hoo-hoo* rang out from the forest behind her. She shivered and ran toward the undercroft. Just as her hand reached out for the door, a voice split the air behind her.

"Annabel. Halt."

She jerked her hand back. Her heart stopped beating then raced so fast it stole her breath.

Lord le Wyse emerged from the trees and strode toward her. She pressed her back against the undercroft door, wishing she could hide. But he had seen her already, his eye focused intently on her face.

He stood two feet from her. "Come with me, quickly."

She followed him as he practically ran up the steep steps that led to the upper hall of the manor house. What did he plan to do? Her behavior certainly was suspicious, and Lord le Wyse had likely seen Stephen with her, or at least noticed someone pulling her along. She couldn't tell him Stephen was with her. He had asked her to swear not to tell anyone, but how could she lie to her lord?

She tried to steady herself as Lord le Wyse led her inside. Standing in the shadow of the doorframe, he glanced outside before shutting the door. He paced off each corner of the room, which was deep in shadows, as if trying to make sure no one else was there. The hall's only light came from one candle on the table across the room and a little moonlight shining through the windows.

Apparently satisfied no one lurked inside, Lord le Wyse looked to Annabel. She simply stood there, praying, *Father God, let it all be a dream.*

He beckoned to her with his hand, and she stepped slowly toward him, her knees weak. He led her to a corner, backing her into it and standing beside the window in such a way to block her view—or perhaps to keep anyone outside from seeing her.

"Who was with you in the forest just now?"

Her heart dropped to her toes. It was against the law to

withhold the truth from one's lord. She searched his face and saw a spark of compassion. "Oh, my lord, please. Please don't ask me." Her words became a whisper as tears clogged her throat. *God, help me. Tell me what to do.*

"Annabel." His voice softened. "You must tell me everything that happened."

She pressed trembling fingers to her lips as the tears spilled down her cheeks. "I'm so afraid."

"What were you doing in the forest tonight?"

"I-I visited the privy." She had to struggle to stop the sob that was emerging from her throat.

"Did you see anyone?"

"Yes, my lord."

"Who?"

She looked down at the dark floor. She wished Lord le Wyse would stir up the embers in the fireplace and light a torch. The darkness seemed to close in around her, reminding her of the forest and the events that had taken place mere minutes before. But Lord le Wyse did not move as he waited for her to answer. *O God, what shall I say?*

"Tell me. Who did you see?"

"I saw—" She shook her head. She couldn't say it. She couldn't say his name.

"You saw Bailiff Tom, didn't you?"

Her tears came faster. "Yes. Is he ...?"

"He's not dead. At least, he was still breathing when I left him. I sent Gilbert Carpenter to get some men to take his body to his sister's house, since it isn't very far away."

The sob broke through and she cried from relief.

Lord le Wyse touched her hand with a handkerchief. "Here."

She took it and held it to her eyes and nose, willing herself to stop crying.

In her mind's eye she saw her father, draped with a linen sheet, after he died from the horrible pestilence. Her brothers had carried him out and had even dug his grave themselves. As her mind reeled, she imagined Bailiff Tom covered in a similar sheet, the priest performing the last rites. Her father died of a sickness, but this ... this death would be by her own knife.

No, she was getting confused. He wasn't dead, she hoped, and it was a rock that hit him in the head. Her insides trembled violently at the memory. But perhaps it was caused by her knife, in an indirect way. After all, if Bailiff Tom hadn't been holding her knife, Stephen wouldn't have thrown the rock. Would he?

Lord le Wyse shifted, drawing her attention back to his looming form. "What happened? Tell me." He reached out and touched her arm with his fingertips, a brief caress.

"It was an accident."

"I know. Only tell me what happened and I can help."

"I'm not sure I should tell you." She felt torn. Her throat ached with held-back tears, making her voice sound rough.

"I know you were there when Tom was injured. And I know someone was with you in the woods. I saw him behind you. You mustn't try to protect anyone, Annabel. It will look bad for you."

The room had started to tilt to one side, then the other. "Truly, I don't want to get anyone into any trouble, my lord. Don't tell anyone I was there. I'm afraid — don't make me tell you — "

She began to sob again. He drew her to the chair by the fireplace and gently helped her sit.

"Annabel."

She looked up at him, hearing the gentle command in his voice.

"If the bailiff doesn't recover consciousness, I must summon the coroner. He's coming anyway to investigate our barn fire. He will make an examination, attempt to question witnesses. If he finds out you were there, you will have to answer a lot of questions. And you cannot refuse to answer. The coroner has the authority of the king."

She felt stunned.

"But if it truly was an accident, you should tell me exactly what happened. No one will be hung for an accident."

Hung? Was it an accident? She tried to sort it all out, tried to figure out how to explain it without it seeming as if Stephen had tried to ... kill Tom.

It sent a pain through her chest and into her stomach to even think the words. She wanted so much to tell Lord le Wyse, but she had to protect her friend. The bailiff might still die.

"You should tell me." His voice was tender and coaxing.

With anxiety wringing her stomach like wet laundry, she said, "If someone tried to protect themselves—or someone else—but they didn't mean to kill the person, only to frighten him away, is it an accident if the person is killed?"

"Are you telling me that the person who was with you was trying to protect you?"

She had said too much. She pressed her hands against her cheeks. *I promised not to tell.* "I didn't say that." She shook her head and turned away. If he continued questioning her, she would end up telling him everything and betraying poor Stephen. Stephen was only trying to defend her.

But she could trust Lord le Wyse, couldn't she? Perhaps he would truly help her and Stephen—would protect her friend. Could she risk it? Nay. The consequences for Stephen were too great; if the bailiff did not survive, Stephen would be tried for murder, she was sure. And if the bailiff lived, he would tell the jury that Stephen attacked him, and who would believe a cripple over the bailiff?

Her head was pounding in her temples, pounding like a thousand drums. She wanted to lie down. "May I go now? I'm so sorry, I ... I need to go."

Chapter
11

Annabel was as transparent as a child as she stood and took a step away from him. She was trying to protect someone. Great anxiety and pain etched lines on her forehead at the thought of betraying this person. Who could it be? A brother? Or maybe Stephen the furniture maker with whom he'd seen her talking when she first arrived. It could be anyone, since she would feel a sense of loyalty to whoever had tried to defend her from the bailiff. He fervently wished he had been the one to help her, wished he had already stripped Tom of his duties as bailiff and made him fear for his life if he dared touch Annabel again.

But what had the bailiff done to her? Tom had been clutching a knife.

Ranulf was seized with a horrible thought. "Did he hurt you?" He stepped closer as his gaze raced over her body, from head to foot.

"Who? No, no. I am unhurt."

But he saw her hand go to her arm and rub it distractedly.

"Tell me the truth. Did he hurt you?" He emphasized each word.

Her bottom lip trembled and she caught it between her teeth. "He hurt my arm, and he hurt my face ... to keep me quiet, so I couldn't raise the hue and cry. But he didn't hurt me in the way you mean. Although he would have had I not gotten away." Tears started to gather in her eyes.

He should have been there. "Let me see your arm."

Reluctantly, she held out her arm. He grasped her hand and pushed up the sleeve of her dress to reveal bruises on her wrist, then more dark fingerprints against the pale skin of her upper arm.

Staring at her arm, he had a sudden yearning to kiss her soft skin—

He let go as if her arm had turned into a hot brand. But it was too late. He should never have touched her. She looked so pale and shaky, so vulnerable. How he longed to hold her.

He was crazed to think this way. He must get hold of himself. Such thoughts could only lead to pain.

He backed away from her. Instead of foolishly thinking about comforting her, he should be thinking of the best way to help her.

It would not look good if she was found alone with him, crying, her face tearstained and lightly bruised.

"Come."

She placed her hand trustingly in his and he led her to the door. "You must go. No one must see you just now." He hurried her toward the door, much too aware of the softness of her small hand in his. "Don't speak of this to anyone. Go down and wash your face then climb into bed and pretend all is well. I will get a message to you if the bailiff dies. Otherwise, you are to assume he is alive and well." He opened the door and stood back in the shadows. "Now go."

As she made her way down the steps, he only saw one person: Mistress Eustacia. She emerged from the kitchen, headed toward the manor. Annabel disappeared into the undercroft.

<hr />

Annabel climbed into bed, her limbs aching and still trembling. Thankfully, no one seemed curious or even noticed that she had been missing. While the other maidens were talking and laughing, she covertly searched each face until she was certain none of them knew about the body of the bailiff lying in the leaves.

Then Maud walked in.

Her stomach sank. Did Maud know her father could be near death?

Dread and fear saturated her senses. Maud looked tired, her eyelids drooping. No one spoke to her as she made her way to her bed and began to rummage through the things stored underneath. Her every movement seemed to convey aloneness.

What kind of father had the bailiff been? Poor Maud had already lost almost her entire family. She had only one sister left, who was married, and apparently an aunt, who lived nearby. Annabel's body seemed to sink deeper into the mattress, weighed down by guilt and regret. *O Father God, what have I done? What did I cause Stephen to do? It's too, too terrible.*

She had felt some brief moments of relief in thinking of the bailiff as unconscious. Perhaps it had been God's will, his way of punishing the bailiff for what he had tried to do to her. But she couldn't think that way now, not when she saw his daughter.

Oh, it was a wretched, wretched, most unfortunate night. She wished she could go to sleep and awaken to find it had all been a dream.

The awful thoughts from the night sank their claws into Annabel the moment she awoke. Mistress Eustacia came early and took Maud out alone, no doubt to tell her what had happened. But no message arrived for Annabel from Lord le Wyse, meaning the bailiff must still be alive. How would Maud react to her father's accident? *What if he regains consciousness and tells everyone that Stephen and I tried to kill him?* She felt her body go cold. Would Lord le Wyse protect them from the bailiff's accusations?

Annabel waited for Maud to return to the undercroft, but she never came.

The news spread quickly that something terrible had befallen Bailiff Tom, and soon every maidservant was talking about it. He had always seemed a kind man, they all said. Everybody liked him. Who would do such a thing? Few speculated he had fallen and hit his head—it seemed more exciting to believe he had been attacked.

Rumors spread, with people saying that he had met the devil in the woods. Others said he woke up long enough to call out his dead wife's name and then fell back into a stupor. Some said he would never be the same even if he woke up, that he would be addlebrained and stupid and would drool.

Annabel tried not to listen to all the talk, but it was impossible not to hear it.

She eventually learned that Bailiff Tom had still not awakened and was lying lifelessly on his sister's bed, and his sister was none too happy about it. The only barber in the village had proclaimed that bleeding him would not help him regain consciousness, and there was nothing that could be done for the bailiff. They'd simply have to wait and see if he woke up. In the meantime, his sister was to pour broth and water into his mouth three times a day and hold him upright until he swallowed.

After hearing the news, a nightmarish fog settled over Annabel's thoughts and followed her every hour. She longed to speak to Lord le Wyse, to find out what he was thinking and if he thought the bailiff would recover his senses. But the only times she'd seen him that day were at meals, and he hadn't said a word to her.

Her mind seemed heavy, tired, and haunted with the image of Bailiff Tom's face as he held her knife in a menacing pose, of her own terror as he gripped her face and hissed in her ear, of Stephen hurling the heavy stone, and of the bailiff's lifeless body. The images seemed to attack her at odd moments as she went about her duties of cooking and cleaning. By late afternoon she was nearly in tears.

Mistress Eustacia came into the kitchen with a basket of onions and set them down on the stone floor. "Child, you don't look like yourself, you don't. Are you ill?"

Annabel turned back to the pot she was stirring over the fire. "No, mistress. I am well."

"I suppose we are all a bit upset, with the bailiff being injured so sudden and maybe on his deathbed. The poor soul. Had no chance at final rites, he didn't. It's almost as if the pestilence has come back. We all remember that dreadful time, we do."

No, he certainly had no opportunity to repent or receive final rites. Annabel felt a stab of guilt, followed by anger. If he'd wanted to repent, he should have, before he got drunk, before he grabbed her in the dark forest and tried to hurt her. She shook her head at the livid thoughts then bit her lip.

"Child, you're so pale. You don't look well at all. Why don't you go lie down in your bed for a while?"

The thought of being alone in the dark undercroft, or any other dark place, made her shudder. Her eyes burned, and her head felt heavy with fatigue. "I'd rather stay here with you, mistress. Truly, I am well." Tears welled up in her eyes, probably because Mistress Eustacia was showing compassion for her—she who didn't deserve it.

Mistress Eustacia watched her with concern in her eyes. She spoke softly. "Tell your mistress what's wrong."

A tear slipped out and Annabel wiped it away. Her heart beat faster as she realized she'd made a mistake by allowing Mistress Eustacia to see her distress. "Nothing is wrong. I'm only sorry for Maud. I know how it feels to lose a father." More tears came and slipped down her cheeks. She wiped as quickly as she could with the backs of her hands.

Mistress Eustacia sat on the wooden bench and motioned for Annabel to sit beside her. The kind woman wrapped her arm around Annabel's shoulders.

She was warm and snug against her mistress's soft, cushiony side, which only made her feel guiltier. What was wrong with her? She'd be inciting suspicion if she wasn't careful. And she appeared to solicit compassion she had no claim on. She tried to force the tears back, but they kept coming.

"You just cry if you want to." Eustacia's voice was kind but firm. "Women cry. Men don't understand it, but crying is what we do."

If she hadn't felt so weighted down with guilt, she might have laughed.

"You'll get married someday, and then you'll be so busy with your husband and children, you won't have time for grieving." Mistress Eustacia patted her on the arm.

"I will never marry." Annabel shook her head.

"Of course you'll marry. Why do you say such a thing?"

"I have always wanted to be a nun. It's been my wish for many years now."

"My dear, the cloister is only for those born to tragedy, it is. Not for sweet maidens like you. Trust me, dear girl, you were born for love, for loving and caring and healing." She pulled away to look at Annabel's face. "Don't you know how beautiful you are?"

Beauty? She was supposed to be happy because she was *beautiful?* What good had beauty ever done her? "Beauty is a curse."

"A curse? How can you say that? Every girl wants to be beautiful."

Annabel didn't know what to say. Mistress Eustacia's words made her feel as if she was being ungrateful for a nice gift. But the bailiff wouldn't have bothered her if she had been plain.

"The convent isn't for girls such as you. In a convent, whose heart would be made glad by your fair smiles?"

"In a convent I can study God's Word and not be harassed and bedeviled by men." She lowered her voice to a mumble. "In a convent I might be safe."

"Who has harassed and bedeviled you? Who?" Mistress Eustacia's face reminded Annabel of a mother badger protecting her babies.

"It doesn't matter." Annabel shook her head, wishing she could take back the words. "No one is harassing me."

"If you mean Gilbert Carpenter, he will leave you alone in time. Things will smooth out for you in the future, you'll see. But you must marry a good man, and you will have your pick of them, my dear. Men always want a beautiful maiden like you to be their wife — one as beautiful of heart as of face. My husband thought I was a beauty once, if you can believe that." She chuckled as a faraway look came over her, and Annabel breathed a grateful sigh that her mistress had moved the topic away from her.

Just then, the door opened and Lord le Wyse stepped inside. He looked first at Annabel, then at Mistress Eustacia, then back. *Did Bailiff Tom die?* The words stuck in her throat.

"I need to speak with you for a moment, Annabel. Mistress Eustacia, can you spare her for—"

"Oh yes, you go ahead. You probably need her to help tend Bailiff Tom. That is a very good idea, aye, indeed it is." She shooed them with her hand.

Mistress Eustacia seemed overly pleased by Lord le Wyse's request, but Annabel didn't have time to linger on it. Worry over what would happen if Bailiff Tom died pushed every other thought away.

Lord le Wyse stepped aside and Annabel preceded him out the door into the hazy late-afternoon sunlight. She held her breath as he began to speak softly, looking at the bush beside him rather than at Annabel.

"I want you to go down the path that leads to the river. Wait for me at the big rock. Do you know the place?"

"Yes. Is he dead?" she whispered back.

"No, he lives. Go now. I'll be only a few moments behind you."

She took a small but well-worn path that wound away from the manor and past the construction of Lord le Wyse's castle, which sat on a bare knoll just above her. Heading toward the river, she tried to walk at a normal pace and settle her breathing, hardly noticing the two rows of linden trees between the fields and the river. She reached the large boulder on the riverbank and sat down to wait, trying not to imagine what Lord le Wyse might say to her.

Moments later, as promised, he was walking down the path toward her, holding his burned arm—she used to think of it as his wolf-attacked arm—against his midsection with his right hand cupping his left elbow. His shoulders and head were high and erect, but his face bore an odd expression, whether of sadness, anger, or frustration, she couldn't tell.

He seemed much older than twenty-five. She tried to imagine him in the fresh glow of youth, smiling and cheerful, but couldn't get a picture of it in her mind.

Lord le Wyse stopped and sat at the other end of the large, flat stone, about two feet away. He didn't look at her, only watched the river below them.

His voice was deep and a bit raspy, as he was trying to speak softly. "The bailiff is no better and no worse. He still hasn't awakened, but we must be prepared for it if he does."

We? She looked at him, wondering why he cared enough to help her.

He cleared his throat. "I feel partially responsible for the terrible way the bailiff treated you."

"Why should you feel responsible?"

"Because you are my servant and under my care, and because he was my bailiff and I knew he had mistreated you on at least two other occasions." He seemed angry, his voice a gruff whisper.

"If and when the bailiff wakes up, I'll tell him he is not to say a word about you, that if he tries to accuse you of being there when he fell and caused himself harm, I'll tell the coroner or the manorial court how he treated you. I'll have him put in the stocks. You won't have to say anything. But if anyone accuses you of knowing something about his ... injury, you are to say you went to the privy that night and then went back to the manor house and to bed."

"Yes, my lord."

"The coroner will be coming. He was delayed by a violent death several miles from here. When he comes to investigate the fire, he will also want to investigate the bailiff's accident. We must continue as usual and try not to excite his suspicions, not let him think we know anything about the bailiff's accident."

"Yes, my lord."

"If the coroner wants to question you ..." He shook his head, staring moodily across the river at the opposite bank. "It can't be helped."

His features softened from their customary hard expression. "I had seen the way Bailiff Tom looked at you and that his presence made you afraid. I should have taken action. I am to blame, and therefore I will take the responsibility for it."

"I don't think you are to blame." Annabel angled her body so that she was facing him. "You couldn't have known the bailiff would—If anything, it is my fault. I'm sure some would say I should have married the bailiff." She looked down at the ground, feeling the tears damming behind her eyes. The pain of knowing her brothers wanted to give her to that vile man ... She had to change the path her thoughts were taking or she'd never stop the tears.

"Nay, you should not have married the bailiff. I'd have sooner paired a dove with a vulture." He took a deep breath and let it out. "You deserve to love and be loved."

You deserve to love and be loved. What did he mean? She had never heard anyone speak of such a thing, although it reminded her of what Mistress Eustacia had said only a few minutes ago. She wrapped her arms around herself, trying to guard herself against the strange longing the gentle tone of his voice and his words evoked.

"You are not to blame." He leaned toward her. There was such intensity in his expression. She wondered if he intended to wrap his arms around her. How would it feel?

But she was being ridiculous to entertain such an irreverent thought. Of course her lord wouldn't do such an improper thing.

His brown hair had fallen across his forehead. She let her gaze travel over his leather eye patch to his cheek and wished she could see him clean-shaven. She didn't think she would mind the scars.

She tore her gaze from his face. *O God, I pray he can't read my thoughts.*

"I am partially to blame for another reason," she said hesitantly. "I was carrying a knife, to protect myself from the bailiff.

While he was dragging me into the trees, I pulled it out of my pocket."

"And he took it away from you." His face was so stern and forbidding, her heart sank. He would see now that it *was* her fault.

⌒⌒⌒

The poor girl had been forced to carry a knife to protect herself. He felt sick, his heart wrenching at the thought of her so frightened. Why hadn't she come to him? Why hadn't she told him how terrified she was? He would have defended her.

But he knew why. She hadn't come to him because he himself had mistreated her. He had been rude and insulting and had assumed the worst.

"I know it was wrong of me to try to use the knife as a weapon—"

"You were only trying to protect yourself." He closed his eyes, groaning inwardly. *God, how can you ever forgive me? How can I ever forgive myself?*

"But the bailiff was holding my knife, and that's why— well, that's why—"

"That's why whoever was with you had to bash the bailiff over the head with whatever it was he bashed him with." Now he was seeing the full picture.

He saw the flicker of fear and sadness in her eyes just before she turned her head.

They sat in silence, listening to the slow-moving river and the birds flitting nearby and overhead in the trees.

Ranulf stared down at his gnarled hand. The fingers and thumb curled inward, the scars and damaged tendons forcing his hand into a claw shape. He was a disfigured man, but he could have, should have protected her from the bailiff.

No matter what it cost him, he would protect her now.

"I won't let anything happen to you." He continued to stare down at his hand. "I will protect you and the person who was with you last night." His voice lowered to a hoarse whisper. "And if you still wish to enter a convent, I will help you."

Annabel's eyes were drawn to his face, and she felt bathed in comforting peace. Her lord would protect her. This was what she had wanted from her brothers, but they had failed to give her—a feeling of protection and security.

A tiny movement in the underbrush near her foot caught her attention. She forced her eyes to focus on it, to see what was moving the leaves. A dark, geometric pattern slithered on the ground not a handbreadth from her foot. A poisonous adder.

She stifled a scream. If she pulled her foot away, it might strike.

"Be still." Lord le Wyse stood.

The adder turned its head toward him, then struck at his leg. He leapt back.

Annabel jumped backward off the rock, landing on the ground behind the boulder.

She spied a fallen limb, almost as thick as her arm. She grabbed it and scrambled to her feet. Lord le Wyse stood beside her, facing the snake, which lay coiled and ready to strike again, a mere six feet in front of him.

He stretched his hand out to Annabel, keeping the rest of his body perfectly still. She handed him the limb. Carefully, he lowered it toward the adder's flat, broad head until the limb rested on the ground in front of the snake. Then, with a sudden flick of the stick, he sent the adder sailing through the air. It plopped to the ground, unharmed, thirty paces away.

Her heart pounded so hard it hurt her chest. She looked down at Lord le Wyse's leg and grasped his good arm. "Are you hurt? Did he strike you?" If he was bitten—*O God, don't let him die!*

"Nay, he missed."

She stared hard at his face. "Truly? I saw him strike! You

could be poisoned! Those snakes are deadly." She gasped as panic stole her breath. "Show me your leg. Let me see."

"I'm telling the truth." A smile turned up the corners of his mouth and he shook his head. "He never touched me."

Annabel took deep breaths to calm herself. She closed her eyes as relief stole through her, relief and gratitude that Lord le Wyse had not been hurt.

Lord le Wyse reached out to her, and before she had time to think, she had leaned into his embrace, resting her cheek against his hard chest as his arms wrapped around her. She was trembling in delayed reaction to the snake, inhaling deeply in an effort to calm herself, and was surrounded by the smell of lavender on his freshly laundered shirt.

She realized she was enjoying his warmth and nearness far too much. Not only should she not be enjoying it, but her lord should not be holding her in his arms. It was highly improper.

She suddenly had a terrifying thought. Was Lord le Wyse holding her because he was having the same feelings for her that Bailiff Tom and Gilbert Carpenter had? Now that she thought about it, why had she agreed to this meeting alone with him? Was she enticing Lord le Wyse? Would he begin to treat her the way other men treated her?

She stepped away from him. He let his arms drop and took a step back as well.

He could probably see the horror on her face. She watched as the tender look in his eye turned hard and cold, and his smile was replaced by a scowl.

"Let us go," he barked, "before someone sees us and thinks we're doing something improper." He seemed to hurl the words at her, putting sarcasm into the last word, *improper.*

She felt stung. Instead of waiting for him to lead the way, she hurried forward, leaving him behind. She was no longer worried about the snake. *Maybe it should have bitten him.* She immediately regretted the thought, but it felt good, for a moment, to get angry at him.

They walked in silence, he slightly behind her. They had

been through so much in such a few days. He had defended her from Tom, had refused to force her to marry the bailiff, and just now had saved her from the snake. He'd been terribly burned in the fire that had destroyed their winter grain. She had tended his injuries. And he had provided her heart's desire when he asked her to read the Bible to him.

A connection had formed between them. But now, with one comment from him, she felt as distant from him as when she'd arrived. The awkward feeling when he yelled at her for looking at his paintings seemed to have returned in full force.

But it wasn't only his angry sarcasm that made her feel uncomfortable. Her own feelings toward him confused her, though she was sure they would go away.

They came into the clearing in front of the manor house. She had let her lord hold her in his arms, and actually enjoyed it. Did he despise her now, thinking she was trying to entice him?

Sir Matefrid said women were a snare. She could see Sir Matefrid's scrunched-up face, his accusing finger pointing at her, as he spoke his familiar sermon, "Woman is the gate of hell."

Sir Clement Tidewell had always been an amiable fellow, with light, straw-colored hair and a hearty laugh. Ranulf remembered him from when they were boys, going on hunts together with their fathers. As adults they had met a few times at weddings, feasts, and the occasional festival. His long history with Sir Clement could work in their favor.

But Sir Clement was also shrewd. Very little escaped his notice, which definitely did *not* work in their favor. Ranulf would have to be equally shrewd, for Annabel's sake, as well as for the sake of the one she was protecting. Because even if that person had attacked the bailiff to save her, he would still have to pay a large fine and possibly be forced to flee from Glynval—and Annabel's reputation would forever be linked to the bailiff's accident. There was no knowing if Tom atte Water would recover, and if he didn't, she would be ostracized by the rest of the village.

She didn't deserve that, or the guilt she would no doubt feel on behalf of her protector.

Ranulf would do his best to protect Annabel, even though she was clearly repulsed by him, repulsed by a simple, innocent embrace. Although, truthfully, he shouldn't blame her for the way she reacted. He was her lord, not a friend or relative comforting her. And he should have shrugged off her obvious rejection instead of lashing out at her—hadn't he learned not to treat her that way? But the look of horror on her face had seemed to stab him in the heart and fire up his old demon temper.

Ranulf would keep Annabel safe from any harm as long as he was able. His conscience demanded it, and his heart wouldn't allow him to do otherwise.

Sir Clement arrived sooner than expected, riding up the next day with the man Ranulf had sent to fetch him. Before even taking a bite of food or swig of ale, he asked to see the barn where the fire had taken place.

"Before you look into this fire, there's something that has happened of even more consequence." Ranulf had resolved that morning to address the issue of the bailiff promptly. Doing otherwise might draw the coroner's suspicion. He went on to explain that his bailiff had been found in the woods with a head wound, lying unconscious. Sir Clement immediately asked to be taken to where the body had been found, and Ranulf led his friend into the woods until they reached the spot.

Both squatting, Ranulf and Sir Clement bent over the ground. Ranulf explained the exact position of the head and the feet while Sir Clement examined everything—the ground, the leaves—and asked questions about what had been found on the bailiff's person. Ranulf couldn't neglect to tell him about the knife, although he would have liked to. He had hoped the coroner would think the bailiff had simply fallen, but with a knife in his hand, things looked much more sinister.

Sir Clement examined the rock lying about two feet from the bailiff's head. When he turned the rock over, a couple of beetles scurried away from their overturned hiding place.

"Hmm," he murmured. "Take me to the bailiff."

"He is still unconscious."

"I realize that, but I need to ... inspect some things."

"Of course." Ranulf prayed the bailiff would still be unconscious when they arrived. If the bailiff told the coroner about Annabel and Stephen, it would be impossible to keep Annabel from becoming embroiled in the investigation.

They tramped to the bailiff's sister's house and entered the dank-smelling wattle-and-daub structure.

Bailiff Tom looked quite pale. A large bump the size of a goose egg rose at his hairline above his left temple, adorned with a smear of dried blood. But other than that, he looked like he was simply asleep.

Ranulf introduced himself and the coroner to Joan Smith. "Has there been any change?"

"No, my lord. My brother hasn't made a sound or a movement since the men brought him here the night before last."

Sir Clement bent over the bailiff. Glancing up, he asked, "Is he wearing the same clothes he was wearing when he was brought in?"

"Aye, sir."

"Nothing is altered? Everything is exactly the same?"

The woman blushed under her leathery skin. "We did go through his pockets."

"What was in his pockets?"

"Only a farthing and some twine. But he did have a knife in his hand."

"This hand?" Clement lifted the bailiff's right hand.

"Aye, sir."

"May I see the knife?"

She brought him the knife, and after looking at it, he handed it back. Next Clement examined the bailiff's feet, asking about his shoes, which were fetched for inspection. After a moment, he went back to examining the bailiff's upper body, and then examined his head, rolling Tom over. Finally, he had Ranulf and the bailiff's sister assist him in taking off all Tom's clothing so he could see if there were any other marks or wounds. After several more minutes of silent examination, the coroner enlisted Joan to help him put the clothes back on the bailiff, and then he dismissed her to tend her garden.

When Joan was gone, the coroner pointed to the bloody spot above the bailiff's right eye. "The only wound seems to be this. Perhaps he tripped and fell, striking his head on the large stone found near his body."

"Yes, that seems likely." Ranulf hoped he didn't sound too eager.

"But the problem with that theory is that the stone seemed to have been recently displaced. It was damp and dirty on one side, indicating it had lain somewhere for a long time before being moved. Perhaps it was moved and then the bailiff stumbled over it. However," Clement continued, "if he stumbled over it, he wouldn't have been likely to strike his head on it, would he? It seems rather more likely that someone hit him with it."

Ranulf raised his eyebrows in an attempt to look intrigued. "I see."

"But the most interesting thing is the knife. Why would the man be clutching a knife? As if he were fighting someone off. Or perhaps attacking someone."

The coroner began searching the bailiff's clothing for hidden pockets or items that may have been concealed, but he found nothing. Next, he lifted the bailiff's empty hand, turning it over. He seemed to start and stare harder, bending low over the man's appendage.

Ranulf kept his eyes fixed on the coroner. "Do you see something?"

"Indeed. There appear to be bite marks here." Sir Clement pointed at the meaty part of the hand between the thumb and forefinger. "If we find who made these teeth marks, we may just find who wanted the bailiff dead."

Ranulf's blood seemed to go cold in his veins.

"You say you are the one who discovered the body?"

"Yes, around vespers Sunday evening."

"Do you know anyone who hated the bailiff and might want him dead?"

Ranulf shrugged. "I have only been here a few weeks."

"Did the bailiff have an argument with anyone recently?"

"Not that I know of."

Sir Clement raised himself to his full height. "It's impossible to say whether the bailiff will recover. If he does, he may not be able to speak or otherwise be able to function normally again. And due to the suspicious circumstances, I shall have to summon the hundred bailiff—you are familiar with the procedure—so he can gather a jury for an inquest. I appreciate any help you can give, Lord le Wyse."

"You shall have my full cooperation, Sir Clement." He bowed respectfully.

"You're a good man. Now I'll have that ale you promised." The coroner smiled, his usual amiability replacing his business face, and they walked together back to the manor house.

He would have to be shrewd indeed to keep anything from Sir Clement.

Chapter
12

After staying hidden in the kitchen all day, Annabel hated the thought of facing everyone in the upper hall for supper. The coroner would be there, and so would Lord le Wyse, whom she hadn't spoken to since he embraced her and then spoke so rudely to her.

She helped Mistress Eustacia set the table with food and drink. The usual frumenty, bread, and ale had been replaced with roast pheasant, pork, and fruit pudding.

As the workers began filing in for their evening meal, Annabel continued filling the cups with ale. Her glance went to the door repeatedly until she spotted Lord le Wyse, followed closely by a sandy-haired, balding stranger: the coroner, no doubt.

Lord le Wyse seemed to look around the room until his eye met hers. With him staring straight at her, the pitcher of ale slipped out of her hand to the floor. The vessel shattered, scattering shards of pottery in all directions.

How could I be so clumsy? Now the whole room would stare at her. And she had wanted nothing more than to go unnoticed.

She bent, her hands trembling, and started picking up the shards.

Adam came running toward her. "Can I help?"

She took one look at his bare feet and held up her hand. "Adam, stop. You'll cut your foot." His father caught him by the arm and pulled the boy back to his place on the bench beside him.

Annabel paid little heed to the sharp edges of the pottery

fragments as she raked them up with her palms and placed them into her apron. Maud knelt to help, picking up a larger piece of broken pottery then mopping up the spilled ale with a cloth. Her hands were shaking too, and her face was red and puffy.

Annabel dumped the contents of her apron into a refuse bucket and hurried over to finish cleaning up the rest of the ale. What should she say to Maud? A wave of guilt pressed down on her as though the stone that had hit the bailiff was sitting on her shoulders.

But Maud's mouth was pinched and set, and she didn't seem in the mood for talk. She grabbed another pitcher, filled it from the barrel in the corner, and topped off the rest of the mugs.

Annabel wiped her hands on her apron, which was now splattered and dirty. A pricking sensation on her leg, like the poke of a thorn, drew her gaze down.

A triangle of pottery was sticking out of her leg, with a trail of blood oozing into her shoe.

"Annabel."

Mistress Eustacia waddled toward her, a clean cloth in her hand. "You're bleeding, lass."

"I know, I'm sorry. I broke the pitcher—"

"Never you mind. Come and let me wrap it up."

They moved to the bench that stood against the wall, and Mistress Eustacia carefully pulled the piece of pottery from Annabel's leg. Getting down on one knee, the older woman wrapped the cloth twice around the leg.

"Oh, pray don't bother with it, Mistress Eustacia. It's nothing." Her vision swam like a fish, and she propped her elbow on her knee and put her head in her hand. This was what she got for not eating anything all day.

Mistress Eustacia patted her shoulder. "You're tired. Go down to the undercroft and crawl into bed, and I'll bring you a choice bit of pheasant and some ale, I will."

She didn't relish being alone in the dark undercroft, but the thought of escaping from Lord le Wyse's and the coroner's presence made the air rush back into her lungs.

"Now, you go and get some rest. I'll accept no argument, I won't."

Her legs a bit wobbly, Annabel headed to the door. Lord le Wyse and the coroner stood directly in her path. She looked down at her dirty apron and prayed, *Let neither of them take notice of me.* She told herself to breathe as she walked past the men and soon was almost to the door.

"Annabel."

She turned quickly then had to blink the black spots away. "Yes, my lord?"

"I would like you to read to us tonight."

"Yes, my lord." She felt her heart lift, and her joy caused the words to come out in a whisper. It was a great relief knowing that he still wanted her to read to him.

She didn't intend to look at him, but she couldn't stop herself from glancing up into his face. He actually had a pleasant face when he wasn't angry, and his features were evenly proportioned, almost regal. His dark hair suited his skin color perfectly. He was quite a contrast to the balding, slightly paunchy coroner.

As she left the room and started down the steps, she had to grip the railing to keep her balance. But her mind was even more unbalanced, or else she wouldn't have been lingering on her lord's features. She was becoming completely daft, with all the horrors that had happened of late.

⁂

Following supper, Sir Clement stretched his legs as he sat in the upper hall of the manor house, sipping his ale while he talked with Ranulf.

Ranulf nodded, his mind wandering away from the fire investigation.

He had probably made a mistake by requesting that Annabel read to them, but his intention was to behave as usual. Or, at least that was one intention. He also wanted to keep her as near to him as he could. He could see she was rattled, even more than he expected, and he hoped to be a calming influence on her.

Truthfully, he simply wanted to be near her.

It was useless to deny it. After his wife's betrayal and death, after being assured that no beautiful woman could love anyone as disfigured as he was, he'd determined to go through life alone, childless, without the heartache of rejection. No woman would touch his heart again. No amorous feelings would complicate his thoughts.

Now he was willing to deceive the king's coroner to protect a beautiful girl.

If he hadn't forced her into the position as a lowly servant, she wouldn't have been so vulnerable to the bailiff's lecherous attentions. She would have been safe at home. Now, she was tormented with fear and guilt and worry, wondering if the bailiff would die, compelled to protect the person who had protected her.

It was his duty to look out for Annabel's safety and well-being, as he would for any servant. His emotions, frustrating as they were, would not and should not be a factor.

He realized he had not been listening to Sir Clement. He blinked at the coroner, who sat staring at him, his tankard of ale halfway to his lips.

"I didn't hear you."

"So I see. Your mind is on something—or someone—else." He grinned and took a large swill from his tankard. "Who is she? The beautiful daughter of a knight? A lady in His Majesty's court? Or a comely lass from the village?"

Ranulf grunted and tried to keep the gruffness out of his voice. "You know that I of all people have no such pleasant thoughts."

Sir Clement raised his eyebrows then frowned. "Nonsense. You're a man of flesh and blood, aren't you?"

"Am I?"

Mistress Eustacia brought a trencher with a large piece of pheasant, as she had promised.

Annabel sat on the edge of her bed and ate, forcing the small bites down her tight throat, while her mistress revived the dying fire in the fireplace at the back wall.

"The coroner is Sir Clement. He seems a kind sort, he does. Knew Lord Ranulf since they were lads together. I'd say we couldn't ask for a better man for the job. He'll soon find out what happened to Bailiff Tom, and then this whole nasty business will be over and done, more's the better."

"Do people think it wasn't an accident, then? That someone was trying to hurt the bailiff?" She glanced up to see Mistress Eustacia's expression.

"Aye, they do—that is, Maud thinks so. She was quite distraught, poor girl." Mistress Eustacia shook her head, her hands on her plump hips.

"Perhaps it was only an accident." Annabel stared down at the piece of pheasant. The last bite seemed to be stuck in her throat.

"'Twill be up to Sir Clement to decide. Come now, finish your morsel of supper and go tend to Lord Ranulf's bandage. He should be nearly finished and waiting for you."

She had forgotten about his bandage. She changed it every night. Why should tonight be any different? She must behave as though everything was normal.

But everything wasn't normal. Besides the fact that Lord le Wyse was behaving strangely, how could she bear the presence of the coroner when the very thought of him made her hands tremble?

She couldn't eat another bite. "Let me go to the well. I must wash my hands and get a drink."

"Of course, child."

As Annabel washed, she took several deep breaths and said a prayer. She tried to think of more words, but all her muddled brain could think to say was "God, help me. Help me."

She willed one foot in front of the other all the way back to the upper hall, then opened the door and stepped inside. Most of the people were beginning to depart, the mood much more quiet and somber than usual. Out of the corner of her eye, she saw Lord le Wyse's gaze lock onto her.

I forgot to get clean bandages and honey from the kitchen store-room. She clenched her teeth to keep from groaning. As she turned to go back out, Mistress Eustacia halted her.

"Where are you going? Lord le Wyse is waiting for you. I have the clean water ready."

"I forgot the bandages and honey."

"Oh, I have those all ready for you. Come."

Annabel obeyed and followed. Her heart seemed to weigh as much as a horse and to take up almost as much room in her chest, forcing her to breathe harder with less intake of air. *Please let me not get dizzy again.* With God's favor, perhaps Lord le Wyse and the coroner would ignore her, as they would a candle or a table or a stick of firewood, and let her work on the burns without engaging her in their conversation. Any other lord would treat her that way all the time. But Lord le Wyse wasn't any other lord. Usually he was kind to her and treated her as if she had intelligence, as if she was more than just a servant.

She had to bring her thoughts back to the here and now, to think only about getting through the next hour, the next minute.

Lord le Wyse and Sir Clement were engaged in conversation alone at the table.

"Anyone could have set the fire, but the evidence appears to have been burned up and destroyed." The coroner rubbed his jaw then took another drink of ale, setting his tankard down with a thud. "I can question the men who were asleep in the barn if you want, but unless someone comes forward saying they saw something, you'll probably never know what happened."

Ranulf nodded.

Not wishing to intrude, Annabel lingered behind Mistress Eustacia as the woman pulled up a stool for Annabel beside Lord le Wyse's chair.

"My lord?" Mistress Eustacia clasped her hands, bending toward him.

He looked up.

"Annabel is here to see to your bandages."

He turned his eye on her. She couldn't help searching his face for signs of his mood, but his features were unreadable. She cast her gaze to the floor before he or Sir Clement thought her insolent.

Lord le Wyse turned to his companion and held up his bandaged arm.

Sir Clement shook his head and waved his hand. "Pray, do not let me hinder you from what you need to do. Pretend I'm not here."

Lord le Wyse turned his chair to face Annabel's stool. She took the bandages from Mistress Eustacia, breathing easier when she saw that her hand did not shake. Surprisingly, a measure of calm descended over her as she drew near to her lord.

She unwrapped the bandage from his arm. Dipping a cloth in the cold water Mistress Eustacia had brought her and holding him by the wrist, she washed the sticky honey from his arm. As ever, Lord le Wyse sat perfectly still.

She held his arm up to the candlelight to get a better look at the burns. Sir Clement said nothing, but Annabel felt his eyes on her. His gaze flitted from Lord le Wyse's face to hers and back again.

She concentrated on her lord's arm as he and Sir Clement began discussing the weather. The burns on his arm still looked far from healed.

Lord le Wyse's left hand was much different from the right—she couldn't help but compare the two. The fingers of his maimed hand seemed smaller, and they were drawn inward. Long, pale scars cut through the dark hair on the back of his hand and halted above his wrist. He had once called himself beastly. But the scars only reminded her of his selfless act, of how he had saved a human being, someone who was beneath his social station.

As she always did, she supported his arm with her left hand while she carefully used her cloth to clean around the edges of the burn, to remove the sticky residue of the honey from the healthy skin. For the first time, she was very aware of his skin on hers. Her palm tingled against the warmth of his arm.

"How does it look?" Sir Clement asked, leaning forward. "Do you think it's healing?"

"It seems to be improving."

She realized she'd begun bandaging his arm and had forgotten to put the honey on first. "Oh." She began unwrapping. Her face grew hotter and her hands shook.

"Honey?" Mistress Eustacia asked.

"Yes." The honey would help keep gangrene from setting in while keeping the scab from becoming hard, making the scarring less severe.

Lord le Wyse didn't deserve any more scars. He'd already been hurt enough.

She clumsily poured the honey over his arm, and a glob dripped off the side and plopped onto the floor.

"I'll clean it." Mistress Eustacia bent and wiped at the mess.

So much for being ignored and treated like a stick of firewood. She was the center of everyone's attention.

Annabel concentrated on wrapping the wound quickly without making any more mistakes. Her lord assisted her by holding his arm higher or lower, as the need arose. But Sir Clement's stares made her wish someone would speak and break the awful silence.

She tied the bandage in place. Her task was finished.

Lord le Wyse turned to Sir Clement. "It is my custom to have my servant read to me every evening."

"By all means, go about your usual activities."

They all migrated toward the fireplace, and Mistress Eustacia pulled up a chair for Annabel. When Lord le Wyse placed the large Bible in Annabel's hands, she opened it to the page where they had stopped the last evening.

Mistress Eustacia quietly backed out of the room.

Annabel began to read, forming the words deliberately and dispassionately, concentrating on reading well for her lord and his guest. Soon, she found herself so immersed in what she was reading she forgot she wasn't alone, until she paused to ponder what she had just read.

She glanced up, catching Lord le Wyse watching her, and Sir Clement watching him. The coroner's expression reminded her of a dog who had cornered a rabbit in its hole.

Peculiar that she should have such a thought.

She read on, stumbling over the first few words before getting into a rhythm again.

Sooner than usual, Lord le Wyse interrupted her. "That will be enough for tonight."

She sent him a questioning look, but he turned away from her.

Trying to fit into her servant role, she waited until Lord le Wyse lifted the book, keeping her head bowed, and curtsied before leaving the room.

⌘

Ranulf waited. Would Clement say what he was thinking or keep it to himself?

"Who is the young maiden?"

"A servant, Annabel Chapman, from Glynval."

"How did she come to be in your service?"

"An unpaid debt her family owed." Ranulf eyed the coroner.

"Very comely lass, isn't she?"

The hair on the back of Ranulf's neck prickled. "She is my servant." He hoped to infuse his voice with just enough warning.

"Is she, perhaps, more than a servant to you?"

"Nay. Why would you ask such a question?" Ranulf kept his voice low.

"No reason."

"She grew up not as a servant but as a merchant's daughter."

"I knew some such thing must be the case, since she is able to read."

"And as her lord, I have a duty to protect her—"

"You need have no fear on that score, not from me." Sir Clement smiled in amusement, his hands motionless in his lap. Only his sharp eyes moved. "As your duty is to provide for and protect your servants, my duty is to ask questions."

"Of course."

Ranulf tried to focus his thoughts and keep alert. Had he already revealed more to the coroner than he'd intended? He should not have allowed Annabel to read to him tonight. The coroner had taken the opportunity to read his thoughts. He should have stared at the floor, anywhere but her winsome face as she read the Scriptures.

"Tell me, what was Annabel's relationship to the bailiff?"

"Relationship? There was no relationship."

"Had either of them spoken to you about the other?"

How could the man know to ask the very question that he couldn't evade without an outright lie, and that would sink Annabel deep into suspicion?

Ranulf had no choice but to answer. "Yes. The bailiff had asked to wed Annabel, but she didn't wish to marry him."

"And this was when?"

"Not more than two weeks ago."

"Did the lass give any reason for her disinterest in the bailiff's request?"

"She did not like the bailiff."

"She said as much?"

"Yes."

"And you said?"

"That she didn't have to marry anyone she didn't wish to."

"And how did the bailiff take the news?"

"He said very little."

"But your impression of his reaction was . . . angry, perhaps?"

"Perhaps, although he didn't say as much."

Sir Clement sighed and pushed himself up from his chair. He took a long swig of ale from his cup before placing it on the table. "Tomorrow I shall wish to speak with the bailiff's family members—I believe you told me he has two daughters in addition to his sister living in Glynval—to ask some questions. And the servant girl, Annabel."

Ranulf's heart skipped a few beats. "Certainly, Sir Clement."

Chapter
13

Ranulf lay motionless as a woman leaned over him. Her face swam in and out of view, her features watery, as though he were looking at her through a fog. She drew nearer and her face gradually came into focus.

"Guinevere."

She smiled her languid smile. As she reached out to touch his chest, her diaphanous sleeve fell away to reveal her bare arm.

"I thought you were—"

"Hush, now." Her smile grew wider as she touched his face, and then she laughed, her head falling back. When she straightened again her smile had turned sinister. She clenched her teeth and face began to turn ashen. With a cackle she lifted something in her hand. A knife. Raising it above her shoulder, she laughed louder.

Ranulf tried to raise his arm to block her blow, but his limbs seemed made of iron. He could barely lift them off the bed.

She brought the knife down, toward his chest, toward his heart, still cackling. She was killing him.

Ranulf woke with a gasp then sat up and looked around. He gulped air as though he'd been running, unable to take in a full breath. The only light came from the barely flickering fire in the fireplace.

It was only another dream, another nightmare. She'd been gone these three years now. Dead.

Her face had been so real, so clear and plain. The memory of her treachery was fresh again, piercing.

Nay, not so piercing as it had once been, when her betrayal had been new, or even a few weeks ago. Certainly not so piercing as when he watched them lower her lifeless body into the ground. Though even then he'd felt a peace, almost a sense of relief that he no longer had to face her disgust. He finally took a deep breath and sighed.

Yes, she was gone, truly gone. Except in his dreams.

He swung his legs off the side of the bed, his feet touching the cool stone. He let his head rest in his hands. True, his wife had hurt him as deeply as if she had driven a knife into his heart. But he no longer felt the pain as keenly. In fact, at this moment, he felt it not at all. When had such a transformation taken place? The memory of her had tormented him, had led him to break down in anguish in the woods only two or three weeks earlier. So why did he feel such peace now, even immediately after dreaming of her?

His mind conjured up a new face. Annabel Chapman. So kind and gentle, with so much warmth and goodness in her mind and soul. A new pain had taken the place of the old one—and like the old, this new feeling was one he did not wish to linger over. Annabel had helped him see the injustice of his own bitterness toward women, but he had failed her—because of him the coroner would ask her question after question, the very thing she had been terrified would happen.

A log crumbled softly in the fireplace, sending up sparks. Another sound caught his attention, coming from the opposite direction. He lifted his head. He could hear Mistress Eustacia snoring softly on the other side of the room, but this brief sound, a scuffling as of bare feet on the stone floor, was much nearer.

A bed had been added to the upper hall for Sir Clement so he didn't have to sleep with the workers. Perhaps Sir Clement was awake.

He called softly, "Who's there? Sir Clement?"

"It is only I." The voice was barely audible. He didn't recognize it.

"Who?"

"Maud atte Water, my lord," she whispered back.

"What are you doing here?" The bailiff's daughter. *What could she need at this hour?*

"I ... I couldn't sleep, and it seems neither can you. We could comfort each other." Her voice broke at the last word, as if she was holding back tears.

Ranulf swallowed past the lump in his throat. If she knew how unwelcome this offer was, she'd certainly never have made it. He tried to wrestle his tone into something akin to compassion, remembering that she was mourning her father.

"I'm sorry, but that would not be my wish. You must go before someone discovers you here."

"Must I?" She sniffed dramatically. "But I could—"

"You must go." He made his words loud and firm, well aware that he was helpless to prevent the girl from putting him in an embarrassing situation.

He had no choice but to awaken Mistress Eustacia. He grabbed his chausses and jerked them on as he came out from behind the screen. The servant girl stood two feet away, hugging herself, her head bent. At least she had on clothing, though it looked like only a thin nightdress.

"Mistress Eustacia will take you down to the undercroft." He stepped toward Eustacia's sleeping area, but the girl caught his arm.

"Nay," she whispered. "Don't wake the mistress." She grabbed his other arm and pulled toward his bed.

Ranulf twisted out of her grasp, clenching his fists. "Mistress Eustacia!" Must he, in his own home, be forced to put up with this nonsense, this disobedience, this impropriety?

A shadowy form rose from Sir Clement's bed against the wall.

"Lord Ranulf?" Eustacia's sleepy voice croaked. Her bed rustled as she moved to sit up.

"I need your help." *Help me, woman, and hurry.*

Eustacia came shuffling over. "Who is it? I can't see a thing in this dim light. Lord Ranulf, is everything well?"

"Please walk Maud back down to the undercroft."

Maud began to cry short, shuddering sobs, with her hands over her face.

"Maud?" Eustacia's voice sounded confused, though less groggy. "Whatever is the matter?"

Maud ripped her hands from her face. "Him." She pointed a finger at Ranulf. "He was trying to take advantage of me, just as he did before my father's attack. Now he wants no part of me."

Heat rushed into Ranulf's face as he understood her meaning. "That is a lie. How dare you tell such a thing to Mistress Eustacia." *And to Sir Clement.* Ranulf watched the man scratch his head.

"I shall tell it everywhere, to everyone. You will be sorry for not—" She stopped herself. "You will be sorry."

"For not accepting your offer, you mean. What you are claiming is a complete falsehood. Sir Clement, you are also a witness."

"So I am." Sir Clement stepped forward into the faint light.

Eustacia hurried to light a candle and carried it back to the small group of people, moving close to Maud, studying her face.

All eyes on her, Maud glared at each person then settled on Sir Clement. "You must force him to marry me. He has ruined me."

"Sir Clement, I've never touched this girl."

"What proof do you have of this claim?" Sir Clement asked Maud.

"My word. Isn't that proof enough?"

"I'm afraid it isn't. What happened tonight carries weight as well."

"Have you no interest in justice? Why are you here, then?"

"I am here to find out what happened to your father."

"You should ask our lord, for he is the one who found the body, isn't he? Should he not be under suspicion?"

"Everyone in Glynval is under suspicion, I assure you. Now I suggest you obey your lord and leave this room at once."

Eustacia placed her hand on Maud's arm, but Maud snatched it away.

"I won't be so easily silenced," Maud hissed. Pure hatred shone on her face. She spun around and stomped to the door, slamming it behind her.

What to do now? If he passionately protested his innocence to Sir Clement, he'd only seem guilty.

"Sir, if you will allow me to speak." Eustacia placed her hand on her chest, staring in Sir Clement's direction.

"You may." It was fine for Sir Clement to sound so calm. He wasn't being accused of bedding a servant he'd never thought of touching.

"The girl's overwrought from her father's injuries. The thing is impossible—I'm here with Lord Ranulf every night. If our lord had crept out to take advantage of her, don't you think I would have known it? My word must surely convince you of Lord Ranulf's innocence."

"Indeed, madam, it does not convince me."

Her eyes flew wide as alarm registered on her face. Ranulf hoped she wouldn't start to cry.

Patting his jaw with a finger, Sir Clement shook his head. "No, you are a hard sleeper, Mistress Eustacia. You did not hear when your lord moaned in his sleep, apparently from a bad dream. And when Maud boldly opened the door and came into the room, you slept on. But no one blames you for any this." He murmured the last statement as he waved his hand.

"I am innocent of these claims, Sir Clement." Ranulf forced himself to breathe evenly.

Sir Clement looked him full in the face, though it was hard to discern the coroner's expression in the dim light. "Yes, I know."

Ranulf waited for him to explain.

"There are several aspects that appear to prove the girl false. For one, why would she come here to accuse you of immorality half dressed and in her nightshirt? And she accused you of trying to take advantage of her tonight. Obviously a falsehood, since I myself heard you refuse to allow her in your bed. But I have another reason that is yet more compelling, which I will keep to myself, for now." He looked at Ranulf with a slight smile. "I again bid you a good night." With that, he returned to his bed and climbed under the bedclothes.

Eustacia stared with her mouth open. And Ranulf decided not to ponder Sir Clement's last reason.

⁘

Ranulf watched as Annabel strode into the upper hall, her back rigid. Her eyes moved, flitting like frightened birds. *Father God, steady her. Give her peace and wisdom.*

At least Sir Clement was allowing him to sit in on the interrogations. Ranulf only wished Annabel wasn't the first person on the coroner's list.

Sir Clement motioned her to a chair in front of one of the long windows — the morning light streaming in made her appear almost unearthly, with her golden hair and wide, innocent eyes.

She clenched her hands together in her lap and stared up at Sir Clement, who fixed her with his own probing stare.

Sir Clement finally broke the silence. "What is your name?"

"Annabel Chapman, sir." Her voice was soft but steely.

"How long have you been in Lord le Wyse's service here at the manor house?" Sir Clement examined his fingernails, as though the conversation bored him.

She blinked and hesitated. "Two or three weeks."

"How came you to be here? You are the daughter of a freeman, are you not?"

"I am, sir. My father died three years ago, and my mother and brothers and I have not been able to pay the censum since then." She took a deep breath and went on. "As we have no money and had avoided fieldwork, the hallmote decided that one of my family must be indentured to Lord le Wyse for three years, the length of time that the censum went unpaid." Annabel finished, expelling a soft breath.

Ranulf swallowed, his throat constricting.

"I see." The coroner stroked his chin, glancing out the window. "How did you feel about coming here?"

"I—" She stopped, her face draining of what little color she'd had. She sat up straighter. "I wasn't eager to leave my home, but I wanted to help my family. One of us had to come. It was only right."

"Why weren't you eager to leave? Were you happy there?"

Annabel stared down at her hands in her lap. She shook her head slightly, almost imperceptibly. "I was not unhappy."

"Was there a particular reason you did not want to come here, to the manor house of Lord le Wyse? Perhaps you had heard your lord was a hard man, unfair, lecherous, unseemly—"

Her head jerked up. "Oh, no! Lord le Wyse is none of those things." Ranulf's heart did a strange stutter at the way she defended him. He longed to intervene, to stop the questioning.

"There is nothing about Lord le Wyse that frightened you? I have known him many years, and he has a nasty temper. And I know the rumors people sometimes spread about his . . . beastliness." Sir Clement gave her a sympathetic look, as if trying to get her to trust him.

Annabel glanced quickly at Ranulf and then looked back at the coroner, "I was a bit afraid of him when I first arrived, but I'm not anymore. His temper is not so nasty, not really. He has a lot of responsibilities, and it's understandable that he might . . . get angry at times. And he is not beastly. That's a terrible thing to say. He is a noble, good lord. No one who knew him could say anything dishonorable about him."

Ranulf's heart swelled at her words. *She thinks I'm honorable.* Her face turned red, her hands fidgeted, and she wouldn't look at him.

Sir Clement was silent for a few moments. "So was there some other reason you did not wish to come to the manor house, to serve Lord le Wyse?"

"There were many reasons. My family depended on me, and I didn't want to live among strangers."

"Strangers? Were you afraid?" As Annabel began to fidget,

a spark lit in the coroner's eyes. "Of whom were you afraid, pray tell?"

"I ... I already said I was afraid of Lord le Wyse."

"But you were afraid of someone else, weren't you?" Sir Clement peered closely at Annabel's face. "Had someone given you reason to be afraid?"

She pressed her lips together, as if struggling not to speak. How Ranulf wanted to protect her from these questions. *O God, help her.* She had no choice but to cooperate with the inquest. And he could do nothing to stop it.

Sir Clement pressed on. "You were afraid of a particular person, weren't you? Was that person Bailiff Tom?"

The light from the window revealed a tear trembling at the corner of her eye.

The coroner leaned forward, studying her hard. "You *were* afraid of Bailiff Tom. Why? What did he do to you?"

"I didn't say — I was afraid — of him." Annabel hiccupped as she seemed to fight back the tears.

"You didn't have to. But I wonder what the man did to you. If you don't tell me" — a warning tone entered his voice — "I shall find out some other way."

Ranulf imagined the coroner asking his probing questions around the village. Soon everyone would find out how the bailiff had tried to force himself on Annabel more than once. She would be embarrassed. He knew how that felt, to have all your neighbors whispering about you, about your deepest pain and humiliation.

Ranulf leapt to his feet. "Is this necessary?"

Annabel felt the tear slip down her cheek as Lord le Wyse shouted the question at Sir Clement. His reaction brought a swell of gratitude for her lord and unleashed the emotion she'd been holding back. Tears coursed down her face and dripped off her chin.

Lord le Wyse thrust his hand through his hair and rubbed the back of his neck. "These questions can hardly serve your purpose. This maiden didn't try to kill the bailiff." His voice was harsh and angry as his gaze flicked back and forth between Sir Clement and Annabel.

The coroner looked up at Lord le Wyse as though surprised. "Forgive me." He spoke softly. "I only have a few more."

Lord le Wyse expelled a burst of air. He glared at the coroner. "I will not allow this ... torment much longer." He started pacing beside them.

"Forgive me, but I must proceed." Sir Clement's voice was smooth, almost mocking. He nodded, as if Ranulf had given him his permission, and turned back to her. "You were afraid of Bailiff Tom, weren't you?" His voice instantly became meek and coaxing.

How could she lie? Somehow, the man already knew about her fear of the bailiff. "He—did something—that frightened me." She glared at the coroner before swiping the tears away with the back of her hand. She hated the man's questions, hated the halting way she spoke, and hated that she couldn't hold back the tears. *O Father God, let me not say something that will endanger anyone.*

"What did he do to you?"

"He grabbed me. He tried to kiss me." Her hands were shaking badly as she pushed a lock of hair off her cheek. "I told him I wouldn't marry him, but he threatened ... to do terrible things to me. I ... I was afraid of him." Another tear slid down her face.

"Where did you last see the bailiff?"

She felt the burn creep into her cheeks and forehead. What could she say now? What did the man know already? Her stomach knotted even tighter as she held her breath, afraid to open her lips.

"Did you see him in the forest?"

She stared past the coroner's head. Perhaps if she said nothing he would eventually ask something else, something she could answer without revealing too much. Her heart thumped painfully as the tears dried on her face, pulling the skin tight across her cheekbones.

Sir Clement came to within inches of her chair. "Answer!" Annabel shuddered, staring up at the towering figure.

"Sir Clement!" Lord le Wyse's voice was as loud as the coroner's. He quickly closed the distance between them and stood glowering at the man, his hands clenched by his sides. "Get away from her."

Chapter 14

Her heart pounded. O God, don't let Lord le Wyse endanger himself because of me! Surely he wouldn't strike the king's coroner, though the two men stood nose to nose. After interminable minutes, Sir Clement took a step away from Lord le Wyse and turned back to Annabel. Her lord took a step back as well, relaxing his fists, but his face was flushed and he continued to scowl dangerously at the coroner.

Sir Clement focused on Annabel. "Did you see the bailiff in the forest?" His voice held a dead sort of calm that sent a chill up her arms and across her shoulders.

She closed her eyes briefly then replied, "Yes."

"Did you strike him with a rock?"

"No."

"Did Lord le Wyse strike him?"

Annabel drew back in horror. "No!"

Lord le Wyse slumped back two more steps, and she met his eye.

"How do you know Lord le Wyse didn't strike him? You saw who struck him, didn't you?"

She realized her mouth was hanging open and closed it, looking down.

"You saw!"

Stephen's face flashed before her; she had to protect him. No matter what Sir Clement said or did, her lips would remain closed and her teeth tightly clenched.

Silence pressed in around her, but she didn't dare look up.

"Then it was Lord le Wyse, wasn't it? He was defending you."

Annabel's head shot up without her willing it. Her throat tightened and her tongue clung to the roof of her mouth. How could he accuse Lord le Wyse? And how could she keep silent?

The coroner is a fiend.

"Nay." Her voice was raspy. She tried to swallow, but her throat had gone dry. "Lord le Wyse is a good man. He would never hurt anyone." Tears pricked her eyes again, she didn't know why. She glanced at her lord and saw his face was flushed. The urge to jump up and go to him was so strong that she grabbed the stool she was sitting on with both hands and clutched the rough wood with all her might.

"So the person who almost killed the bailiff was not a good man?"

"I didn't say that. Oh, how would I know?" Annabel bit her lip, feeling she had slipped and said the wrong thing. But she couldn't let the coroner think Lord le Wyse was guilty.

Sir Clement rubbed his chin again, staring blankly at the wall. "You must understand, Lord le Wyse's involvement makes sense. After all, he's the one who found the body. It's only a matter of time before the people of Glynval start pointing fingers in his direction ..." He let his voice trail off.

His words chilled her. Naturally, some people might suspect her lord. Few had seen beyond his scars and rough demeanor to the man inside. But everyone knew the bailiff, and he seemed well liked, though she couldn't imagine why. If they knew how Tom atte Water actually behaved ... How could she allow people to accuse Lord le Wyse?

Her mind went back to the first time he allowed her to read his Bible. And when he'd burned himself saving the ewe lamb, how her heart had gone out to him; and he'd borne his injury with such patience, never complaining. How could she allow anyone to falsely accuse him? She couldn't bear the thought of him being hurt again.

"Lord le Wyse is innocent."

"The only way you can prove that is to tell me who struck the bailiff."

"I cannot tell you that."

"Then I cannot be sure your Lord le Wyse is innocent, can I?" The coroner began pacing toward Ranulf, intent in his eyes.

"It . . . was an accident."

The coroner turned abruptly. "So you did see it. What happened?"

Annabel pressed her lips together so hard she tasted blood.

"Did you want to kill him?"

"No!"

"Who did?"

"He didn't mean to do it." Her voice was a whisper.

"Who was it?" the coroner hissed.

"I will not tell you. But he never intended to kill him."

"Perhaps you will tell the jury that is being summoned by the hundred bailiff. Hmm?" He raised his eyebrows at her, and a slight smile lifted his thin lips.

He then turned to Lord le Wyse. "I think I'll take a walk. I shall return shortly, and then I'd like to speak with this Maud, the bailiff's daughter."

The coroner brushed by Lord le Wyse, whistling as he flung open the door and disappeared outside.

So it was over—for the moment. She had revealed so much! Too much. The coroner now knew that she had seen who struck the bailiff. How could she have allowed him to wrench that much of the truth from her? But at least she hadn't betrayed Stephen—not yet. She would still have to face a jury and the entire village of Glynval.

Her hands shook. The shattered look on her lord's face squeezed her heart. Was he angry that she had not revealed the identity of the person who struck the bailiff? After all, she was allowing suspicion to fall on him—the jury was sure to accuse Lord le Wyse as Sir Clement had. She had the power to clear her lord's name forever, but she had chosen to protect someone else.

Her chest ached. She couldn't bear to think she had hurt him, or that he might be angry with her.

Her words came out halting and slow. "I am—so sorry. Pray—forgive me."

"Forgive you?" His brow creased.

"For not telling—who—struck the bailiff."

Lord le Wyse let out a shuddering breath and passed his palm across his eyes. He looked at her with so much sympathy, he seemed to draw her to him.

Annabel slipped her trembling fingers into his large, warm hand, and he gently pulled her to her feet. "I forgive you," he said, "and I understand."

Without thinking, she leaned against him, pressing her forehead against his shoulder. They stood like that, unmoving, while Annabel concentrated on calming her breathing and forcing away the tears that still threatened. She smelled the familiar lavender, which Mistress Eustacia placed inside his clean laundry, but also a warm, masculine smell that was distinctly Ranulf's. She felt soothed, safe, and she never wanted this moment to end.

<hr />

Ranulf stared down at Annabel's tearstained face. He closed his eyes against the sight of her, savoring the feel of her hand in his.

His eyes flicked wide as he felt her body lean against his. *Sweet agony.* He hesitated to touch her, but finally he put his arms around her and drew in a deep, ragged breath. "Holy saints above," he whispered.

"Jesus, help us," she murmured in reply, no doubt sincerely praying about their situation.

He felt her relax against him, taking deep breaths, one hand hanging onto his shoulder. Her eyes were closed, her lips slightly parted as she rested against him.

She suddenly dropped her hand from his shoulder and pulled away.

He loosened his hold but was reluctant to let her go. Her

eyes flicked nervously from his face to the floor. She muttered, "Forgive me. My behavior is ... unseemly."

"No, not at all." He cupped her elbows in his hands to keep her from turning away from him.

Annabel stared up into his face. Her cheeks blushed red. "I must go."

She turned and practically ran from him.

❧

Grateful to find the undercroft empty, Annabel flung herself onto her bed.

It was the worst morning of her life. By accusing Lord le Wyse, the coroner had wrung much more information from her than she'd been willing to give. Sitting alone now, she wondered if the vile man had mentioned her lord only to trick her. Annabel wrapped her arms around herself, still feeling Lord le Wyse's warmth. *I touched him. I pressed my forehead against his shoulder. What must he think of me?* She wouldn't have done it if he hadn't looked at her the way he did. But she had wanted to be in his arms. In fact, she had wanted it ... and enjoyed it ... far too much.

While she had stood, soothed by the rhythm of his beating heart against her ear, she had remembered the way Lord le Wyse had tried to defend her from Sir Clement's harassing questions. The thought had stirred her heart and caused her breath to hitch in her throat.

When she looked up at Lord le Wyse, something about his expression — seeking, tender, intense — caused something to ignite deep inside her. The feeling intensified when she realized she enjoyed his comfort, enjoyed being close to him.

And that terrified her.

She knew with all certainty that it wasn't the way a servant should feel toward her lord. Her heart was still pounding from the effect of it. Was she as bad as Beatrice?

"O God, send me away. Send me away to a nunnery, please. I want to get away from here, from this turmoil. Save me from the coroner, and don't let me betray poor Stephen. O God, send me away. I'm so confused."

⁂

Maud's surly attitude toward Sir Clement infuriated Ranulf. She mumbled her answers, glared openly, and all but accused Ranulf of attempting to murder her father, though she gave no proof for her assertions. He'd apparently made an enemy of the maiden when he spurned her late-night offers.

Maud sat stiffly. Sir Clement asked, "Did your father have any enemies?"

"Nay, everyone admired my father. He was friendly with everyone."

What would Maud do if she found out what her father had done to Annabel? Or even that Annabel knew who struck her father? He prayed that Sir Clement would keep that small piece of information to himself. But why should he? The jury would need to know all the facts they could get in order to decide whom, if anyone, to accuse in the attack on the bailiff, and then everyone would know the facts. And that Annabel had hid them.

His breath shallowed at this new thought.

Annabel was not safe. He had to get her out of Glynval altogether. And soon.

Maud glared at him from across the room. The coroner was asking her something, but her eyes were locked on Ranulf, her expression overflowing with hatred. One thing was now clear: if Maud found out Annabel had actually seen what happened to her father but was refusing to tell, she'd rip her apart with her fingernails.

He would write to his aunt, the abbess at Rosings Abbey, and send the letter by messenger today. He resolved to speak to Sir Clement as well and beg him to keep what he knew about Annabel a secret. As Maud's examination continued, a plan formed in Ranulf's mind. He had been trying to get Annabel to confide in him before, and he still intended to find out whom she was with that night; he would merely tell Sir Clement he needed more time to draw the attacker's name from Annabel's lips. Knowing Clement, the man's curiosity would win out and Annabel would be safe for the moment.

If she revealed to Ranulf who struck the bailiff, would he tell Sir Clement? She would feel betrayed, but it might be the only way to clear her—and him—of suspicion.

He was sure of one thing: he couldn't let Sir Clement know he was sending Annabel to the abbey.

Annabel, locked away at an abbey. He wouldn't be able to see her or speak to her ever again. But she would be safe from the inquest, and safe from Maud.

The hundred bailiff wasted no time in gathering a jury from Glynval and a few neighboring villages. That afternoon, while they were alone in the upper hall, Sir Clement read the names of the jury to Ranulf. He didn't know any of them, of course.

"You're frowning," Sir Clement remarked. "Do you disapprove the selection?"

Ranulf cleared his throat, trying to think before he spoke. "It isn't for me to approve or disapprove." He rubbed his temple. "Sir Clement . . ."

"Yes?"

"The young maiden, Annabel, has revealed some important information to you, I believe."

The coroner blinked, his face suddenly alert and trained on Ranulf. "Indeed."

"Under distress, she has divulged that she saw what happened to the bailiff and the person responsible."

"True."

"But she did not betray the person who struck the bailiff, whether accidentally or intentionally, though she claims it was accidental."

"That is correct."

"Now, it would be important to you, would it not, to find out the identity of this person?"

"Yes, of course."

"Since I would prefer that no one harass or harm my servant, I ask that you not breathe a word of what she has told you, or insinuate that she knows aught. Meanwhile, I shall try to extract the information from her myself."

Sir Clement's eyes narrowed. "I see." He looked away, staring out the window at the gray mist.

It had been a chilly day. Autumn was getting nearer, and the rain, which had been so scant for a year, had been threatening to fall all day.

"You are right to try to protect her this way." Sir Clement turned on his heel. "But the truth must come out, and if you're unable to extract it from her, I'm afraid I shall be forced to ask the jury to question her."

So he was agreeable to the plan. "Of course, Sir Clement. I understand."

Sir Clement crossed his arms in front of his chest and a strange smile pulled at the corners of his mouth. "Why don't you just marry the girl, Ranulf? She's of age."

Ranulf swallowed hard. When he was able to speak, he asked, "What do you mean?"

"She's a lovely one and would make a sweet wife."

His face went hot. "I don't wish to discuss this with you."

"Oh, come, Ranulf. I mean no harm. We're old friends and should be able to speak freely with one another. Unburden yourself. My lips are secure, you know. Why don't you marry her?"

"She doesn't love me, and it's none of your business." He didn't care if his voice sounded gruff.

"How do you know that? She's a kindhearted girl. She'd come to love a good man like you."

"Like me?" Ranulf felt the ire rising in his throat and spun away from Sir Clement, staring now at the shadowed wall and trying to calm himself before he said things he would later regret. "I do not wish to marry again."

In a suggestive voice, the coroner responded, "I suppose you wouldn't have to marry her."

Ranulf turned and glared at Sir Clement. "Sir, you are determined to anger me."

"Nay, nay." Sir Clement smiled and shook his head. "Forgive me. My task makes me prone to say the very thing that will elicit the most information. Forgive me, my friend. I am merely trying to understand."

"Understand this. Annabel doesn't love me and isn't interested in men or marriage. And I will never again marry a woman who doesn't love me."

Sir Clement's face sobered. He pursed his lips in a frown. "I do understand."

Yes, he surely did. The rumors had spread far and wide about how the young lord's beautiful bride had scorned him for the company of the third son of a baron, whom she'd been in love with before she agreed to marry Ranulf. Everyone had known of her affair — except Ranulf. Once they were married, she made no secret that she despised his scars and didn't love him. At first he believed he could win her heart — and then he'd caught them together.

And what had she done then? Laughed.

His gut twisted at the memory.

"But I think you are wrong about one thing."

Ranulf looked at him wearily. "And that is?"

"You said Annabel wasn't interested in men." He tapped his chin with his finger and watched him. "Most men, perhaps, but ... she trusts you."

"All my servants trust me." A flicker of hope ignited inside him. *I am a fool.*

"But not all your servants look at you the way she does, I'll vow."

Sir Clement hadn't seen the way she'd looked at Ranulf when he embraced her after the viper frightened her. She'd looked horrified, repulsed. She did come into his arms willingly enough this morning. *But she doesn't love me.*

The coroner tapped his chin again. Abruptly, he turned to face Ranulf. "I will do as you have asked and not speak of what

Annabel knows. And I will expect to hear that you have found out the mysterious attacker's identity."

"Of course."

Annabel tried to avoid Lord le Wyse's gaze at supper, but she knew she would need to change his bandage after the meal was over. Once the table was cleared, she took the honey flask and bandages and waited beside his chair. He waved her to a stool and she sat.

She concentrated on unwrapping the bandage while Lord le Wyse listened to Sir Clement and Gilbert Carpenter speak about the problems caused by the recent drought.

Her fingers fumbled with the sticky bandage more than usual, but his burn once again showed no signs of becoming worse. She began to wipe his arm with a wet cloth and bit her lip in consternation at the way her hand trembled. What was wrong with her?

Annabel cleaned his arm as quickly as she could. As before, she encountered an old scar leading up to his burn. She knew the scar was from the wolf attack several years before, when he was only a youth. How brave he had been . . .

She found Lord le Wyse watching her, but his expression seemed guarded.

She was almost finished with the task. Sir Clement stood. "Gilbert, could you take me to see how your building is coming along?"

Gilbert Carpenter rose and followed him out. Mistress Eustacia, the last person left in the upper hall, slipped out the door after them. Wondering why they had all left her conspicuously alone with her lord, she finished wrapping his burn, tying the bandage in place.

Lord le Wyse said nothing. She tried to avoid looking at his face, but she felt him watching her as she gathered all the bandages and supplies and began putting them away on a shelf nearby.

Would he want her to read to him tonight? When he didn't say anything, she picked up the bucket of scraps from their evening meal and turned to take them outside.

"Don't go." Lord le Wyse laid a hand on her wrist. "Stay and read."

He removed his hand as she set down the bucket. Why wouldn't her heartbeat slow? Her wrist still tingled pleasantly from where he'd placed his hand.

She waited as he pulled the most comfortable chair near the fire and nodded at her to sit. He retrieved the large Bible from the chest behind the screen and laid it in her lap. Annabel shivered.

"Are you cold?" Lord le Wyse's forehead creased.

She shook her head but wrapped her hands around her arms.

"Are you feeling ill? If you don't wish to read tonight —"

"Nay, I'm well. I do wish to read." At that moment, she wanted to read the Holy Scriptures more than anything in the world.

He turned and disappeared behind the screen. When he came back he carried a brightly colored blanket with silk embroidery. She could only watch as he took the book from her lap with one hand and laid it on the table then unfolded the blanket and spread it over her. He retrieved the Bible and placed it back in her lap.

Annabel was surrounded now with the scent of the blanket, her lord's own scent of lavender and warm masculinity. "Thank you."

She wanted to look at him but didn't trust herself. Instead, she opened the Holy Writ and turned to the section she had marked the last time they read by placing a feather between the pages. It was Romans chapter eight, and she began to read. "Therefore, there is now no condemnation for those who are in Christ Jesus, because through Christ Jesus the law of the Spirit who gives life has set you free."

She sighed and relaxed into the chair, feeling warm and safe.

Chapter
15

Ranulf's heart seemed to beat slower as he listened to Annabel read verses from the letter to the Romans, even though he was only able to concentrate on the words in snatches. He knew he needed to tell Annabel of his plan to send her away to the abbey, and Sir Clement had left them alone so she would reveal who struck the bailiff, but he couldn't do it. He would do it tomorrow, but right now ... he couldn't justify it, but he simply needed to be with her, to hear her read.

In the morning he would find some way to coax her into telling him who threw the rock. Once he had that information, he could send her away quietly, thus fulfilling her wish and keeping her safe at the same time.

"... Now if we are children, then we are heirs—heirs of God and co-heirs with Christ, if indeed we share in his sufferings in order that we may also share in his glory. I consider that our present sufferings are not worth comparing with the glory that will be revealed in us."

Father God, let my sufferings not be for nothing. And don't let Annabel suffer any longer. Help her realize none of this is her fault. Protect her.

His chest ached at the thought of sending her away, but he wouldn't think about that tonight. Besides, she wanted to go. It was her wish to devote herself to a life of prayer, study, and service. If he could do nothing else for her, he could give her this wish.

"... And we know that in all things God works for the good of those who love him, who have been called according to his purpose."

She stopped after reading that verse and stared at the page.

"Annabel? What are you thinking?"

"I was just thinking about all these things that have been happening lately and wondering how God could work them out for our good."

He waited for her to go on.

"You didn't deserve to have your arm burned. How could that be a good thing? Or the grain crops getting burned up, or Sir Clement's questions ... How could all that be good?" She shook her head and looked down. "I suppose I shouldn't say such things."

"It doesn't say it's all good. It only says that God works in all things for the good of those who love him."

She seemed to think for a moment. "Do you love God, my lord?"

"Yes, of course."

"Then I suppose we must believe that all this can be, and will be, worked out for your good."

"And for your good."

"Yes." She seemed afraid to look at him tonight. Had he frightened her that much when he held her in his arms this morning? She hadn't seemed repulsed by him, had laid her cheek against his chest ... but then she'd seemed to realize what she was doing and ran away.

Finally, she did glance up at him, but her gaze darted around so that she never looked him in the eye. "God wouldn't want us to disbelieve him," she whispered. "So we must believe it will all ... be well in the end." She sighed.

He reached out, on impulse, and grabbed her hand. "It will be well. I promise." He squeezed her fingers and let go.

Staring down at her hand, she nodded. After another minute, she continued to read, her voice shaky.

The next morning Ranulf found Annabel in the kitchen. *It has to be done.* "Will you take a walk with me?"

She looked startled, even a little afraid, but she nodded and laid aside the bread dough she was patting into a loaf, wiping her hands on her apron. Mistress Eustacia gave Annabel a look that made him wonder what they had been talking about.

She followed as he strolled toward the clearing where the work was going on for his new home. After several moments of silence, she asked, "How is the construction of your castle coming along?"

"Castle? Is that what you call it?" He smiled in amusement. "I suppose it must look like a castle, but castles are fortresses for the politically ambitious. This house won't be built for defense. If someone wishes to do me harm, I'm afraid they'll encounter little resistance."

"Oh."

"We have finished the foundation. I hope to move in most of the household by All Souls' Day—which is appropriate, I think."

All Souls' Day came almost two months before Christmas, the day when everyone said prayers to help extricate the dead from purgatory. He only hoped by then he could keep his heart out of the purgatory of loving beautiful women who didn't love him.

As they drew nearer, the clang of the smiths' hammers rang out, as well as shouts from the various workers. Soon they were able to view the whole scene on the swell of land above them. Carters hauled stone up the hill and up the ramps built along the sides of the walls. Masons laid the stones with mortar while a nearby lime burner made more.

The trenches for the foundation had been dug, the foundation laid, and the walls were rising quickly. Lead workers, carpenters, and roof tilers all performed their various skilled tasks, with laborers assisting, carrying, and fetching.

"Oh." Annabel stood still, watching the scene with wide eyes. She looked so fascinated, Ranulf couldn't help but smile.

"What do you think of my 'castle'?"

"It's nearly finished!"

"Only the front section. I shall move into it in a few weeks." And she wouldn't even be around to see it.

"I can hardly believe how much has been done. They've worked quickly, haven't they?"

"It's quite an army of men," Ranulf acknowledged.

It was certainly a stately home, even he had to admit. The stone front rose two full stories, its gray stone formidable. The wooden front door was wide enough for three people abreast, with long, black iron hinges reaching across it. The roof came to a point, and dipped and rose again at the two round towers on either side. Generous glass panes gave it a peaceful look, as no fear of besiegers had dictated the size of the windows. The beauty of it was undeniable, if he did think so himself, and there was much more house to come, extending far to the rear and to the north from the main section.

Annabel was one of the few people from Glynval who had been to London, and so would have seen other buildings — churches and a few castles — to rival its eventual size, but even she seemed impressed.

Ranulf led her to a felled tree in a shady nook where they could observe the builders without being noticed themselves.

He took a deep breath and began, "We are friends, are we not?"

"Yes, my lord."

"You are not an ordinary servant. You're the daughter of a wealthy merchant."

"Perhaps at one time, but my father is dead and his ships were all lost. He died a poor man."

"Nonetheless, you grew up in a wealthy home. You are educated. You learned languages, learned to read and write. You've traveled to large cities. None of the other villagers can boast of these things."

Annabel questioned him with her eyes as she perched on the tree trunk a couple of feet away.

"What I'm trying to say is that there is no one here for you"—he swallowed, having a hard time getting the words out—"for you to marry." *Except me.* But he was foolish to even think those words. "And you told me once that you didn't wish to marry. You wanted to become a nun. Is this still true?"

"Yes, my lord."

"Then I shall send you to Rosings Abbey. I know the abbess there. In fact, she is my mother's sister. I have written to her and expect to receive her reply any day. Does this please you?" He did not allow any emotion to show in his face as he searched hers.

Her expression showed interest—and joy. "Oh, yes, my lord. It pleases me. But are you sure you want to send me away? I was indentured to you for three years. My service has hardly begun."

Ranulf again had to swallow the lump in his throat before he could speak. "I don't want to send you away, but I want you to be safe. You see, I will be sending you away in secret. Not even Mistress Eustacia knows my plans. If Sir Clement finds out you are going to an abbey before his investigation is over, he will prevent you."

"Oh." Sober-faced, she stared out into the milling workers.

"I wish to help you escape any repercussions from people here in Glynval once they find out you know who struck the bailiff. It is the only way to keep you safe from the jury's inquest."

"Won't Sir Clement come to the abbey and force me to tell what I know?"

"Nay, you will be safe as long as you stay within the walls of the abbey." He tried to take a deep breath, but his lungs were too tight. "And as for your service to me, you have done more for me in a fortnight than most other servants do in three years."

She blushed and looked confused. She stared down at her hands fidgeting in her lap.

He wanted to tell her so much more, how she had convicted him of his bitterness toward women and how unjust that had been. She made him realize there were good people in the world. And though it was bittersweet, at least he knew he was no longer dead inside. He couldn't tell her, but he enjoyed being with her, talking with her, seeing the sincerity of her feelings and the purity of her thoughts. God was obviously alive, alive in her. Hearing her thoughts as they read the Bible together had given him joy he had seldom known before.

Perhaps he should tell her this, but it would only strain their friendship. She would be afraid of him if she knew the depths of his feelings.

He sighed. He'd told her his plan. Now he must fulfill his promise to Sir Clement of trying to pry the identity of the bailiff's attacker from her.

"Annabel."

"Yes, my lord?"

"Sir Clement and I know you saw who struck the bailiff. From what you say, he didn't intend to kill him, but the bailiff still has not regained consciousness. I need you to tell me who you were with that night."

"How could I hurt him in this way?" She turned toward him, her forehead creased, her eyes pleading with him. "I have no right to keep the information from you, but how can I do such a traitorous thing to a friend who was only trying to defend me from Bailiff Tom?"

Ranulf felt the heat rise up his neck. Once again, he wished he had been the one with her, the one to help her.

"Annabel, if you tell me now, I will only tell the coroner after you've gone to the abbey. And I will make sure Sir Clement and the entire village knows that this person was defending you from the bailiff." She seemed to be considering it, not looking quite as perplexed as before. "I promise I'll do all I can to keep the person safe from repercussions. No one can blame him when they find out what the bailiff was doing to you."

"I don't want you to be blamed, either." Her lip quivered and tears swam in her eyes. But she swallowed and blinked the tears away. "I will tell you, but please promise me that you won't reveal it unless you have to, to keep yourself safe from blame."

"I promise. But I need you also to tell me everything that happened. Don't leave anything out. Then when this is all over, if the bailiff recovers, he can be properly punished."

She stared down at the ground, pursing her lips and blinking rapidly. His longing to reach out and comfort her was so strong it was a physical ache. But he held back.

She took a deep breath and began telling about walking through the woods to the privy. She didn't look at him, just stared at the ground while she talked.

"He grabbed me. I tried to scream, but he put his hand over my mouth. I bit him on the hand, but he just held me harder, hurting my face. He dragged me off the path and into the woods."

She continued talking in a monotone voice, until she said, "He managed to take my knife, but I got away from him before he could really hurt me." Anxiety seeped back into her voice as she said, "I tripped and fell, and I was so terrified." She lowered her voice to a whisper as she said, "Then someone came and lifted me up."

"Who was it?"

She didn't say anything. A tear dripped from her eye.

"Was it Gilbert Carpenter?"

She shook her head.

"Was it Stephen Blundel?"

She bit her lip and nodded. "He'd heard me try to scream. I told him to run, but he picked up the rock to defend us from the bailiff. He threw the rock and it hit the bailiff in the head. And that's all. If Stephen hadn't been there, the bailiff might have caught up with me, and ... he would have ..." She shook her head and wiped her face with her hands as tears began streaming down her face.

"So it was Stephen."

She nodded, her head down as she tried to hide her tears from him.

The young furniture maker. He finally knew the protector's identity, but seeing Annabel's distress, he was almost sorry he had forced her to tell and to relive that terrible night.

She leaned forward and grasped his wrist. "Please don't tell anyone. He begged me not to tell. He begged me. Please don't tell."

<hr />

She was suddenly gripped with guilt. Had she done the right thing? *Oh, Stephen, forgive me! I'm a terrible, traitorous friend.* What would happen if the bailiff died and the coroner found out it was Stephen? Would Stephen be executed? Would he have to pay a heavy fine to the king and to the bailiff's remaining family?

He'd told her he had some money, and he was saving it to build a house for himself and his mother. His plans would be destroyed. What would he think of her?

Compassion was clearly etched on Lord le Wyse's brow. He slid closer. "I'm so sorry." He placed his arms around her and pulled her to him.

She let him hold her against his chest. She was getting his shirt wet with her tears, but he didn't seem to mind. When she started to sob, he held her closer, his arm cradling her shoulders.

She should pull away, stand out of his reach, but instead, she leaned against his solid chest and let the warmth and comfort of his arms flow through her. But the worry over what would happen to Stephen came back.

She lifted her head from his chest and grabbed his arms, holding him away from her. Choking back tears, she said, "I bind you, sir, to what you said before—that you are my friend. Please help Stephen if Sir Clement finds out about him."

"Please don't worry. I will take care of Stephen and help him every way possible."

She sagged in relief, and Lord le Wyse pulled her back into his arms. Her head fell weakly against his shoulder.

She should push him away. His arms were strong, but he would not force her to stay.

But she didn't want to push him away. He promised he would keep Stephen safe, and she realized she trusted him to do that. She heard his warm, deep voice say, "Don't cry. All will be well."

She closed her eyes, savoring the warmth and closeness of him. She sniffed, and Lord le Wyse handed her a handkerchief.

"I'm sorry." She pushed back to wipe her nose and her eyes. She shook her head. "I-I shouldn't be crying in your arms. It's wrong. Please forgive me."

"I do not feel wronged."

His voice was so altered, so raw, Annabel looked up. Lord le Wyse's expression was strange again, the way he had looked when she drew away from him in the upper hall after Sir Clement had finished his questions.

Slowly, he reached his hand toward her face. Her heart trembled in her chest as he placed his palm gently against her cheek. His thumb caressed the damp skin under her eye. "I will miss you," he whispered.

Her skin tingled beneath his touch. She stared at his lips. They looked so inviting, so enticing. What would it feel like to kiss them, to feel loved? Before she could stop herself, she reached out and touched Lord le Wyse's cheek with her fingertips, staring into his warm brown eye.

The rough texture of his beard against her fingers seemed to bring her out of the fog in her mind. She pulled her hand away and leaned back.

"Sweet saints above," she whispered. Her heart hammered faster than any smith's mallet as Lord le Wyse removed his hand from her cheek but continued to capture her gaze with his.

Now what had she done? What did it all mean? They both sat, pretending to be calm, but she saw something in his eye that told her he was reining himself in ... No, she was imagining things. Her lord would never ... think about ... what she was thinking about. He would never think about kissing her.

Lord le Wyse closed his eye, breaking the connection. He turned his head slowly, as if the motion caused him pain, and stood to his feet.

Annabel also stood. "I must go. Mistress Eustacia—"

He nodded without looking at her. "You may go. Don't worry. I won't tell your secret unless I know I can keep both you and Stephen safe."

"Thank you, my lord." She hesitated, not willing to leave him. His shoulders were slumped and he seemed to be watching the laborers as they worked on his house.

After a few moments it seemed plain that he wanted her to go, so she turned and walked away.

He was sending her away to live with the nuns. She would be away from the inquest, away from Sir Clement's questions, and away from Lord le Wyse and the disturbing feelings he stirred within her.

She couldn't get to that abbey too soon.

Chapter
16

Annabel's thoughts skittered everywhere while she tried to help Mistress Eustacia cook. She dropped the basket that held the peas, strewing them all over the stone floor. She dropped the water bucket, spilling water over her feet. She dropped everything she touched until Mistress Eustacia sent her to the mill to inquire when the flour would be ready.

As Annabel walked along the dirt trail carved by cart wheels, a heaviness filled her chest. *Forgive me, Father God. I didn't mean to betray Stephen. And as for Lord le Wyse, I shouldn't be feeling this way about my lord.*

But soon she'd be at the abbey, away from him and away from these strange sensations. *Then I'll be good again, God. I'll read your Holy Writ and pray every waking moment.* She couldn't disappoint anyone there. At the abbey she'd be away from people, and away from temptation and these troubling thoughts. *Lord God, why does Lord le Wyse look at me in that way that makes my heart flutter like birds' wings? Why did he touch my cheek? Forgive me, God, but it felt so good.*

She closed her eyes for a moment, remembering as her cheek tingled.

"Annabel!"

She stopped abruptly. Stephen stood only an arm's length away. A shudder convulsed her as she realized how close she'd come to smacking headfirst into her friend. She'd been walking with her head down, so lost in her thoughts . . .

"You didn't even see me." Stephen's look of amazement made her aware of how odd her behavior must appear.

She shook her head, unable to make the effort to smile. "I was thinking, not watching where I was going. Forgive me. Are you well?" Cold fingers wrapped around her throat. What would Stephen say to her if he knew she'd betrayed his secret?

"I am. How do you fare?" He looked at her so intensely, and leaned toward her so near that she took a step back.

"I am well." What would he think when she went away to the abbey in a few days? She couldn't tell him, of course. Lord le Wyse had told her not to, and she couldn't betray two people in one day. She would simply have to leave him a note.

Stephen stared at her again with that strange look. He swallowed, making his Adam's apple bob up and down, as though he were about to say something, then he closed his mouth.

Finally, he spoke. "I hear the bailiff's condition hasn't changed. He's still asleep."

Annabel nodded. "No one knows if he will recover." That was why he was behaving strangely. He was thinking of the bailiff. Should she tell him that the coroner had questioned her? She never kept secrets from Stephen, but she was too ashamed of how much she had revealed to Sir Clement.

"I-I try not to think about it, but I dream about it every night." That was when she noticed the dark circles under his eyes.

"Oh, Stephen, please don't worry so much. I truly believe everything will be all right." *After all, Lord le Wyse promised to protect us, both of us.*

Stephen fidgeted, shifting his weight from one foot to the other. "I know it was the bailiff's fault for trying to hurt you, but I hope he doesn't die. I don't want that on my conscience."

"I know, but I'm sure God will forgive you. He will, Stephen."

He looked uncomfortable and changed the tone of his voice when he asked, "How are you faring with Lord le Wyse? I hear he has a horrible temper."

"Oh, no, he doesn't."

Stephen gave her a quizzical look.

"I mean, sometimes he can be harsh, I suppose, but he is good and fair and I can't imagine he would ever mistreat anyone." She thought about how kind he had been to her, how gentle, how he even comforted her . . .

"You like him, don't you?" A look of surprise and amazement spread over Stephen's face.

"W-what? Like him? Whatever can you mean? He is my lord. How can you suggest such a thing?" She clamped her mouth shut. She was protesting too much, as she inwardly cursed the blush that was heating her face.

A slow smile came over Stephen's face. "I've been wondering if you would ever notice a man. Now I see —"

Annabel snorted. "You see nothing. I am only his servant."

"But he is a kind man? I am glad of that." Stephen winked.

Annabel opened her mouth to say something, she wasn't sure what.

"I met a girl named Abigail," Stephen said with a sheepish half smile. "She's from Lincoln. Do you know her?"

"Oh yes, she seems nice."

Was Stephen actually blushing? "She is nice."

"Why, Stephen! Are you sweet on this girl?"

"Shh!"

Annabel looked for the source of Stephen's sudden panic, and saw a woman was coming down the road toward them: Margery, the miller's young wife. Annabel quickly turned to Stephen. "We'll talk later, but please believe me when I say that everything is going to turn out for our good. And I know God forgives you." She gave him a quick embrace before Margery got close enough to hear what they were saying.

Annabel continued down the road toward the mill. Seeing she couldn't avoid Margery, she plastered a smile on her face and greeted the busybody blonde.

"Oh, Annabel! I haven't seen you since the day before you went to work as Lord le Wyse's servant. Are you well? Has it been simply horrible?"

"No, of course not, Margery. I am very well."

"I told you then that you should marry. I couldn't believe you refused to marry Bailiff Tom! And now he's—no one knows if he'll ever be well again. So many terrible things happening in Glynval. Everyone says"—she lowered her voice and glanced over her shoulder—"that the new lord is cursed. He brought all these hardships on us."

"Cursed? That's nonsense."

"Well, just look at him! With that claw for a hand and only one eye. If I ever saw anyone who looked cursed, it would be him. Although I can imagine he was quite handsome before— But that temper! Everyone says he's a perfect beast, yelling and growling at people."

"Margery." Annabel felt the anger rising inside her and struggled to stifle the ugly things she wanted to say. After taking a deep breath, she said, "I think it is a terrible thing to speak so of one's lord."

"But I—"

"Even if you are the miller's wife, Lord le Wyse is still the lord of this demesne, and as such you should respect him enough not to spread nasty rumors about him being cursed. Cursed! That's silly. And he is not a beast, he is a man, and a very kind lord."

Margery narrowed her eyes. "You seem quite enamored with our new lord."

"Don't be foolish." Annabel glared back at her.

"I still say he's cursed, and you should have married the bailiff." Margery looked away with a smirk. "But at least the hard work hasn't affected your looks. You're still as pretty as you were." She looked down her nose at Annabel. "But I don't know what good it does you if you stay an indentured servant and refuse to marry."

"That's nothing for you to worry about, Margery. Perhaps you should worry that the powerful Lord le Wyse will find out what you've been saying about him, spreading wicked gossip about him being cursed. If I were you, I'm not sure I could even sleep at night." She smiled, wide-eyed, at Margery as she skirted around her and continued on her way.

She held back a chuckle at the fear that flickered over Margery's face.

"Mistress Eustacia, do you think you would have been happy if you'd never gotten married?" She and her mistress were alone, indulging in a real bath at the stream—possibly their last good dunking before the weather turned cold—and it seemed like a good time to ask the question that had plagued her since Lord le Wyse mentioned the abbey. All the other maidens seemed so sure marriage was central to a woman's happiness.

Mistress Eustacia stopped in the middle of washing her hair with the special hair soap Lord le Wyse insisted on sharing with his servants. Annabel had used the liquid soap before, as her father had imported some from India the last year he lived. Grabbing the flask, she lathered some into her own hair. She loved to rub it into her scalp then dunk her head, feeling as though all the impurities of the world were floating away downstream. And in this moment, the feeling was more welcome than usual.

While massaging in the hair soap, she kept her chin half-submerged under the water as she waited for Mistress Eustacia to answer. She held her breath, afraid Eustacia would ask what had prompted the question.

Instead, Mistress Eustacia stared downriver, as though she was seeing into the past. "I heard a priest once say that marriage was instituted by God for procreation, so we could have children. But that's not the only thing marriage is for."

The older woman became quiet and began splashing water on her neck. Annabel busied herself by scrubbing her own face and then her toes.

When Annabel finished, Mistress Eustacia was looking down at her. "Women want a husband of their own, someone to love them and protect them. Men want a wife to cook and clean for them, and the other privileges of marriage." The mistress winked.

Annabel had to duck her head under the water to cool her face. She came up sputtering and asked, "Why did you marry? Was it for love?"

"For that and more. It's a natural thing to want to be married, to want a husband and children."

"Were you happy when you were married?"

"Aye, I was happy." She smiled wistfully. Annabel knew Eustacia had borne four children, and one had died as a baby. "A good husband is a blessing, and children are a gift from God. My children and my husband were my whole life, along with helping care for Lord Ranulf and his brother and sister."

"Lord le Wyse has a brother and sister?"

"He did have. They are gone now, poor things. His brother, the oldest and the heir, died of a fever several years ago, and his sister died in the Great Pestilence. When his brother died, Lord Ranulf's life changed, of course. Around that time he was pursued by Guinevere—the woman he married. She only wanted him for his wealth and power." Eustacia's mouth twisted in distaste.

Annabel felt a pain in her stomach thinking about Lord le Wyse being treated badly, especially by his own wife. She submerged her head underwater and rinsed away the remains of the hair soap. Mention of the lord's wife brought to mind the lord's paintings, especially the one of the woman and baby lying dead in coffins. How much pain her lord had suffered! She tried to scrub away the images.

Clearly, marriage could bring pain as well as the happiness Mistress Eustacia had known. In going to live at the abbey, women would be her only companions, women she hoped were as kind as Mistress Eustacia and who only wished to live for God and His purposes. She wouldn't have to be tormented with confusing thoughts or marriage proposals or violent attacks or inquisitions. God was finally saving her from all her troubles.

The only thing that gnawed at her was Lord le Wyse. He said he would miss her when she left. She remembered the way he had touched her cheek, so tenderly . . . but she was only a servant to him. He wasn't in love with her. She didn't even want him to be. Did she?

She shook her head. She didn't know the answer to that.

❧

When Annabel sat down with the Bible that night to read, Sir Clement and Mistress Eustacia quietly left the room. She opened her mouth but was only able to get out the first word before Lord le Wyse interrupted her.

"I have something to tell you while we're alone."

"Yes, my lord?"

He sighed then said, "I received a missive from my aunt, the abbess at Rosings Abbey. I'm afraid you won't be able to go as soon as I had hoped."

Annabel was surprised not to feel some disappointment at his news. She waited for him to go on.

"My aunt tells me there is an illness that has spread through the abbey. No one has died yet, but it involves fever and a rash. She begs me to wait until she is able to send word that the illness is over."

"Very well, then."

Lord le Wyse's expression was sober. "I'm afraid you will not be able to avoid being here when the jury begins their inquiries into the bailiff's injuries."

"I see." This was grave indeed. She stared down morosely at the open Bible. The prospect of standing before the jury, in the presence of everyone who knew her and hated her family, terrified her.

"I will do my best to keep Sir Clement from revealing what he knows, and I won't betray your secret."

Annabel nodded.

"I'm very sorry you can't leave yet." Lord le Wyse looked grim, almost angry. "I know you're eager to go."

"It isn't that. I'm afraid of having to answer the jury's questions."

"Of course." The angry tone was gone, but now he looked despondent. "I will protect you as much as I can."

"I know. All will be well." She tried to look hopeful, to turn him from sad thoughts. His melancholy moods always made her want to cheer him up. "God works out everything for our good, remember?"

He stared back at her and half frowned. But how could God work this out? She had no idea.

"But sometimes I wonder if he's angry with me," she confessed, "and that is why this is happening."

"Angry? With you? Why?"

She shook her head. "I did a terrible thing by possibly bringing about the bailiff's death. He may not have been a good man, but I should never have reacted as I did."

"But you didn't—"

"No, I didn't throw the stone, but what happened to him was my fault." She looked up and pressed her hand against her chest, trying to push back the pain and guilt that seemed to suffocate her now as it did when she was lying in bed at night. "I am to blame for his death if he dies."

"How?" By the look on his face, he clearly didn't believe her.

"By carrying a knife around—out of fear! Shouldn't I rather have trusted God to save me? I pulled out that knife and held it as though I meant to do him harm with it. But I was the fool, because it was no good to me at all. He had no weapon. He took mine from me." Her breath was coming shallow and her temples throbbed. "If he dies, it will be my doing."

"No, Annabel. It will not." Lord le Wyse's words were firm, but they only seemed to stir up more anguish in her. She felt the perverse need to convince him of her culpability.

"Yes, it will! I should have screamed. I should have screamed and screamed until help came. Why should I ... think ..." Oh, what was the use in talking about it? She pressed the heels of her hands into her eyes.

"Annabel, listen to me. It was not your fault. You struggled. You tried to scream. You did all you could. I heard you when I was on my walk, but I didn't reach you in time. Stephen heard you too, and he was closer. You have to stop torturing yourself."

"But God must be angry with me. He intends to punish me."

"No. A verse from First John reads, 'If we confess our sins, He is faithful and just and will forgive us our sins, and purify us from all unrighteousness.' Are you saying you don't believe He will forgive you when he has plainly said He would?"

Peace washed over her. "You're right. I'm sorry."

They sat looking at each other for a long time.

"The verse says, 'If we confess our sins,' so I must confess. I didn't trust God as I should have."

"And God forgives you."

But does he forgive me for wanting you to hold me in your arms? For thinking about kissing you? Annabel shuddered at the thought of her lord finding out.

"What is it?"

"Nothing. I-I just wonder if God's tired of hearing all my confessions lately."

"I don't think God gets tired of hearing you. I never could."

The light was so dim she couldn't read his expression, but his words made her heart flutter. As she watched the candle and firelight flicker over his face, she was struck with the thought that she knew little about him, about his family or past, except for the wolf attack and his wife's unfaithfulness. "You said the abbess is your mother's sister. Is your mother still alive?"

"She died seven years ago. My father died last spring. My brother and sister have been gone a few years as well. The worst may have been my sister—she died the same week as my wife and child."

"I'm so sorry. That is grievous indeed." He was all alone. "Were you married long?"

"Two years." He blinked twice, as though he were erasing all emotion from his face and voice. "But there was no love between us—at least, not on her side. She never cared for me."

Annabel swallowed. Her heart seemed to expand toward him, reaching out to him. He had endured so much pain. She longed to do or say something to comfort him.

"In truth, no one knows if the child born to her was mine or ... his. Though I was determined to claim him for my own. After all, it wasn't the child's fault his mother was ... as she was."

"You speak of it as if it is no longer painful, but I know you must have suffered." If ever anyone deserved a noble, loving wife, it was Lord le Wyse.

"Time," he said, pausing and leaning back in his chair. He stared into the fire. "Time blunts the pain and creates a mist over one's memory—at least in the case of death and sorrow. Other types of pain linger longer."

No doubt he was thinking of his wife's betrayal. How could anyone be so false? Annabel hated her with an intensity that took her breath away.

"Perhaps time is an inconsistent healer," he said, "but God can purge even the most painful memories."

What was Annabel's most painful memory? Her father's death? Bailiff Tom's lifeless body in the forest? Nay, it was the terrifying moment when she realized the bailiff wanted her to marry him and was willing to resort to violence. Raw fear had shot through her stomach as he grabbed her and kissed her. Fearful thoughts dogged her steps from that moment to this.

But God had taken care of her. When the bailiff was near, a protector was always there as well. Usually it had been Lord le Wyse, and Stephen had appeared the final time.

Lord le Wyse's questioning look brought her out of her reverie.

"Shall I read?" she asked.

"As you wish."

The book opened to the second epistle to Timothy. Her eyes centered on the verse, "For the Spirit God gave us does not make us timid, but gives us power, love, and self-discipline." *Forgive me for my timidity, God. It did not come from You. I pray you will cast out this spirit of fear. And replace Lord le Wyse's pain with a spirit of joy.*

Chapter
17

*Three days later, Sir Clement and the hun-*dred bailiff went through the village of Glynval and neighboring villages gathering the men and women who would form a jury for the inquest into the attack on Bailiff Tom. Come morning, the inquest would begin.

Sir Clement had already spoken to the jury about the evidence the body presented. Ranulf had only tonight to evade Sir Clement's questions about whether he had extracted the name of the bailiff's attacker from Annabel, and to convince Sir Clement not to question Annabel before the jury.

With these thoughts swirling in his mind, Ranulf came around his dressing screen as the coroner stopped at the fireplace to warm himself. "Sir Clement, do you have a moment?"

"Ah, Lord Ranulf. I was hoping to see you tonight. Have you discovered whom the maiden Annabel is protecting?" He smiled and rubbed his hands before the warmth of the fire, but Ranulf saw a sharp eagerness in his eyes that contradicted his casual stance.

"I have." Ranulf stepped forward and leaned against the side of the stone hearth.

"Who is it?" Sir Clement was all attention once he turned his body to face his friend.

Ranulf considered each word before speaking. "It is someone who was protecting Annabel."

"Protecting her? From the bailiff?"

"Yes."

"So the teeth marks *are* Annabel's."

Ranulf winced as he realized this might create a direct link placing Annabel in violent conflict with the bailiff. If the jury asked her if they were her teeth marks, she would have to say yes.

"The point I would like to make to you, Sir Clement, is that this person is no man of violence. He was simply trying to keep the bailiff from hurting Annabel. He is a man ... that no one would ever think ..." How should he say this? "His heart is pure, and the assault of the bailiff was an accident resulting from a man's desire to protect a childhood friend."

"Accident or not, I need to know this man's identity, to question him. The truth must come forth, Lord Ranulf, for truth is paramount." The coroner spoke softly, as though trying to lull him into a sense of trust. "Who is he?"

But Ranulf couldn't betray Annabel. "I will not tell you."

"Then the jury and I will be forced to question her tomorrow at the inquest."

"Sir Clement, believe me, this was a terrible event, but it will serve no purpose to reveal the person, who no doubt feels very badly about what he had to do to protect an innocent maiden. I ask you, pray, do not press it further." He had vowed not to get angry but to speak calmly and pray for God to touch Sir Clement and bend him not to question Annabel. But Ranulf could already feel his face growing warm and his jaw beginning to clench. "Why must you put this village through more anguish?"

"For the sake of truth, my friend. Truth and justice. Justice is everything."

"No, justice is not everything. There are more important things than justice."

Sir Clement frowned. "What is greater than justice?"

The answer came to Ranulf in a blink, as though whispered to his spirit by a familiar voice. He murmured, "Faith, hope, and love, but the greatest of these is love."

"What did you say?" Sir Clement leaned forward, his eyes fastened on Ranulf's face.

"Mercy. Love." His heart thumped then seemed to soar above him to the very clouds, but painfully, like a bird with a wounded wing. His breath went out of him as he spoke the words. "Mercy and love are greater. For us mortals, love is greater than justice."

Annabel stood in the courtyard with Mistress Eustacia. The goats that usually grazed there had been shut in their pen as people descended onto the open space, talking low among themselves. She watched them, her heart pounding against her chest.

Two of Lord le Wyse's men hauled a table and some stools out of the manor house and set them up on the grassy court, which had lately turned brown with the coming frost. The coroner's clerk, Ralph Abovebrook, who had arrived the night before, sat on the stool and unfolded his leather case, from which he drew out a pot of ink, a quill, and a long sheet of parchment.

The stools were set up for the twelve members of the jury, arranged in a circle on the yard. Soon she might be forced to stand in that circle, to answer the coroner's questions in front of the jury; indeed, in front of the entire village, which was gathering around to witness the proceedings. She wanted so much to run away and hide. How could she possibly allow Sir Clement to ask those questions he was sure to press her with? She had prayed and prayed for a miracle, a way out of this terrible mess. Surely God would rescue her somehow.

When she saw the twelve men of the jury sit on the stools, she groaned, drawing a look from Mistress Eustacia. *O God, please don't place me in front of all those men. What will happen if I am forced to tell Stephen's secret? God, save me! Don't make me do this.*

"Child! Are you ill?" Mistress Eustacia's voice registered alarm, breaking into Annabel's fevered prayer. "You're so pale."

"I am well, I am well." She forced herself to stop wringing her hands and instead clasped her arms around herself, willing herself to be still, if not calm.

"Annabel."

Stephen stood at her left elbow. "Oh!" She jumped then placed her hand over her heart, wondering if it would thump straight out of her body. "What are you doing here?" She lowered her voice, hoping that even Mistress Eustacia, who was beside her, wouldn't hear. She stepped away with Stephen a few feet and leaned against the cold stone of the manor house, beside the undercroft door.

"I know I shouldn't have come, but I couldn't help it. Do you think they will question you?"

Her lip trembled, and she bit it to make it stop. "I am almost certain of it."

"Don't worry. I won't be angry with you, even if you tell them everything."

"Oh, Stephen. Please forgive me ... if I do."

"I will."

"I will do my best. I promise." Tears stung her eyelids as she tried not to think about what might happen to Stephen. "I have to go." Not wanting people to see her and Stephen together, she turned and fled back to Mistress Eustacia, plastering herself against her mistress's side.

⁂

Ranulf caught sight of Sir Clement standing by the corner of the manor house and started toward him, but Sir Clement was intent on watching two people several feet away—Annabel and Stephen.

Annabel looked pale and distressed. But Sir Clement's eyes were trained on Stephen, his head cocked as though listening intently. Annabel ran away, eliciting a grim expression from the young woodworker. However, Ranulf was interested in Sir Clement's expression. His brows had pulled together to form a V between his eyes, and his mouth was slightly ajar.

When Sir Clement turned his gaze on Ranulf, the coroner hurried over to him. "Ranulf, who is that man yonder with the impaired legs?"

"That is Stephen Blundel, a furniture maker and woodworker."

"Call him over here, and the maiden Annabel."

Ranulf hadn't obeyed anyone since his father died. But he had little choice now.

"Stephen." Ranulf beckoned with his hand then strode to where Annabel stood with Eustacia.

"Annabel." He spoke her name softly, but still she started and turned. "Come with me for a moment. Sir Clement wants to speak with you and Stephen."

Her cheeks were already devoid of their usual color, but she lifted her chin and followed. She must have known as well as he did that she had no choice.

Stephen's face was almost as pale as Annabel's. *Like sheep to the slaughter.*

Sir Clement focused on Stephen's face. "Do you know who I am?"

"You are the king's coroner."

"And you must answer me truthfully. Where were you the night the bailiff was struck in the head, rendering him senseless to this day?"

"I was here."

"Did you see what happened to him?"

Stephen stood still and silent. Even his eyes didn't blink.

"Did you strike him?"

"I was trying to protect Annabel. I wasn't trying to kill him. That is all."

"What did you hit him with?"

"He was holding a knife and was trying to hurt an innocent maiden." Defiance mixed with the fear in his eyes.

Stephen shifted his weight awkwardly, placing his hip at an abnormal angle that drew the coroner's notice.

Sir Clement's lips parted, obviously deep in thought. His voice was somehow softer when he resumed. "You were protecting Annabel?"

Stephen didn't reply. His throat bobbed as he swallowed.

"Yes." Sir Clement answered his own question then rubbed

his palm over his cheek and chin. He stared in the direction of the circle of jurors across the yard, but his eyes were vacant.

Shouts came from the direction of the lane that led to the village. Adam came running into the yard, panting and out of breath, with his father rather far behind him, also running.

"Bailiff Tom is awake!"

Several people exclaimed, "What?"

"He's awake," Adam repeated. "My father sent me to fetch the coroner."

Annabel looked at Lord le Wyse. He gave her a grim smile and a nod. While she still appeared fragile, a new strength seemed to enter her as she returned his smile.

Tom was alive. And awake. *I'm glad he's survived, God. I pray he will repent of his evil ways.* But what would this mean for Annabel? Would he say that Stephen threw the rock, that Stephen tried to kill him? No doubt Annabel would be forced to tell what the bailiff had done, and had been planning to do, to her.

But at least Stephen wouldn't be hanged for the bailiff's death.

***

Ranulf hurried down the road, with Sir Clement close behind him. He was well aware that the entire village, which had turned out for the jury's inquisition, was following close on his heels.

When they arrived at Joan Smith's house, Sir Clement demanded that the rest of the village go back to the manor, but he allowed Ranulf to go inside with him. They found the bailiff in a half-sitting position, eating some oat and pea pottage that his sister, Joan, was feeding him. He looked very weak, his head propped up with blankets and a pillow.

"Good morning, Bailiff Tom," Ranulf greeted him, fighting to keep the disdain from his voice.

The bailiff stared blankly back at him and swallowed a mouthful of pottage.

"Tom, this is Sir Clement, the king's coroner."

The bailiff stared at him as well.

"Tom? Can you hear me?"

"Aye, I can hear you," he said weakly.

His sister shook her head as she looked up at them. "He don't know you, don't know me, don't know anybody."

Better and better.

Sir Clement stepped toward the bailiff. "I wonder if you could tell me how you got that wound?" Sir Clement pointed to the front of Bailiff Tom's head.

The bailiff slowly raised his hand to his head, feeling gingerly at the bump that had receded so much as to be barely visible. "No, I don't know."

"What is your name?" the coroner asked.

The bailiff opened his mouth, but his eyes went blank as he stared past the two men. Finally, he said, "I can't remember."

Sir Clement stepped back. "That's all right." He nodded at Joan. "Thank you. We won't need to ask any more questions. Good day."

They left the house and walked slowly. Several villagers looked at them, obviously wanting to know what happened and what the bailiff had said to them.

What would happen now? Ranulf wondered just as much as the villagers. But Sir Clement was silent all the way back to the manor house courtyard.

⌘

Annabel didn't have to wait long for the coroner and Lord le Wyse to return. When they arrived, the jurors went back to their places on their stools, and the clerk sat back down and took up his quill.

Sir Clement stood in their midst. When everyone was perfectly quiet and every eye was on him, the coroner announced, "Praise be to God, who orders all our days, Bailiff Tom atte Water is awake and recovering from his injury. I've just spoken with him, and he is speaking as clearly as I am speaking to you now."

A cheer went up—a rather half-hearted cheer, as many had already heard this news and were more interested in how the inquest would proceed.

"I am sure we all want to thank the hundred bailiff for coming and assembling this special jury to inquire into the suspicious circumstances surrounding the bailiff's serious injury. And we want to thank the jurors who were willing to come and do their duty to their fellow man. However ..."

What had Bailiff Tom told him?

Everyone, Annabel included, seemed to hold their breath, waiting for the coroner to continue.

"Bailiff Tom, we all hope, shall recover from this injury. When he grows stronger, we pray he remembers all that happened."

Does he not remember?

"And when he remembers, you may either summon me to return, at which time the hundred bailiff and jury may be reassembled, or you may assess this matter in your own manorial court with your own jury, as you please, since this is not a death inquest." The hundred bailiff nodded around the circle at the gathered assembly. "Good day to you all."

With that, Sir Clement turned and strode away.

As he came near to where Stephen stood, he nodded to him, and as he passed Annabel he nodded to her as well. He headed up the manor house steps, Annabel supposed, to collect his things.

So, Sir Clement intended to conceal the fact that Stephen was the attacker and that Bailiff Tom had been trying to assault Annabel. He wouldn't force Stephen and Annabel to tell what happened after all.

He chose mercy instead of justice.

Thank you, God.

Annabel closed her mouth and looked at Lord le Wyse for confirmation. He simply stared back, the lines in his forehead relaxing and his jaw going slack.

Relief flooded her body, buckling her knees. She held on to Mistress Eustacia's arm to steady herself. She wanted to go to Stephen and hug him, but instead she smiled across the way at him. He simply lifted his brows, as relieved as she was, and wiped his forehead with his sleeve.

But their relief might only be temporary. The bailiff could regain his memory, as Sir Clement had implied, and when he did, he might accuse both Stephen and Annabel of trying to kill him — his word against theirs. But at least there was no threat of Stephen being hung.

Lord Le Wyse gave her a whisper of a smile.

As Annabel began to relax, Maud rushed to the middle of the disintegrating circle. "What of the teeth marks on my father's hand?" Her brows were lowered in a fierce scowl, and she directed her question to the members of the jury, turning her body to look each person in the face.

Sir Clement stopped at the top of the manor house steps and turned to listen.

"Teeth marks don't appear by accident," Maud continued, her cheeks red. "And the knife in his hand? What of that?"

The other jury members squinted, looked away thoughtfully, or nodded.

"Someone tried to kill my father. What do you say to that, Sir Clement? You are the king's coroner. Shouldn't you investigate?"

Annabel's stomach sank.

Sir Clement shrugged and gestured with his hand, his eyelids half closed as though Maud's outburst concerned him not at all. "As I clearly said, when your father is stronger, and remembers what happened, your jury may question any and all that you wish."

"No. The inquest jury is here. Why should we wait? My father may never remember what happened."

A murmur of approval went around the circle.

Sir Clement hesitated then nodded to the hundred bailiff. "There is your hundred bailiff. Let him decide."

The crowd began to reassemble into a tighter circle, suddenly attentive and murmuring approval.

"I agree with this young woman," the hundred bailiff said. "Let the jury question those they wish to question."

The jury foreman stood. He cleared his throat, and when the assembly had grown quiet again, he said, "The first person we wish to question is the bailiff's daughter, as she claims to have information to offer. Maud atte Water, come forward."

The crowd turned as Maud made her way through the press of people. Her lips were pursed together, barely able to cover her prominent top teeth, and her eyes glinted with malice. Maud moved to the middle of the circle as if she were on stage.

"Maud, who do you think tried to kill your father?" the jury foreman asked in his loud voice.

Sir Clement interrupted from the manor house steps. "This is not the time to speculate about who, if anyone, tried to kill the bailiff. You may question Maud about where she was the night of the bailiff's death or about what she saw. Nothing more."

The jury foreman gave a slight bow to the coroner. "Maud, did you see anything the night of the bailiff's death?"

"I saw him" — she pointed a finger at Lord le Wyse — "coming out of the woods behind the manor house."

Chapter
18

The murmuring and whispering rose to a high pitch.

"He knew my father would protest him seducing me and then refusing to marry me."

Loud gasps and cries arose with this declaration. Annabel's face burned and her stomach turned. Lord le Wyse and Maud? The mere thought made her want to retch. But no, he would never do such a thing. *I don't believe it. I won't believe it.*

In a clear but monotone voice, Lord le Wyse replied, "That is a lie." His face turned pale, but there was no other outward reaction from him. He remained expressionless, his eye unblinking.

For her to tell such a lie, and in front of the entire village! A fire burned inside Annabel as she glared at Maud.

A rumble of thunder, as if triggered by Maud's expression, vibrated Annabel's breastbone. The crowd lifted their eyes to study the clouds.

Neither the jury foreman nor Maud reacted to the noise or the coming storm.

The foreman continued with his questions. "Did you see the knife the bailiff had in his hand when he was found?"

"Aye."

"Had you ever seen the knife before?"

"Nay. It wasn't my father's."

Annabel's insides turned cold.

Sir Clement came closer and joined the hundred bailiff

standing near the jury. The coroner absently chewed a length of straw. He drew it out of his mouth and proclaimed, "You have yet to establish that the bailiff was attacked or that any foul play was involved. This jury needs to be about the business of finding facts. Maud atte Water, do you have any facts to offer?"

Maud's tiny black eyes stared back at the coroner defiantly. Her hands were drawn up into fists at her side. "Someone tried to kill my father." She stepped in Sir Clement's direction and screamed, "I have nothing else to say!" A vein stood out, red and bulging, in her neck. She spun around and stalked away on stiff legs.

The foreman then announced, "The jury now wishes to summon the one who discovered the bailiff's body. The jury wishes to question Lord Ranulf le Wyse."

Annabel's gaze flicked to Lord le Wyse, but his face was unreadable. *O God, please be with him. Don't let him take the blame.*

Lord le Wyse stood before them all, looking both stoic and calm.

The foreman looked a bit nervous and cleared his throat, his shoulders rounding a bit as he faced the lord of the demesne.

Lord Le Wyse's dark brown hair was skillfully cut and combed into place, though his black eye patch gave him a look of danger. His beard was, as always, neatly trimmed, and he wore his finest silk doublet—sapphire blue with gold embroidery— along with a purple velvet robe with an intricate border along the hem, fastened at his right shoulder with a jeweled pin. He would have been welcome anywhere in that attire. *Anywhere except, perhaps, here.*

In stark contrast, the jury foreman, as well as the other members of the jury, wore the typical dress of the villagers. The foreman's dull-brown hood hung down his back, its folds draped around his neck and shoulders. His hay-colored hair was stiff and in need of a scrubbing, but his brown tunic was clean. It hung down to his knees over his dull earth-colored hose, and was cinched with a belt at his waist.

The foreman cleared his throat again, looked down at the

ground, then finally raised his eyes to meet Lord le Wyse's. "Did my lord find the body of our bailiff in the woods?"

"Aye, I did."

"And was my lord the first to discover him?"

"As far as I know."

"Had you heard the bailiff set up the hue and cry?"

"No."

"Then how came you to be in the woods at that time of evening?"

"I was on the path to the men's privy. You do know that some people use the privy?"

This drew several chuckles from the crowd.

The foreman didn't even smile. "Did you find anyone there with the body?"

"No."

Maud cried out from the inside edge of the circle of spectators. "Did you kill my father?"

"I did not."

Turmoil erupted as the hundred bailiff and Sir Clement said, at the same time, "Girl, you may not speak."

"You are out of order, young woman," the hundred bailiff said.

Maud ignored him, never taking her eyes off Lord le Wyse. "Then how came my father to lie on the ground with a knife in his hand and teeth marks upon him?"

"I have no explanation to offer."

"My father was in perfect health!" Maud screamed even as two men grasped her arms and tried to remove her from the gathering. She broke free from the men's hold and spun away from Lord le Wyse to look at the jurors. "Now my father doesn't even know who he is! Since this man came to our village we have had nothing but bad fortune. There is a curse upon us! A drought has ruined most of our gardens and pastures. Fire destroyed our grain crop!" She pointed at Lord le Wyse. "This man has brought this curse upon us. I charge you, look upon him! See that he is accursed!"

Annabel cried out in distress, but she was hardly heard above the muffled exclamations of the crowd. How dare Maud say such things? She clutched her hand over her mouth as she stared at Lord le Wyse, almost expecting to see him laid open and bleeding from such a violent, unfair assault. Her only thought was to go to him and shield him, defend him and lash out at this ludicrous attack. She stepped forward.

"Nay, Annabel. You mustn't." Stephen caught her by the arm and pulled her back.

She shook off Stephen's hand and crossed her arms, her eyes fastened on her lord's face.

Gradually the crowd quieted, and the hundred bailiff spoke quite loudly. "Jury, you are to assess a fine to this woman for this disturbance."

Maud allowed herself to be taken outside the inner circle of the court without further struggle while the jury conferred about her fine.

In a few moments, the jury foreman said, "For contempt of the court, the jury fines Maud atte Water fifteen pence."

The hundred bailiff then addressed Lord le Wyse. "Would you like to respond to the accusations?"

From between clenched teeth, Lord le Wyse ground out, "Superstition shows ignorance. I neither caused nor could I have prevented any of those events. It's her spite that drives her to cast suspicion on me. And I may be accursed, but at least I don't tell lies under oath."

Annabel wanted to cheer. The crowd around her mumbled and whispered to each other.

Maud's cheeks turned fiery red.

The jury seemed to pretend nothing out of the ordinary had happened as they called two other people forward and questioned them, but neither had any new information to share.

The hundred bailiff spoke. "If no one has any factual information to offer this inquest, I am forced to declare the injury of Bailiff Tom atte Water an accident, unless he, of his own accord, decides to make a complaint."

Annabel watched Sir Clement's face. He knew everything and yet he wouldn't reveal the truth.

The clerk, sitting at his tiny desk, wrote while the hundred bailiff spoke, and while dipping his quill in the ink, he neither lifted his eyes nor his head.

"May the bailiff recover and God's grace shine upon him and the village of Glynval," Sir Clement concluded.

At that moment, the skies began to release their first raindrops, and the people scattered, hunching their shoulders as they hurried away to find shelter from the storm.

Sir Clement went over to help his clerk by rolling up the parchment and tucking it into a bag to keep it dry while the clerk packed up his things.

Annabel's eyes flicked to Maud, standing in the rain, and she could have sworn she saw steam rising from the girl's head. The way Maud narrowed her eyes at Lord le Wyse before turning away sent a shiver through her. Annabel should have been relieved at the way things had concluded, but her insides still trembled with foreboding.

A hand closed around her elbow. She jumped and turned her head.

"Oh, it's you, Stephen." She threw her arms around his neck. "God saved us, didn't He?"

"He did indeed."

Annabel pulled away. "You should get out of the rain."

Stephen nodded. Annabel turned and ran to the manor house.

⚜

Maud left Lord le Wyse's service that day, clearing her things out of the undercroft. Annabel didn't see her after the inquest, but some of the other maids said she was to live with her sister in a nearby village. Annabel prayed for her but was relieved she no longer had to see Tom's daughter.

Beatrice's duties as a dairymaid increased. On the first day of Maud's absence, she sat at one end of the upper hall churning butter as Annabel swept the floor. The girls chatted, until Lord le Wyse came through the door and walked across the nearly empty hall to the screened-off corner of the room where his bed and trunks were stored. Annabel glanced at him as he passed by her.

Beatrice was watching him as well. She smiled her biggest, toothy grin. "Good morning, Lord le Wyse."

He mumbled, "Good day."

The fact that he didn't even glance in Beatrice's direction gave Annabel an unaccountable feeling of joy.

"Is there anything I can help you with?" Beatrice asked. Her smile was wasted, as Lord le Wyse was hidden behind his screen.

He didn't answer her, and with a small smile of her own, Annabel went on sweeping. Then she heard a quick series of loud thuds. She looked up to see Beatrice sprawled on the floor, her head and shoulders pinned against the wall by the heavy butter churn. Her stool lay overturned beside her. *She certainly has persistence.*

"Help me! I can't move!" Beatrice whimpered dramatically, struggling feebly on the floor.

Lord le Wyse emerged from behind his screen. Annabel hurried to help, but Lord le Wyse was closer. He reached down and lifted the stone churn off of Beatrice then held out his hand to her.

"Oh, thank you, Lord le Wyse." She clasped his hand and let him help her up, then pretended to stumble into him, throwing her arms around his neck.

Annabel felt her face get hot. Could Lord le Wyse see what Beatrice was doing? And did he think Annabel had done the same thing when she had cried in his arms?

Lord le Wyse patted Beatrice on the back with one hand but didn't embrace the girl. He looked over her shoulder at Annabel. "Could you set that stool up?"

She righted the stool and Lord le Wyse promptly lowered Beatrice onto it, holding her by her arms. Beatrice continued to cling to him.

"I've hurt my ankle again. Oh, Lord le Wyse, I don't know what I would have done if you hadn't been here. You saved me again."

Lord le Wyse gently extricated her hands from around his neck and pulled away from her as soon as he was free. "I'll go get Mistress Eustacia to come look at your ankle."

He turned and strode across the room and out the door.

Annabel frowned down at Beatrice.

Beatrice smirked at her. "Picking up ideas of your own, Annabel? With all that time you spend with him every night, I would think you would have already found a way to his heart. But maybe you're too prudish."

She stared at the girl's big nose and rude sneer. "I'd rather be prudish than throw myself at my lord, like you, Beatrice."

Beatrice rose to her feet. "'Maybe you're afraid of Lord le Wyse. Is that it? Does he scare you, Annabel?" She laughed.

Beatrice stepped toe to toe with Annabel, their noses almost touching. Punching Annabel's shoulder with her fingernail, she said, "I want you to stay away from Lord le Wyse. He's mine. You will tell him that you can't read to him anymore, that it's improper. Do you hear me?"

Annabel's face grew hot and a red fog seemed to descend over her vision. "I will not. I do not take orders from you, and if you do anything to hurt Lord le Wyse," Annabel hissed in Beatrice's face, "I'll give you a bloody nose you'll never forget."

Annabel tried not to show it, but she was shocked at her own vehemence. What had come over her? She was shaking all over as she stared at Beatrice's stunned expression.

Mistress Eustacia hurried into the room, asking Beatrice if she was all right. Annabel turned and left the room.

That afternoon, as Annabel took a break from her labors in the kitchen, she walked to the edge of the courtyard and breathed in deeply of the fresh, early autumn air. Birds twittered nearby, and Annabel took several deep breaths, still thinking of what had happened during the special court session.

Gilbert Carpenter approached her, striding across the courtyard.

"Hello, Annabel." He nodded to her.

"Oh, hello, Gilbert. How is the building coming along?"

"Very well. Lord le Wyse is pleased." Gilbert moved closer and smiled.

This is it, time to be honest with him. "I feel I need to tell you something. I'm not going to be able to marry you." Annabel made her tone as gentle as possible. "You see, Lord le Wyse has kindly arranged for me to enter a convent. As soon as the sickness that is plaguing the abbey is gone, I will be leaving."

Gilbert's posture softened.

"I'm sorry," she went on, "but I know there is some worthy woman out there waiting for a man like you. You'll make her very happy, I'm sure."

Gilbert smiled wanly at her. "I thank you for telling me. Lord le Wyse will be allowing me to go back to Lincoln in a few weeks. Adam will find me a wife there, don't you think?"

Annabel smiled back. "I'm sure he will. He is a wonderful little boy. I know you're proud of him."

He smiled broadly and nodded. "I'll see you tonight at supper then." He turned and walked away.

That was nearly painless. She was surprised that being honest was easier than pretending she might come to love the man just to keep from hurting his feelings.

Annabel hummed as she hung the sheets on the line. The wind at her back sent the chill of coming winter across her shoulders as she hurried to finish her task and return to the warm kitchen.

Six weeks had passed since the coroner's inquest, and Beatrice, instead of harassing her about staying away from Lord le Wyse, had actually been friendlier with her. Ever since the day Annabel stood up to her and told her she wouldn't stop reading to Lord le Wyse, Beatrice always spoke to her with respect, asking her opinion and listening to her, daring anyone else to disparage what Annabel said. Life in the undercroft had become downright pleasant.

Beatrice still flirted with Lord le Wyse, though she was more subtle about it. Instead of hanging all over him and pretending to hurt herself, she smiled at him and always had something to say to him whenever he was nearby. Annabel sometimes wondered if Lord le Wyse would grow to like her attention. Would he think she was a sweet girl? Could he ever think of marrying her? Certainly the girl seemed to adore him. Any man would want that, she supposed. But those kinds of thoughts always made Annabel uneasy, even sick inside, so she pushed them away.

Standing in the clearing beside the manor house, she slipped another bedsheet onto the clothesline. Hammers and chisels rang out from the small hill, and the loud voices of the laborers could be heard beyond the trees. Lord le Wyse's new home was rising to life. The front wing of the stone structure was complete enough that her lord would be moving in today. Now he had the privacy he'd lacked since his arrival in Glynval.

A crackling sound behind her caught her attention. Someone was walking toward her. She spun around.

"Forgive me if I startled you."

"Lord le Wyse."

She began to smile but faltered when she noticed his slow, purposeful stride toward her. His brown eye was fixed on her face.

"I have two things to tell you." He sighed and motioned to two tree stumps, just the right height for sitting.

Annabel stopped hanging the laundry, and they both sat.

"My aunt has written to me again. She believes it's safe now for you to go to the abbey." His expression was solemn as he spoke in a soft voice he seemed to use for no one's ears but hers. "And the second thing is that Bailiff Tom came to me this morning. He remembers everything that happened that night."

"Oh. What will he do?" Annabel whispered back, her heart in her throat.

"He had some idea to bring you and Stephen to court, but I told him I would expose everything he had ever done to you, including the violence of what he was trying to do to you that night, and that he would lose any fight of that kind. I also told him I was relieving him of his bailiff duties, and if he complained to anyone about it, I would not give him the six months' pay I was planning to settle on him."

Annabel nodded. "Th-that is good." She was surprised at how nervous just talking about Bailiff Tom still made her. She squeezed her hands together. "Did he agree? Was he angry?"

"He agreed, and I'm sure he was angry. I have already told the most loyal of my men to watch out for him, and if they see him coming around here, to have him followed and to come and tell me."

His words and actions made her dizzy with gratitude.

A muscle in his jaw twitched as he went on. "Not that you will need to worry about Tom any longer, as you'll be going to the abbey tomorrow. I give you leave to go to your home and gather what possessions you left there. Gilbert is waiting for you at the manor house and will escort you there and help you carry your things."

"Oh." So it was to happen so quickly? Was she to say good-bye to him now? Here?

He looked straight into her eyes. "Please come back and stay one more night here, if you wish, so that you can start your journey at first light. Gilbert will accompany you to the abbey. It's only a day's ride."

The breath she'd been holding rushed out. She still had until morning with Lord le Wyse. They would be able to spend one more evening together.

"Very well, my lord." She curtsied.

He turned without a word and strode away from her.

Strange that she didn't feel any sense of loss at parting from her own mother and brothers, but the thought of putting so much distance between herself and her lord made her wonder if she was doing the right thing.

When Annabel went to see her family, she found the three of them pretty much as she'd left them. Edward still planned to go to London, Durand sat around looking listless, and her mother seemed falsely cheerful.

"Mother, Lord le Wyse is allowing me to go to Rosings Abbey. He's sending me there tomorrow."

"But why?" her mother exclaimed.

"How did you manage that?" Durand asked.

"What did you do to make him send you away?" Edward looked at her with an evil sneer.

"I've always wanted to live in a nunnery and study the Bible," Annabel told them. "You know that. Lord le Wyse ..." How could she explain? She couldn't tell them that she was possibly in danger from the bailiff over his accident. "He found out I wanted to go to an abbey, so he is sending me."

Edward shook his head. Mother passed a hand over her hair. "You could have made a good match," her mother said sadly. "If your father had been alive, he would have taken you to London and found a wealthy husband for you, and then our family wouldn't have the troubles we now have."

"Why would you ask him to send you to a nunnery?" Edward demanded. "You must be daft. How does that benefit anyone? If he is sending you there, he must be sending money as well. You should have asked him for money instead. That would have at least benefited someone."

"They do have good herbal healers at nunneries." Durand's face brightened. "Perhaps I can come visit you and you can tell the nuns with the greatest healing gifts about my illnesses, and the pains in my head. They might prescribe a remedy for me."

Edward closed his eyes in disgust. "Didn't you think at all of your family? You're selfish. You're a selfish, conceited sister." Edward flung the words at her and stalked away down the hall, slamming his bedchamber door.

Her mother cried, sniffing and wiping her eyes, but didn't say anything else. In fact, her family made little comment as she gathered her remaining possessions. Hadn't they missed her?

Didn't they wonder how she had gotten along at the manor house with all the other servants? Did they assume all had been well with her, or did they simply not care?

Dusk of her last day in Glynval was only a few hours away as Annabel plodded along beside Gilbert, who carried the two bags that contained all her earthly possessions. Tomorrow she would be on her way to the abbey.

She was no longer sure why she was going.

She had wanted to enter an abbey so that she might read the Holy Scriptures. And she had wanted to get away from Bailiff Tom. But she was already reading the Holy Scriptures. She and Lord le Wyse had made it through the entire New Testament in the last few weeks. And as for Bailiff Tom ... if he revealed what happened that night in the forest, she might have to admit to the entire village how he had tried to take advantage of her. But if Lord le Wyse was standing near her, even that might be bearable.

Certainly her reasons for cloistering herself in an abbey were fewer and less urgent than they had once been, but the fact remained that she had no wish to be coerced into marriage by her life situation. The whole concept of marriage had always seemed somewhat unappealing to her ... And yet, hadn't she felt something, some new feeling she'd never felt before, for Lord le Wyse in the last few weeks?

She felt repulsed by the thought of marrying Bailiff Tom, or anyone else. Anyone else, that is, except Lord le Wyse.

She didn't like the path her mind was taking. Her lord was a good man, chivalrous and honorable and worthy of her respect. He'd helped her in so many ways. It was wrong to think about him this way.

She pressed her hands against her burning cheeks.

Annabel stumbled over a root in the pathway. Gilbert glanced at her. "Are you well?"

She nodded.

Strange that she was having these thoughts now, when her ultimate goal was about to be achieved. She would be safe from all the grumbling and anger lingering around Glynval since the coroner's abandoned inquiry, and since Maud claimed that their lord was cursed and was causing Glynval's troubles.

But as she pictured the abbey, a huge gray building with smaller buildings surrounding it, and a high wall around the entire compound, it didn't give her a feeling of safety. Instead, loneliness, sameness, and solemnity seemed to emanate from the cold stone walls.

Safety was being near Lord le Wyse, hearing him say he would protect her, and feeling his arms around her.

Nay! She wiped a hand across her forehead, trying to wipe away the unbidden images and sensations. *O God, take these thoughts from my mind. I have no desire to transgress against Lord le Wyse in this way. He's my lord and should not be—that is, it is wrong to have such— O God, save me.*

Annabel felt listless as she helped prepare for the evening meal. Not even Mistress Eustacia's chatter in the kitchen could lift her spirits.

She was turning a pig on a spit over the fire when the door opened and Lord le Wyse stepped inside, letting in the chill wind of fall.

A smell, an intangible feeling, was in the air. Perhaps a storm was coming. It had been so dry since the fateful day of the inquest, a storm would be welcome. But a shudder passed over her shoulders as the chill seemed to pass through her bones.

She had never seen her lord's face looking so pale. "Is something wrong, my lord?"

He ignored her question and focused on Mistress Eustacia. "Annabel is leaving us tomorrow morning. I wish for you to accompany her and Gilbert on the journey to the abbey. That is all." He bowed slightly and backed out the door.

The two women stared at each other.

"What does it mean, child?" Mistress Eustacia's eyes were wide with wonder.

"I'm entering the abbey. Though I don't know why Lord

le Wyse wants you to go with me." The foreboding feeling expanded inside her. Something was wrong.

"The abbey? Why, child—but I'd hoped ..." Mistress Eustacia pursed her lips and turned away.

Now her mistress was angry with her for not listening when she told Annabel that the abbey was not for her, that she should marry.

Annabel thought she would be full of joy when she was finally able to leave Glynval and go to a nunnery. But the expression on Lord le Wyse's face, the way he ignored her question and wouldn't even look at her ...

Was she doing the wrong thing?

Ranulf stared out the glass window from the second floor of his new home. Some movement at the edge of the cleared area in front of the castle caught his eye. Tom atte Water and several other men crouched behind some bushes fifty feet from the steps leading up to the front door.

Tom and the men squinted up at the stone edifice, toward Ranulf. Then they ducked their heads, speaking to each other and gesturing. Each man held a weapon—a knife, a spear, or a longbow with a quiver of arrows over one shoulder. They seemed to be on a hunt—and he was their prey.

It was beginning. He'd been half expecting it. He went to look for his sword and found it, as well as a crossbow and several arrows, an old battle ax his father had once carried, a shield, and a spear. If it was a fight the villagers wanted, so be it.

His new home was only partially complete, but even if it were, there were no real defenses planned in the design: no protective wall, no crenellations to hide behind, no gatehouse or guards to keep out intruders. He was vulnerable to attack, and it looked as if Tom had already stirred up the people against him.

He rubbed his eyes and sighed heavily. He hadn't hired a new bailiff yet, and none of the men he'd brought with him were fighting men. They were builders, carpenters, laborers.

He looked out the window again. Tom and the men of the village were retreating. It would soon be dark; perhaps they wanted to wait until morning.

He would have to round up the men he'd brought from Lincoln and tell them what was happening. At least they were loyal, and they were strong. As they had to be, for they would probably be outnumbered two to one.

If it came down to it, Ranulf would rather die alone than get any of them killed. But at least Annabel and Eustacia would be out of Glynval at first light.

He stared at the rose on the mantle of his new home, in the vase Eustacia had been filling with fresh flowers for several weeks. The rose that was in the vase now was wilting fast. Several petals had already fallen off. It was almost as if the rose was commiserating with him, as the spirit of life prepared to depart from them both.

Chapter
19

As they ate that night, Annabel's eyes skirted to Lord le Wyse, sitting at the head of the table. He kept his head down and said nothing. The quietness of the workers increased her feeling of foreboding. She'd never seen the people so hushed, as if they shared a secret and dared not talk for fear of divulging it. Their gazes darted from person to person, to Lord le Wyse, and back to the food on their trenchers. No one hurriedly ate and left either, but all lingered, as though expecting something to happen.

Was she imagining it? All day it was as if little bugs were jumping under her skin, making her rub her arms to try to get rid of the feeling. Now, as she looked around the room at her fellow workers, she was sure something was about to happen. But what?

The only person in the room who didn't seem anxious was Lord le Wyse, though every time she tried to meet his eye, he refused to look up at her.

God, what is happening?

Annabel left her food almost untouched. How could she eat when her stomach was twisting like a contortionist? She began cleaning up, hoping to inspire the others to get up and leave. She had no idea what she would say to him, but she wanted time alone with Lord le Wyse the way a thirsty man wanted water. How could she leave tomorrow without speaking with him one last time? A twinge of fear pinched her at what he might say tonight, fear about whatever was making him avoid her eye. Still, she couldn't resist the craving to look into his face—and have him look into her eyes and speak to her one last time.

She should be concentrating on her new life, on getting away from the place that had caused her pain, on finding peace and tranquility in the house of God. Prayer and contemplation would be the tasks of her day. She would be happy in her new home. Her life would change for the better and she would have no more reason to fear.

Finally, a few people shuffled out the door, looking over their shoulders. She longed to ask someone what was afoot. Beatrice had a wide-eyed, expectant look, but when Annabel caught her eye in hopes of asking her what was happening, Beatrice just turned away.

At least everyone was finally leaving. Mistress Eustacia was one of the last to go, and she gave Annabel a sad, backward glance, pursing her lips together as though she was holding back tears.

At least she could account for her mistress's sadness. Mistress Eustacia would never see her again after tomorrow and would miss her. Annabel would miss her too. The realization struck her so forcefully that tears pricked her eyelids and she had to blink several times to drive them away.

Lord le Wyse was watching her, his face suddenly alert.

"My lord, may I read to you tonight?" She was surprised at the way her voice shook as she looked into his eye.

He regarded her for a moment without speaking, staring intently, as though he was trying to sear her face into his memory.

"Do you wish it?" His voice was deep but barely above a whisper, and yet his words seemed to bounce off the stone walls of the empty room.

Of course she wished it. "It is the last time I will be able to read to you."

The line of his mouth hardened. He turned his head and seemed to focus on the darkest corner of the room. "Very well then."

Her heart sank at his obvious bad mood. She swallowed before settling into her usual chair by the fireplace. Had she displeased her lord by asking him if she could read? Perhaps he wanted to be alone tonight.

A sudden pain squeezed her chest and inexplicable tears pricked her eyes again as Ranulf set the Holy Writ on her lap. She took a deep breath to calm herself, opened the book, and began to read. At once it felt like the fifty other times she'd read to him, and nothing at all like any time before.

Certainly she would have a Bible available to her at the abbey. So why was she hardly able to blink back the tears at this moment? Why did they blur her vision so much that it was impossible to read on? *Because I will never be with you like this again?*

She squeezed her eyes shut while catching the tears in her hand, horrified at the thought that they might fall on the precious pages and damage the book. How could she explain this embarrassing show of emotion? She should be showing her gratitude for all her lord was doing for her, not crying because he had given her what she wanted.

"Forgive me." Annabel wiped her face as quickly as she could.

"Pray, don't read tonight." Lord le Wyse's voice was deep and ragged. His face was contorted, as if he was in pain. "I'm not in a humor for listening. Just sit here with me." His voice trailed off so that it was hard to catch his last words.

She sat still, watching her lord's features relax in the flickering firelight. He was now staring down at the floor off to his right, lost in thought.

His was such a kind, masculine face. She still wished he would shave his beard, wished she could see his face smooth, as it had been before the wolf attack. She couldn't imagine a more pleasing face on any man, ever. He didn't realize his own appeal.

He glanced up at her and then away. He stood up and paced away then back again. He sat down and studied her, his expression intense. She wished she could read his thoughts. There was such a tortured look on his face. Did he not want her to leave? The protracted silence made her squirm then run her hands along the cover of the Bible.

He stood and came closer to her, his gaze never leaving her face. "Truly, you believe you'll be happy at the abbey? You are content to live alone there?"

"I-I . . ." His intense stare unnerved her so much she seemed to stop breathing. "I believe . . . I mean, I know not . . ."

He seemed desperate for her to say something, but she had no idea what.

He took her hand off the Bible and held it gently between both of his. She loved the way his hands felt, sending warmth all through her. "Are you sure this is what you want? If you are unhappy about the prospect of going there, among strangers, you don't have to go."

"I'm—I'm not sure how I feel." She watched his face carefully for any sign that she had said the wrong thing. Could he see how his touch affected her? But his features seemed frozen.

He released her hand and stood up slowly, woodenly. He walked to the window facing the moon and stared out. His broad shoulders slumped, his bad hand tucked against his stomach.

Annabel's head started to pound along with her heart. She had hurt him, she was sure of it.

"Did I say something wrong? I'm so sorry. Please forgive me, my lord. Please tell me what to say to make you feel better." She held her breath to stave off the threatening tears. She couldn't part with Lord le Wyse knowing he was upset with her. *It will be hard to leave him at all.*

He turned toward her, throwing his face into shadow as the moonlight streamed over his shoulder, illuminating his hair and creating a sort of silvery halo. He sighed. When he finally spoke, his voice was soft and deep and barely above a whisper. "You have done nothing wrong. Go to bed. You have a long day of travel tomorrow."

Ranulf's heart pressed against his chest like a boulder that blocked the air in his throat.

Annabel looked troubled. *But not because she doesn't want to leave me.* She simply was afraid she had offended him, or thought he had changed his mind about letting her go.

Nay, he was convinced now. She wanted to go. A marriage proposal from him would not tempt her. If he asked her to marry him, she would only hurry away faster.

She doesn't love me.

The heavy weight in his chest grew more painful. But he wouldn't lash out at her. It wasn't her fault she didn't want to marry him. How could she fall in love with a beastly looking man like him?

He would take his leave of her just as he had planned.

He took a step toward her. "I wish you to have this." He closed the distance between them and placed his hand on the Bible in her lap.

"Your Bible?" She stared up at him with those luminous blue eyes, which were now swimming with tears, sparkling in the light of the moon. Her lip trembled, and a pain pierced straight through the heaviness in his heart.

He looked away, unable to bear her tears. But how could he bear not to drink in the sight of her while he could? This was the last time he would behold her face or see the light in her eyes.

"You mustn't give me your Bible, my lord," she whispered.

"Why ever not? I can get another one. You'll want it at the abbey."

"You mustn't, my lord. You have need of it. I —"

"Nay, I will get another. Besides, there will be no one here who can read it to me." He heard the note of bitterness in his own voice and clenched his jaw. He didn't want to ruin their last moments together.

She tried to push the huge tome into his hands, but he refused to take it. "I want you to have it, Annabel."

Her head remained down so that he couldn't see her face. Then he noticed her shoulders were shaking, and a sob escaped her.

"What is amiss?" He bent lower, trying to see her face.

She shook her head. "I know not. I'm ... I'm confused." Her sobs mingled with her words, and she sniffed and took deep breaths, as though fighting to gain control.

He wrapped his arm around her trembling shoulders, the bulky book between them. Her soft hair brushed his chin. The painful pressure in his chest eased a little as he bent and pressed his cheek against the top of her head. *Soon you will be gone.*

"Fly away and be safe."

She sniffed loudly and straightened, pulling away from him. "Will I never see you again?" Her voice was ragged with tears. "Will you never come to visit me?" Her eyes were red, her lashes dark and wet.

He stifled the moan that rose in his throat and shook his head. "Nay. I would not be allowed, as we are not blood relations."

"I will miss you, Lord le Wyse." She sniffed again and started walking away.

"Annabel."

She turned and looked at him.

He was about to say, *If you ever need anything, send for me.* But after tomorrow, he didn't know if he could lend assistance to her or anyone else—ever again.

"I ... I want you to be happy."

She gazed back at him. Her brows drew together and she bit her lip. "I want you to be happy too."

Then stay with me. Nay, he couldn't say those words to her. He was wrong to even think them. To stay here would only mean danger to her.

If she loved him, they could run away together. Even now there was probably time for them to escape. But she didn't love him. She'd never agree to run back to Lincoln and marry him.

"Farewell, Annabel."

"Farewell, my lord." She slipped out the door and was gone.

Annabel woke with an unsettled feeling, as though she'd forgotten something, or made some sort of error, and the consequences were about to manifest themselves. But surely it was only because she was leaving today. Such a complete life change was bringing about this feeling that she was making a terrible mistake.

Leaving Glynval and going to the abbey was what she had always wanted, wasn't it? Besides, there was no one in Glynval who cared for her, not even her own family. They hadn't even come to visit her during her stay at the manor. And what friends did she have? Even her friendship with Stephen felt different now that they had this terrible secret between them. Perhaps he would marry Abigail and have a family. He'd have no time for her then.

The only other friend she'd be leaving behind was Mistress Eustacia.

And Lord le Wyse.

She couldn't deny that he cared for her after the way he'd looked last night, when he gave her his Bible.

With effort she pulled the great book out from under her bed and held it in her lap. How many times had she sat, alone with her lord, and read to him from the Holy Writ? She could hardly bear the thought of never reading to him again. Would he be all right? Who would take care of him if he got hurt again?

He was the lord of the demesne. He had servants to take care of him. Why was she having these strange thoughts? Perhaps she was only afraid of leaving home and going somewhere new, living among strangers. She couldn't change her mind now, could she? Especially after last night.

How would he feel if she told him now she didn't want to go, that she would miss him and would worry about him too much? That he made her feel safe?

She couldn't make such a declaration.

She put the book down and scrubbed her face with her hands, as though to rub away the disconcerting thoughts of Lord le Wyse. She pulled the rest of her belongings from under the bed as the door to the undercroft creaked open behind her.

Night still blackened the world as Mistress Eustacia stepped into the room. She held a candle that lit up her face. As the other maids breathed heavily in sleep, she made her way toward Annabel.

"Time to go, child. Are you ready?"

"Yes, Mistress Eustacia." With the mistress's help she wrapped the Bible in a cloth, and together they carried it along with her two bags and headed out the door.

Gilbert jumped down from his horse and helped tie down Annabel's bundles, one on her mare and the other and the Bible to his own horse. Then he helped both women mount their horses, and they were off.

No one spoke as they began their journey, which first took them at a slow walk toward the village. The sun was just turning the sky pink, and villagers were coming out of their homes and congregating in the tiny open area in front of Butcher Wagge's shop.

People were putting their heads together and whispering, with Tom atte Water at the center of them. The sight made her heart beat erratically against her ribs. Mistress Eustacia had her head down and didn't notice, but Gilbert's face seemed a mirror of her own unease. He slowed his horse and dismounted.

Annabel slid to the ground and joined him. His eyes were focused on the huddled group, and he took a step toward them.

"Wait." She grabbed his arm, stalling him. "If you simply walk up, they'll recognize you, and you won't be able to find out what they're saying. Let's hide our horses and sneak up to them."

He frowned down at her, hesitated, then nodded.

They started walking the horses back toward the cover of trees near the side of the road.

"What's amiss?" Mistress Eustacia demanded.

"Gilbert and I are going to find out what those people are saying."

Just as they reached the trees, Beatrice came running down the road. Annabel waved at her and caught her attention, and Beatrice ran over.

Beatrice huffed and puffed, trying to catch her breath. "Something is happening." Still breathing hard, she bent over and propped her hands on her knees.

"What?" Annabel demanded. "What is happening?" Gilbert and Mistress Eustacia stood at her side, listening and staring hard at Beatrice.

"I waited up for you last night, but I must have fallen asleep before you came to bed. Tom is stirring up the people against Lord le Wyse. They're planning to attack his new house this morning."

"But why?" Annabel exclaimed.

Mistress Eustacia and Gilbert both asked questions as well, but Annabel waited for Beatrice's answer.

"He says it's Lord le Wyse's fault the drought came and that the barn burned, that the lord is cursed and he's bringing ill fate on our village, and it will only get worse. He also said Lord le Wyse is to blame for what happened to him. He incited the villagers to get rid of Lord le Wyse."

Beatrice swallowed hard, her throat bobbing, and stared at Annabel with wild eyes.

Mistress Eustacia started making panicked exclamations. Annabel motioned for her to stay quiet and to follow her into the trees to hide. Then she turned her attention to the small, huddled group down the road, which was becoming more animated. Tom raised his voice—and his arms—and soon the men were pumping their fists in the air. A cry gradually grew louder, and she made out the words "cursed" and "put an end to" and "Lord le Wyse."

Abruptly, the group disintegrated as they each went in a different direction.

A woman and her young son walked by and were stopped by Margery, just in front of where Annabel was hiding. Annabel inched closer as Margery asked, "What's amiss?"

"Bailiff Tom and the men are going to burn the lord in his castle."

Annabel clapped her hand over her mouth.

"Burn the lord's castle?"

"Aye. Tom's stirred them all up. The men have gone home to get whatever weapons they can find—and torches. Today is the end of our lord. If he isn't killed, they'll at least run him back where he came from. I suppose he deserves it ..."

Annabel didn't wait to hear the rest. She turned to her companions. "We must go back to the castle. Lord le Wyse is in danger."

"I couldn't hear," Mistress Eustacia cried. "What did they say?"

"The people want to kill Lord le Wyse. They're going now to burn down his house with him inside." Even as Annabel said the words, a fire rose up inside her. *They will* not *hurt Lord le Wyse!* A strange calm came over her as she thought about what to do.

"How could anyone ...?" Mistress Eustacia clutched at her throat, looking pale, even as sweat broke out on her forehead.

The grim set of Gilbert's jaw told Annabel he was with her. Annabel grabbed his arm. "Let us make haste!"

Slowly, he shook his head, increasing the roar in her ears. Why wouldn't he hurry?

"I will go, but you and Mistress Eustacia should stay here. I promised the lord I would keep you safe. Besides, there is naught you could do against an angry mob."

Did the man think she would do nothing while Lord le Wyse was being attacked?

She turned away from him. Mistress Eustacia wouldn't be any help; her panicked questions were a mere noise that never developed into comprehension. Annabel leapt onto the back of her horse and urged her mare into a gallop toward the lord's home. But instead of going to the front of the house, she steered the horse to the back, where the male workers were bedded down in an old shed. She rode right up to the shed and slid off her horse. Banging on the door, she yelled, "Lord le Wyse is in danger! Please help!"

She continued to pound until one of the laborers opened the door.

"What? What's amiss?"

"The villagers are trying to kill Lord le Wyse," Annabel announced, loudly enough for the rest of the men inside to hear.

A few shouts broke out as she heard scrambling and thumps from inside. She had to step out of the doorway as they came barreling out. A few of the men carried weapons—longbows and crossbows and knives—as if they had been prepared.

She didn't stay to observe them. She mounted her horse again and urged it across the clearing behind the lord's house. Her heart pounded with the horse's hooves. *O God, don't let them hurt Lord le Wyse. Help me, God. I have to save him.*

Why? the voice in her head asked. *Why do you have to save him?* The voice answered itself. *Because you love him.*

I do! O God, I do love him.

She'd loved him for a long time, and she suddenly wanted to tell him so, more than anything. But first she had to get to him before anyone else—before it was too late.

Annabel held on tight to the horse's reins, clutching its mane in her fists as she drove the mare harder, up the grassy hill toward the completed section of the house.

What would she say to Lord le Wyse? *I love you? I've wanted to kiss you for weeks?* She almost laughed. Obviously she was hysterical.

As she rounded the side of the stone building, however, those thoughts abruptly left her. On the lawn, spread out on the hillside, were villagers, not only men but women as well. Every one of them held a weapon—an ax, a longbow and arrows, a spear—and several carried torches.

To her right, a man stood holding a longbow with an arrow at the ready, the string pulled taut. Then she saw whom he was aiming at. Lord le Wyse stood in the doorway of his home, the heavy wooden door open behind him.

"No!" she screamed. The archer let the arrow fly, and her heart stopped beating. With a sickening, high-pitched *whoosh*, it sliced through the air toward Lord le Wyse and struck his leg, propelling him back against the door.

Chapter
20

From where she was at the bottom of the hill, Annabel could see the bright red blood on his leg.

She screamed, and Lord le Wyse looked away from the mob.

"Annabel!" he yelled savagely. "Get away from here!"

She ignored his command and pushed her horse up the hill, ignoring the shouts from the angry villagers. At the top, a few feet from the front door, she jumped from the horse's back. Lord le Wyse's hose was torn at his outer thigh. Blood trickled out from the tear. She flung herself at him, grabbing his arms and tugging him inside. She kicked the door shut behind them.

Dropping to her knees beside his injured leg, she ripped the hole in his hose wider. "Oh, thank you, God." It was only a nick, not very deep.

"Annabel, get up and get out of here." His voice was gruff. He grabbed her by her elbows and pulled her to her feet. "Get away from here before you get hurt." His face was dark and angry.

"No. I won't let them hurt you."

"You will, because it doesn't matter." He let go of her and turned away. His features were anguished as he ran his good hand through his hair, and his voice was rough. "You should be on your way to the abbey by now. I don't want you injured because of me." He turned back to her and grabbed her shoulders. "Don't you understand? They have come here to kill me. There is nothing you can do."

251

"Your men are coming. I told them to come with their weapons—"

"I will stop them." He took a step to the door and started to open it.

"No! They'll kill you!" She grabbed his hand to stop him.

"They will kill my men! I can't let them do that."

Without any clear plan, Annabel jerked the door open and stepped out.

"Stop, Annabel!"

She ignored Lord le Wyse's command. Men were streaming out from the trees and from the road into the glade below, brandishing weapons and torches. The workers also came, flooding in from around the back of the house, their own weapons at the ready.

Annabel stood with one hand palm out and the other on her hip as Lord le Wyse came to stand beside her, his hand on her arm, probably ready to yank her back inside at any moment.

The villagers' faces twisted with hate and anger. Their teeth showed as they shouted epithets of rage toward her and Lord le Wyse. The workers raised their various weapons over their heads, but it was clear Lord le Wyse's fears were founded. The workers were outmatched and disorganized.

Annabel cried out in her loudest voice, "Desist! I have something to say!"

The shouting quieted, but the looks of rage remained.

"What are you doing here with your torches and implements of war?"

Tom atte Water strutted forward, thrusting his torch over his head. "We are here to right the wrongs made against us by this man, Ranulf le Wyse. He deserves to die!"

The men roared behind him as they all raised their weapons and shouted their agreement.

In a strong, steady voice, she yelled, "Your lord has done nothing worthy of death."

A few of them roared back at her, Tom the loudest, his curses and sneers personal.

God, help me. What shall I say now?

Her brain registered the words, *I will be with you. For it is not you who shall speak.*

"Will you kill your own lord for crimes he has not committed?" She stared them down, making eye contact with one villager, then another. "Will you kill a man who had been kind to you? Who of you has not benefited from your lord's kindness? Who among you was able to replace the grain burned in the barn fire? Your lord did this — the man, Ranulf le Wyse."

They lowered their weapons and torches. Some of the men's faces softened. Annabel drew courage and went on.

"Would a man who had burned your grain buy new grain so you wouldn't starve? Furthermore, has our lord not rescued you from the dishonest conniving of both the miller and the butcher? Who of you has not benefited from paying a fair price for your bread, for the first time in more years than any of you can remember? God has helped you — through Lord le Wyse!"

"Are you going to listen to this — this chit?" Tom yelled, turning to face the mob. "What has God done for you? For any of you?"

"Pray, let me speak!"

"Let her speak!" a carter from the village shouted.

Without waiting for further permission, Annabel pressed on. "Tom atte Water has spoken evil of your lord, and wrongly! You have let him lead you astray. If you were injured, had lost your eye in an accident, would you want someone saying you were cursed?"

A few murmurs went through the crowd. Tom turned and sneered at the men around him. "Don't listen to her!"

The workers shouted at Tom, stepping closer to him. Lord le Wyse pulled on her arm. "Come inside, now."

Mistress Eustacia and Gilbert had arrived on horseback and were starting up the hill toward her. She ignored Lord le Wyse's plea and motioned with her hand for Gilbert and her mistress to stop and stay where they were.

Annabel went on in a clear, strong voice. "Tom has lied to

you, and he's lying now. Lord le Wyse is an honorable man. To the pure, all things are pure. But to the corrupted, nothing is pure. Tom's mind is corrupted and he is trying to corrupt you."

A few shouts rang out, and Tom scowled and cursed.

"Tom wants you to think that God doesn't care about your wellbeing, but it isn't true! God saved all of you from the pestilence. Are you not alive? Can't you be thankful for that, at least? God is not trying to kill you, or trick you, or send your souls to hell. God loves His children. Will you kill the man God sent to bless you?"

Her voice reached a fevered pitch with the last word. Her hands shook violently, and she clasped them to her chest to still them.

Slowly, one by one, the men lowered their heads. No one, except Tom, would meet her eye. Two of them pushed their torches in the dirt and snuffed them out. Then three more followed suit.

"Don't listen to her! She lies!" Tom's face was as red as a geranium. "You believe God cares about you? Or Lord le Wyse cares about you? You're fools! God didn't send this man to you! He's from the devil!"

The men turned away and began walking toward the road that led back to the village. That was when she saw Edward, her brother, walking with them, looking sheepish as he tried to hide the torch in his hand.

Tom waved his arms wildly. "Where are you going? Be men! Are you going to listen to this girl? You're all fools! Fools!"

More of the men turned to leave. Tom caught one by the shoulder and spun him around. The man drew his fist back and hit Tom in the face.

Tom staggered, clutching his cheek. "Cowards!"

The entire mob left the hillside. Tom followed after them, yelling foul threats and accusations. Soon they all disappeared from view.

Annabel went weak with relief. She stepped inside and Lord le Wyse followed her, closing the door with force.

She threw her arms around him. Then she remembered that he was bleeding. "Let me take care of your leg." She took his hand and led him to his large chair, the one she always sat in to read to him. She knelt beside him.

His eye focused on her face. His lips curved up ever so slightly at the corners. "You shouldn't have come."

She forced her face into a scowl. "A fine thing to say to me when I just saved your life."

A sigh escaped his lips. "I didn't want you to come back. I didn't want you to get hurt." He stared away from her, at the floor, at nothing.

Why didn't he look at her? "I'm not hurt. Didn't you see how God turned the hearts of the people from their anger and caused them to cease listening to Tom?"

"You were amazing." The slight smile graced his lips again. "I thank God you're safe."

Why was he behaving this way? So listless? "Does your leg pain you?" Annabel bent and examined his leg. The bleeding seemed to have stopped. "Shall I bandage it for you?"

"Nay. You must go now. Go on to the abbey. Your work here is done." His words sent a pain through her heart, but the bitter note in his voice gave her hope. She understood it now.

"I don't wish to go." Still on her knees, she leaned against the arm of the chair, her side pressing against his knee.

"Don't wish to go?" He sounded gruff, and his brows lowered. "Why?"

She shook her head. This was harder than she had thought. But she had come so close to losing him, she couldn't stop now. Picturing the arrow racing toward him as he stood outside his front door, remembering the absolute terror she'd felt at the possibility of him being killed, she felt courage surging through her. She leaned closer, wishing he would sit up and put his arms around her. But he only regarded her from beneath a half-closed eyelid.

She wouldn't let him send her away without telling him she loved him. If he cared for her at all — and it was possible she had misread him—he might think her confession of love brazen and unseemly, or worse yet, he might think she was offering herself to him in a sinful way. He had never said he wanted to marry her. But she found those risks were meaningless.

"Answer me! Why don't you wish to go?" His voice sounded angry now.

She swallowed nervously. "I-I don't wish to leave you."

"Don't wish to leave me?" His voice was softer and shook slightly. "Why not?"

His eye sought hers. He leaned toward her until his face was only a handbreadth from hers. "Tell me the truth, Annabel. Do you want to be a nun?"

She didn't even have to think about it. She shook her head. "No, I don't. Please don't send me away, my lord." She clasped her hands in front of her in a pleading gesture.

He sat back in his chair, drawing back again and looking away. He spoke in a lethargic voice. "Sir Clement said truth and justice were the most important thing. But we both realized it isn't. Love and mercy are much greater." After a short pause, he met her gaze again. "Love tears out your heart, but pain is better than bitterness."

The look on Lord le Wyse's face revived her hope. He did love her. Oh, he must! Why else would he look that way? He needed her love. But whether he did or didn't, she wouldn't hold in the truth any longer. She had to speak or her heart would leap out of her chest.

She seized his good hand, caressing his large fingers between her palms, and spoke quickly. "I love you. I'm so sorry I didn't realize it before. Pray, don't send me away. You're the dearest person in the world to me." She raised his hand to her lips and kissed it reverently.

His shoulders straightened. His gaze bore into her, as though he hadn't seen her until that moment. His forehead creased in a pained expression. "You love me? How . . . ?"

"I do love you, I do." She blinked rapidly to keep the tears from flooding her eyes.

"What about this?" He held up his crippled hand.

She grabbed it and pressed an eager kiss into his palm. She leaned closer, rising from her knees, and pressed his hand to her cheek, her heart fluttering at the warmth of his skin against hers.

"Annabel." His voice was low and rough.

"Your scars only make you dearer to me, reminding me of what a hero you are. My eyes behold the most handsome man in the world. I love you. Please say you love me too." Her voice broke. She bit her lip and held her breath as she waited for his answer.

He leaned toward her, his face only a breath away. His intense look captured her fully.

His words rumbled from his chest. "If you love me, kiss me."

Her stomach leapt. Even so, she didn't hesitate. If he wanted proof, she would gladly prove her love with a kiss. She clutched his upper arms and pressed her lips against his.

His mouth was warm and moved ever so slightly beneath hers, creating the most pleasant sensation she'd ever known, radiating all the way to her fingertips. Her insides melted like butter over the fire.

Breathless, she pulled away. His expression was pleasant surprise mingled with gentle longing. He focused on her lips. The request was plain. She leaned forward and complied, kissing him again.

His arms went around her and pulled her against his chest. Her feet no longer touched the floor, but she hardly noticed. His hand sank into her hair at the back of her head as his lips moved over hers, kissing and enticing her to kiss him back, to deepen the connection between them.

Thank you, God, for this. Thank you that I'm no longer afraid.

Ranulf poured his soul into the kiss. His arms shook as he held her close and he had to force himself to pull away and look at her. Her hair fell about her cheeks. Her lips parted and her expression was one of mingled shyness and wonder.

She whispered, "You do love me, don't you?"

He moaned. "I love you—" Unable to go on, he took a few raspy breaths as he gazed into her blue eyes. "I tried not to love you, but ... even a man with a heart of stone, like me, couldn't resist you."

Her eyes glistened, and she placed her palm against his beard. He turned his head and kissed her fingers.

"You never had a heart of stone."

"You must admit, I wasn't kind to you at first."

"But why?"

"I was bitter. I didn't believe any woman could love me, as disfigured as I am, and especially anyone as beautiful as you are, inside and out. I still can hardly believe it." He stroked her cheek with two fingertips, his breath catching in his throat at the softness of her skin. He pulled her down into his lap. Instead of resisting, she snuggled against his shoulder.

She lifted her head enough to gaze into his eyes.

"I thought the way I was feeling about you was wrong because you were my lord and I was only a servant, and I thought I wanted to go to the convent and never marry. But now I know I never would have been content at the abbey, after knowing you and loving you. I loved being close to you and talking to you."

He pulled her closer, and she rested her forehead against his neck.

"I wasn't sure I could ever give love to a man, after what Bailiff Tom did." She placed a hand against his chest. "But you ... you were so noble, so kind ..." She stroked his beard with her fingertips. "I want to make up for every cruel thing that has happened to you."

Her words seemed to come to him through a dream. They filled his heart with a strange peace.

"You make me feel so safe." She brought her knees up and tucked her head beneath his chin, curling up like a kitten on his chest.

If he died now, he would die happy. His chest expanded and his whole body felt alive with pleasant sensations. He could be content to stay here, without moving, forever.

She lifted her head and leaned into the crook of his arm. "We shall marry?"

"Tomorrow."

"We can't marry tomorrow." She smiled. "We'll have to wait until the banns have been cried. That will take three weeks."

"We will be married in three weeks, then."

"Three weeks, then." She sighed, her eyelids lowering.

Saints surround us, she was staring at his lips. He would surely awake from this heavenly dream, but he hoped not too soon. She kissed him.

She sat straighter and tugged lightly at his beard. "Pray allow me one request."

Anything.

She stroked the hair on his cheek and jaw, wrinkling her charming little nose. "Let me shave your beard."

"My beard?"

"Pray allow me, my lord. I long to see your face. And your beard prickles me." She smiled, raising her eyebrows in a shy, hopeful way. "You won't deny me this small request, will you?"

He couldn't deny her, but he had to swallow the uncomfortable lump that had formed in his throat. The beard was the only thing hiding his scars.

"Aye."

"Thank you." She threw her arms around his neck and pressed her cheek to his. "Ow. You see? My husband needs to be clean-shaven."

Her wily smile made his chest ache with the longing to kiss her perfect lips again. He was contemplating doing just that when he heard shouts coming from the front door.

His arm tightened around Annabel's waist. He stood to his feet, lifting her with him. He stepped in front of her, expecting the worst—that the villagers had returned.

Mistress Eustacia and Gilbert burst into the room.

Chapter
21

"My lord." Mistress Eustacia's bosom heaved with her heavy breathing, one hand pressed against her heart. "I was so frightened for you both. But we waited outside for everyone to leave. Everyone is at peace, I do believe, except for the old bailiff, Tom."

Ranulf pulled Annabel to his side.

"Oh, thank God you are both well." Eustacia covered her face with her hands.

"My lord, forgive me," Gilbert put in. "I tried to stop her—"

Ranulf interrupted him. "I need you to ride to the church and find the priest. Tell him there will be a wedding as soon as possible."

"A wedding, my lord?"

"Yes. He must proclaim the impending marriage between myself and Annabel Chapman. Where are the servants? Did anyone get hurt?"

"I-I believe they are all well and have gone to the manor house to get breakfast."

"Good. You may go to the priest."

"Yes, my lord." Gilbert's eyes were wide as they flitted from Ranulf to Annabel. He lingered, as though hoping for an explanation. Receiving none, he spun on his heel and departed.

Annabel left his side and hurried to Eustacia, who threw her arms around his future bride. Her mistress exclaimed her joy in high-pitched accents.

After she had calmed a bit, Annabel asked, "Mistress, does my lord have a shaving blade and hair shears?"

"A shaving blade? Whatever for?"

"He wishes me to shave his beard."

That wasn't completely true, but she was determined and he wouldn't stop her. Besides, it would bring her in close proximity to him again, and nothing could please him more than that.

Eustacia stared quizzically at her. Annabel whispered in her ear and they embraced, then the two of them hurried off to who knew where.

He sat down to wait for them.

A strange day indeed. An hour ago he'd believed it quite likely that he was about to die, knowing his villeins were bent on killing him. Now he was anticipating not his demise but his wedding — to Annabel, the most beautiful, virtuous, courageous creature he'd ever known.

"I'll get some hot water," Eustacia called as Annabel entered the room, smiling with her whole face. In her hands Annabel carried his shaving blade and hair shears.

"Now, my lord, this chair won't do. Come sit on this stool."

Ranulf sat on the high stool, eyeing the way she slipped the blade from its leather holder and placed it on a bench. Then she stood before him with the shears in her hand.

"May I ask if you have experience in the realm of shaving men?"

"You may, and I do."

He'd never seen such a confident, impertinent smile on her face. He frowned. "You're enjoying this too much."

"Forgive me. I am simply happy. Now hold still so that I don't cut you."

Not even married yet and already she's taking liberties with me. But he sat perfectly still, feeling like a sheep at shearing time as she clipped his beard. He could have taken the shears away from her and told her he could do this part himself. He was accustomed to trimming his own beard. But he would be a fool to protest, not when he could drink in her nearness, the way she kept placing her hand against his face to tilt him, or touching his forehead to tip his head back to reach the hair under his chin.

He closed his eyes and breathed in her feminine smell of roses, dried lavender, and fresh air. He remembered all the times she had touched him in the past, changing his bandages, even putting her arms around him a few times. He no longer had to steel himself against her touch. Now he could enjoy it, revel in it, encourage it.

In three weeks they would be married. Was such an event possible?

Mistress Eustacia brought the steaming water in a pot and set it by the shaving blade. Annabel dipped a cloth into the water, squeezed it out, then placed it over his face, pressing it against his beard.

The heat from the cloth sent a soothing warmth through him, relaxing his shoulders. He gazed deeply into her sky-blue eyes, trying to see inside her heaven-born soul. She seemed to see inside his too, into the most intimate part of his heart, where all his longings fed upon her gentleness, her softness, and her beauty.

"Oh, my dear Lord Ranulf." Mistress Eustacia jarred him from his exquisitely pleasant thoughts. "Pray allow me to wish you joy in your marriage to this dulcet maiden." She ended her statement with a half laugh, half sob.

He intended to say, "Thank you, Mistress Eustacia." But the cloth around his face, covering everything but his nose and eyes, prevented him.

Smiling widely, Eustacia nodded. "I knew you would love her, my lord. I knew she was the one who would make you happy."

Annabel put the cloth aside and picked up the shaving blade. "Now stay still."

Mistress Eustacia left the room and they were alone again.

Annabel began to shave his right cheek. "I used to shave my father all the time." She rinsed the blade in the warm water and resumed her labor. "I even shaved my brothers. So you see, you're in safe, experienced hands."

He didn't answer. He was enjoying a close examination of her features, her hair, her skin, her eyelashes. The feather softness of her breath on his cheek drew his gaze to her lips, which were parted slightly in her concentration.

She said nothing until she finished the right side and started on the left cheek. His scarred side.

How hideous would he look with his scar exposed? Would she be repulsed?

She didn't say anything for a while as she shaved, but her eyes were cloudy with her thoughts. Finally, she murmured, her face opening up like a rosebud in the sun, "You look so different ... so handsome." She reached out and ran two fingers along his jawline, caressing his cheek and then his chin. "You always were handsome ... manly ... but now ... you look so young. Your skin ... it's so smooth. Without the beard, your scar is hardly noticeable at all." Tears welled in her eyes.

"Mistress Eustacia!" she cried. "Bring a mirror."

Mistress Eustacia hurried back into the room and gasped as she stared at him. "Your scar has faded to almost nothing." She handed him a mirror.

He was startled to see himself without a beard for the first time after so many years. As he held the mirror closer, his left cheek was streaked with a pale line. But it was quite faint and looked nothing like it had when he'd grown his beard.

He glanced at Annabel, then Eustacia. They both stared with wide smiles. "So handsome," Eustacia murmured.

"Yes indeed," Annabel answered. Eustacia excused herself from the room, winking at Annabel.

Annabel placed her hand in his, and a reverence came over him, as though he were on holy ground. "Will you kneel with me?"

They slipped to their knees on the floor. Facing her and clutching her hand, he bowed his head. "Thank you, God. Thank you for protecting Annabel when she spoke to the angry villagers, and that they left peacefully. And thank you for taking away my scars." His voice broke, but he forced himself to go on. "Thank you for showing that you do love me." *O God, I can hardly believe Annabel is mine, a gift beyond what I deserve. You are so good, God. You truly do love your children. Forgive me for doubting it. All the painful memories are nothing compared to the surpassing joy I feel at this moment.*

A tear splashed onto his hand, and he wasn't sure if it was his or Annabel's. He lifted his eyes and caught her watching him. She scooted forward on her knees and took his face in her hands. His heart pounded faster. Slowly, reverently, her eyes half closed, she kissed his eyelid, brushed her cheek against his, then kissed his chin and jawline, her lips igniting a burning deep inside him. He pulled her close and their lips met.

What could be more miraculous than that?

Justice and love had both won this day.

Epilogue

"*Adam shall carry the bridecup,*" *Mistress* Eustacia declared as they prepared to walk to the church. Adam smiled.

Ranulf's shoulders were erect and his head high as he watched the lad pass through the massive wooden door. Annabel took Ranulf's arm and they followed Adam out onto the top step.

A large gathering of villagers stood on the lawn before them. As soon as they stepped out, the crowd saw them and fell silent.

Ranulf's whole body tensed, and Annabel took a step back.

The scene brought back the memory of the morning, three weeks ago, when the villagers stood defiant and angry, holding up weapons, yelling and cursing as they followed Tom atte Water across the yard.

"What is it you want?" Ranulf asked them.

A carter named Henry in the Lane stepped forward, pulling off his tippet to bare his head. "If it please you, my lord, we have come to ask forgiveness for what we did, or were about to do, when we followed Tom." He kept his head half bowed, not daring to lift his eyes.

"It was a grave sin to come to our lord with intent to harm." The group around him kept their heads bowed as well, most of them nodding quietly to agree with his words. "We all know that the merchant's daughter, Annabel Chapman, was right in all that she said. We were led astray by Tom atte Water, who has now reaped the just reward for his sin." He crossed himself then added, "May God have mercy on his soul."

Ranulf asked, "What happened to Tom?"

"He was taken ill of a sudden, my lord. A fit of rage came over him after everyone went home, and he fell down as though dead. He never moved again, and this morning the breath of life left him. He's dead."

So Tom was gone forever, and the people were sorry for what they'd done. *O God, let me not rejoice in anyone's suffering, but I thank you for the peace this news brings to our wedding day.*

"You are forgiven," Ranulf said evenly.

"You are most kind, my lord." Henry in the Lane crushed his cloth hat between his hands, bowing low.

The people randomly offered words of thanks. "Thank you, my lord." "May our lord be ever blessed." "May you live long and have many children!" A cheer rose up from the crowd at this last shouted sentiment.

Gilbert Carpenter stepped forward and announced in a loud voice, "Your lord is getting married today. Let us give honor to Lord Ranulf le Wyse and his new bride!"

A much louder cheer arose. All the people's faces had changed from fearful submission to joyful exultation. Ranulf held out his hand to acknowledge their expressions of elation.

"Long live our lord's bride, the most beautiful maiden in the land!"

Another cheer. Annabel seemed unable to stop smiling as she curtsied to the crowd. Ranulf turned to her and elegantly kissed her hand.

They made their way down the steps, Annabel being careful of the hem of her dress, and the crowd parted for them.

Soon they were on the road to the church. Some of Ranulf's men played instruments, including the lute and shawm, as they followed them down the road. Adam, holding the bridecup out in front, led the entire procession.

As they neared the village, young children, both boys and girls, fell into line in front of the couple, skipping and dancing, twirling ribbons in the air. But Ranulf hardly noticed anything except the maiden on his arm. She looked so striking in his mother's court dress. The soft blue color brought out the creamy tone of her skin and golden hair, which hung in ringlets about her face.

Soon she would belong to him, and he would cherish her with every beat of his heart.

The stone church loomed ahead of them. Sir Matefrid stood on the steps, waiting to bless their union and to celebrate Mass with the wedding party. He wore the white wool tunic Ranulf had sent to him for the wedding, along with a white stole embroidered with red, gold, and green thread around his neck, hanging to his knees, and a great hat more than a foot tall.

Their vows to love and honor and obey, in sickness and in health, in wealth or in want, in good times and bad, were spoken before the silent throng behind them. Then the priest blessed them and led them all into the church for Mass.

Emerging from the church with Annabel beside him, he stared for a long time into her eyes. The overcast sky hung low and was strangely gray. But the lack of brilliance in the sky did not dim her beauty in the least. She seemed to glow with a light from within.

He felt moved to declare, "God is good."

"Aye, my lord. God is good." She squeezed his arm and pressed closer.

He looked out over the crowd of people. The servants had gone to lay out the food for the wedding celebration, which would take place in the courtyard of the manor house. All those who now stood before them, who had witnessed their sacred union inside the church, no longer looked like his enemies. They smiled. Many of them carried cakes to stack on top of each other, a traditional way of wishing them good favor. A few of the villagers looked sheepish and avoided his gaze, but no one fled. No one crossed his arms in anger or resentment.

They had all accepted his forgiveness. They all wished them well.

This — *this* was what he had wanted when he came to Glynval, though he never imagined himself marrying again. He was starting anew, among strangers.

A white flake floated down from the sky. Then another and another, until everyone noticed and looked up.

"It's snowing." Annabel raised wide eyes at him and laughed. "It's snowing before Saint Catherine's Day."

The snow raced down in a thick sheet of white, dusting everything and everyone. Children whooped and held out their tongues to catch the flakes. Smiles grew wider on every face. Ranulf said a silent prayer of thanks for the unusual gift then led the whole company toward the manor house.

The irony struck him that he was celebrating his wedding feast in the same place where the jury had accused him of both murder and lechery.

But today it looked different, not like the same place at all. The beautiful blanket of white quickly covered the courtyard, making the town clean and new.

Several voices began to chant, "Kiss! Kiss! Kiss!"

Annabel pulled on his arm, and he turned his attention to her. Snowflakes stuck to her eyelashes and made her blue eyes sparkle. He kissed her.

Cheers went up from the onlookers. He pulled away as music trilled behind him. A lively tune jounced to the beat of a tambourine.

Annabel murmured, "Shall we dance?"

"We shall."

~ THE END ~

Author's Note

Researching for a historical novel is always an adventure, and this book was no exception. I am very grateful for the wonderful research books that are widely available in my library and online bookstores, written by many knowledgeable scholars. I am especially grateful to Frances and Joseph Gies, who wrote, among other works, the fascinating and helpful *Life in a Medieval Village*. I learned a wealth of information from this book about the judicial system in place in England during the Middle Ages. Often this information came from actual surviving documents quoted by the Gieses. Their meticulous research was just what I needed to piece together my own fictional hallmote and trial, events that are as authentic as I could make them. But any inaccuracies are solely the fault of me, the author of this fictional work.

I would also like to note that at the time of the setting of this story, mid-1300s England, the only translation of the Bible in wide use was in Latin. I chose to use the NIV translation in the scenes in this book, since the NIV most closely mirrors the way I have my characters speak, and also because I don't understand Latin and I assume most of my readers probably don't either.

I have always loved the classic *Beauty and the Beast* story in which the characters fall in love with each other's inner beauty in spite of outward appearance. I also wanted to explore how it would feel to desperately desire to read the Bible, and to finally get the opportunity to read it for the first time. I explored concepts of discrimination, of unfair treatment based on a person's appearance, and the interesting concept of owing respect and honor to an earthly lord, as well as a heavenly lord. When I write a book, ideas and issues come into play during the development of the story that I hadn't planned, and that was certainly the case with *The Merchant's Daughter*. So I pray this work of fiction not only entertains you but makes you think—especially about the nature of true love and true beauty.

God bless.

Acknowledgments

Once again, I want to thank my brilliant editor, Jacque Alberta, for her skill, wisdom, and meticulous hard work in editing *The Merchant's Daughter*. Her insight and suggestions made this a much stronger story. Words can't say how blessed I feel to have Jacque as my editor.

I want to thank Linore Burkard, Debbie Lynne Costello, and Heather Burch for their input, critiques, and encouragement.

I also want to thank Linore and Debbie Lynne for being my accountability buddies, critique partners, and BFFs, and for knowing more about me than just about anybody else and not running away screaming! And Julie Lessman, who is my emotional twin, God love her. And Mary Connealy, who always knows the answer to my questions. It's so good to have writer friends who can relate to the ups and downs and sheer craziness of trying to succeed and be a blessing in this business.

I want to thank my mother, Voneice Lee, for being such a great word-of-mouth publicist (and just because I can); my husband and children for supporting me, even though they have to sacrifice so much for me to do this "job"; all the members of ACFW who, over the years, have answered countless questions from me, including how a second- and third-degree burn looks a week, two weeks, and a month later; and Jordyn Redwood for helping me and other authors get their medical facts straight. I'm also thankful to all my medieval-writing friends who let me bounce ideas off them and keep my medieval facts straight. Thanks a million!

I want to say thank you to the sales team and the marketing team at Zondervan, especially Candice Frederick and Sara (Maher)

Merritt for all their marketing and publicity efforts on behalf of *The Healer's Apprentice* and *The Merchant's Daughter*. Marketing is so different from writing, and I'd be sunk without you.

I want to thank the creative team at Zondervan and Mike Heath of Magnus Creative for the amazing work they've done on the covers of *The Healer's Apprentice* and *The Merchant's Daughter*, as well as the trailers. Covers are so important, and I am still stunned at how wonderful these are, how perfect for the stories, and how awesome from a design standpoint. As an author, I feel like I've won the cover lottery! Thank you so much!

I especially want to thank all the wonderful readers who let me know exactly what they thought about Wilhelm, Rose, Hildy, Rupert, and Hagenheim from *The Healer's Apprentice*, and sent me encouraging messages through my website, *www. melaniedickerson.com*, and through Facebook. I love my readers, and I love hearing from you and interacting with you. God bless you all.

Check out this excerpt from
Melanie Dickerson's

THE
Healer's
APPRENTICE

Chapter

1

Spring, 1386. Hagenheim. The Harz Mountains, Lower Saxony.

The townspeople of Hagenheim craned their necks as they peered down the cobblestone street, hoping to catch a glimpse of the Duke of Hagenheim's two handsome sons. The top-heavy, half-timbered houses hovered above the crowd as if they too were eager to get a peek at Lord Hamlin and Lord Rupert.

Rose shifted her basket from her left hip to her right and wrinkled her nose at the stale smell of sweat from the many bodies pressed close, mingled with the pungent scent of animal dung. Chickens and children skittered about, the clucking and squealing adding to the excited murmurs.

"I'll wait with you to the count of one hundred, Hildy, then I'm leaving." Rose couldn't let Frau Geruscha think her apprentice was a lazy dawdler.

"Are you not curious to see if they've changed?" Hildy asked, her green eyes glinting in the sun.

"No doubt the duke's sons have developed into humble scholars after two years at Heidelberg's university." Even as she spoke, she glanced up the street. In spite of wanting Hildy to think her indifferent to the young noblemen, Rose was glad she had a good view.

Rose's dog, Wolfie, began barking so zealously his front paws lifted off the ground.

"Hist. No barking." Rose leaned down and rubbed the ruff of fur at the back of his neck.

"Rose!"

Her heart leapt at the horrified tone in Hildy's voice, and she stood and faced her friend.

"You didn't even wear your best dress!"

Rose glanced down at her green woolen kirtle. "Oh, Hildy. As if it matters."

"At least your hair looks beautiful." Hildy ran her hand down Rose's loose mane of brown curls, only partially hidden by her linen coif. "How do you ever hope to get a husband if you don't pay more attention to your clothing?"

Rose scowled. "I don't hope."

How many times would she have to explain this to Hildy? When Rose was a little child, Frau Geruscha had taken a liking to her. Now that Rose was grown up, the town healer had chosen Rose to be her apprentice—an honorable life's work that would prevent Rose from being forced to marry. Frau Geruscha, having grown up in a convent, had not only taught Rose about medicinal herbs, but also how to read Latin—a skill Rose was very proud of. But it was a skill most men would hardly value in a wife.

"You don't fool me, Rose Roemer. Every girl wants to be married. Besides, look across the street at Mathias." Hildy pointed with her eyes. "He speaks to you every chance he gets, and he's quite handsome."

Rose harrumphed at Hildy's dreamy tone. "The blacksmith's son?" *With his lecherous grin?* "He only wants one thing from me, and it isn't marriage."

"How can you be so sure ..."

Hildy's voice trailed off at the crowd's whispered exclamations as six men on horseback came into view around the bend in the narrow street.

Hildy grabbed her thick blonde braid and draped it over her shoulder then chewed on her lips to redden them. "You should at least try to catch their eye."

Rose shook her head at Hildy. "You know Lord Hamlin is betrothed—as good as married—and Lord Rupert must marry an heiress." Rose took hold of her friend's arm. Someone had to be the voice of reason. "I hate to dampen your excitement, Hildy, but if either of the noble sons takes a single look at us, I'll be vastly astonished."

Hildy smirked. "I won't be."

The approaching clop-clop of hooves drew Hildy's gaze back to the street. "Shh. Here they come." She set her basket of beans, leeks, and onions on the ground behind her and smoothed her skirt.

The throng of people fell silent out of respect for their young lords.

The duke's elder son, Wilhelm, Earl of Hamlin, led the way down the street on his black horse. His younger brother, Lord Rupert, rode beside him. Two bearded knights on cinnamon-colored horses followed three lengths behind the young men, with two more bringing up the rear.

The knights were simply dressed, but the noble sons were covered from neck to toe in flowing robes. Rose stifled a snort. They were only returning home. Did they think they were on their way to the king's court?

Yet as he drew nearer, she saw that Lord Hamlin wore not a robe after all, but a plain cloak of dark wool. His bearing and the proud tilt of his head were what made him look so regal.

In contrast to his brother's outerwear, a fur-trimmed surcoat of lustrous sapphire silk hung over Lord Rupert's lean frame, with only the toes of his leather boots peeking out. The disparity between the brothers went beyond their clothing. Lord Rupert's light brown hair was long and curled at the ends, and a blue ribbon gathered it at the nape of his neck. A jaunty glint shone from his pale eyes. Lord Hamlin's black hair hung over his forehead, and he seemed oblivious to the crowd. He focused his gaze straight ahead, toward Hagenheim Castle, whose towers were visible over the tops of the town's tallest buildings.

No, she'd say they hadn't changed at all.

"*Willkommen!*" Hildy called out. "Welcome back, my lords!" She waved her hand high, as though hailing a messenger.

All eyes turned to Rose and Hildy. A spear of panic went through Rose. She wanted to hide, but it was too late. Lord Hamlin's eyes darted in their direction, alighted on Rose, and held. His expression changed and his features softened as he looked at her. Then his gaze swept down, taking in her basket and her dress. He quickly faced forward again.

He realizes I'm nobody, a peasant girl. Heat spread up Rose's neck and burned her cheeks.

Lord Rupert's huge blond warhorse walked toward Rose and Hildy as the crowd suddenly took up Hildy's cheer. "*Willkommen!* Welcome back!" The horse came within three feet of the girls and stopped, stamping its hooves on the cobblestone street and sending Wolfie into a wild fit of barking.

Rose threw her arms around Wolfie's neck to hold him back. Her temples pounded at the sight of the warhorse's powerful legs.

The younger nobleman swept off his plumed hat, bowing from his saddle. His eyes roved from Hildy to Rose, then he winked. "I thank you, ladies, for your kind welcome." He grinned and swung his hat back on his head, then spurred his horse into a trot and caught up with the others.

"Did you see that? Did you see it?" Hildy pounded on Rose's shoulder.

Wolfie calmed as the men rode into the distance. Rose let go of him and stood up, glaring at Hildy. "I can't believe you called out to them."

"Lord Rupert actually spoke to us. *To us.* And did you see how Lord Hamlin looked at you?" Hildy clutched her hands to her heart, gazing at the clouds. "Are they not the most handsome men you've ever seen? I could hardly breathe!" She turned and smiled at Rose. "I knew they'd like what they saw once they caught sight of you."

"Would you keep your voice down?" Rose urged Hildy to start walking toward the *Marktplatz.* She glanced around, afraid the towns-people would overhear their embarrassing conversation. She imagined the miller's skinny wife, who walked ahead of them, snorting in deri-sion at Hildy's compliment. The shoemaker's buxom daughter, striding down the other side of the street, would laugh out loud.

Hildy and her romantic notions of love. She was a candle-maker's daughter, dreaming about the local nobility as if she had any chance of inspiring a serious thought in them. As a woodcutter's daughter, Rose held no grand illusions about her own prospects.

Hildy's chatter faded into the background as Rose wondered at Lord Rupert's flirtatious wink. But what stuck in her mind was the way Lord Hamlin had looked at her. Thinking of that, her face began to burn once again. She'd encountered her share of leering men and their crude comments, but Lord Hamlin's look was different. It had made her feel pretty—until he noticed her clothing.

She should have worn her good dress, the crimson one with the bit of white silk at the neck and wrists that Frau Geruscha had given her. Hildy said it brought out the red tint in her chestnut hair. But how could she have known Hildy would draw the attention of both Lord Hamlin and Lord Rupert and that they would look straight at her?

Realizing her train of thought, she snorted. What difference did it make which dress she wore? Everyone knew Lord Hamlin was betrothed to the daughter of the Duke of Marienberg. But betrothed or not, he'd hardly be interested in her. And Lord Rupert, as the younger son, would inherit none of the family's wealth and so would need to find a rich heiress to marry.

If, as an apprentice, Rose could impress Frau Geruscha with her skill, she would become the next healer—needed, respected. She could avoid the indignity of marrying someone out of desperation.

So she'd never experience love. Most married people didn't, either.

Rose dipped her quill in the pot of ink and concentrated on scratching out the next sentence of the tale she was writing. Frau Geruscha encouraged her to write her stories, although she said it was probably best if she didn't tell anyone about them.

Shouts drifted through the open window of the healer's chambers. From her vantage point in the southwest tower of Hagenheim Castle, Rose peered out, seeking the source of the commotion.

"Make way!"

Two men hastened across the courtyard. They carried a boy between them, using their arms for a seat. A woman ran behind them.

Rose scrambled to hide her parchment, pen, and ink in the small trunk beside her desk. "Frau Geruscha! Someone's coming!" She snatched up a gray apron that lay nearby and slipped it over her head.

Wolfie adjusted his grip on his bone and growled low in his throat.

"Wolfie, stay."

The dog's lips came together, sheathing his fangs, but he focused his eyes on the door.

Frau Geruscha entered the chamber from the storage room, her wimple bobbing like the wings of a great white bird.

The two men carrying the boy burst through the door, the woman following close behind. Rose recognized one man as a farmer who lived near her parents' home. The boy was his son, perhaps eight years old. He wore ragged brown hose and his torn shirt drooped on his thin frame. Bright red blood covered one of his sleeves. His lips were white, as if all the blood had drained out of his body.

Here was her chance to show Frau Geruscha she was a competent apprentice. She would strive to appear calm and ready to help. She was thankful she had already braided her hair that morning and covered it with a linen cloth, as her mistress had instructed her.

"Frau Geruscha!" Fear and panic lent a high pitch to the woman's voice. "Our son fell on the plow blade."

The healer's wise face wrinkled in concentration as her gaze swept the boy from head to toe. She pointed to a low straw bed against the wall, and the men laid the child on it.

Pain drew the boy's features tight. Rose longed to comfort him, but she didn't want to get in Frau Geruscha's way.

Frau Geruscha sat on the edge of the bed. She showed no emotion as she pulled back his sleeve, revealing the gaping wound.

"No!" The boy screamed and shrank away from her. He held his arm against his chest and drew his knees up like a shield.

Rose turned her head. *O God, don't let me get sick.* She had to prove herself.

Frau Geruscha glanced back at Rose. "Fetch me some water from the kettle and a roll of bandages."

Rose scurried to the fireplace and grabbed a pottery bowl. Using a cloth to hold the lip of the iron kettle, she tipped it to one side and poured hot water into the shallow vessel. She carried it back to Frau Geruscha then dashed to the storage room to get the bandages.

"Don't touch it!"

Rose tried to force the boy's terrified voice from her mind. When she returned, Frau Geruscha was washing the blood from the wound. Rose held out the roll of fabric.

Her hand shook. She had to get control of herself before her mistress noticed.

Frau Geruscha took a section of the clean linen and used it to soak up the blood and water around the wound. "Rose, get him some henbane and wormwood tea." She turned to the parents. "The herbs will help ease his pain."

Biting her lip, Rose ran into the adjoining storage room again. She should have guessed Frau Geruscha would want that tea. She should have already gone for it instead of standing there with her mouth open. So far she wasn't proving herself very competent.

Shelves of dried herbs lined the walls. She grabbed the flasks labeled *henbane* and *wormwood* and scooped a spoonful of each into a metal cup, then used a dipper to ladle in steaming water from the kettle.

She hurried back and placed the cup in the mother's outstretched hands. The woman held it to her son's lips.

Frau Geruscha made the sign of the cross and laid her hand on the boy's arm. She then closed her eyes. "In the name of the Father and of the Son and of the Holy Ghost, we ask you, God, to heal this boy's wound in the name of Jesus and by the power of his blood. Amen."

The smell of blood, warm and stifling, mingled with the odor of sweat. The bowl of water was now bright red, and Rose caught another whiff of the familiar, sickening smell.

Frau Geruscha opened her eyes and crossed herself again. She reached into her box of supplies and held up a needle. The tiny metal object glinted in the morning light.

The boy locked wide eyes on the needle and screamed, "No! No! No!" His father moved to hold him down.

Rose fled into the storeroom, her bare feet noiseless on the stone floor. She leaned against the wall and sucked in deep breaths. Her head seemed to float off her shoulders, as light as a fluff of wool, while her face tingled and spots danced before her eyes.

How childish. Rose pressed her face into her hands and stifled a groan. Had Frau Geruscha seen her flee the room? She must get back in there and overcome this squeamishness.

She drew in another deep breath. The earthy odor of the herbs that hung from the rafters was stuffy, but at least it didn't trouble her stomach like the smell of blood. Rose focused on the sights around her—the rushes strewn over the stone floor ... low shelves packed with flasks of dried herbs ... the rough stone wall poking her back. The screaming drifted away.

The tingling sensation gradually left her face and she breathed more normally.

She entered the room again, stepping carefully so as not to rustle the rushes on the floor and draw attention to herself. The boy's eyes were closed and his lips were the same ash gray as his face. He must have lost consciousness, since he didn't even wince as the needle pierced his skin.

Frau Geruscha quickly finished stitching the wound. After she tied the last knot and clipped the string of catgut, she wound the remainder of the bandage around his arm and tied a thin strip of cloth around it to hold it in place.

Finally, the people left, carrying the limp boy with them.

Rose hurried to clean up the water spills and the bloody linen. Her stomach lurched at every whiff of the metallic odor, but she had to pretend it didn't bother her, to hope her mistress didn't notice how it affected her.

"Are you well?" Frau Geruscha's gray eyes narrowed, studying Rose. "You looked pale when you ran into the storage room."

So her mistress had noticed. "I am very well."

How could she be so pathetic? She had to find a way to prepare herself for the next time she must face the blood, screams, and smells.

Ravenous after his long journey from Heidelberg, Wilhelm attacked the roasted pheasant on his trencher. A page, a lad of less than ten years, leaned over his shoulder to refill his goblet. The boy lost his balance and teetered forward. Wilhelm grabbed him around his middle and righted him, but the goblet overturned onto the table.

The boy's face flushed red. "Lord Hamlin, forgive me. I —"

"No harm done." Wilhelm gave the boy an encouraging smile.

With a quick bow, the boy refilled Wilhelm's goblet and moved on to the next cup.

The Great Hall looked exactly as Wilhelm remembered it. Flags bearing the family colors of green, gold, and red jutted out from the gray stone walls on wooden poles, and several hung like banners on either side of the large mural painted on the wall. His father still spoke sternly, and his mother still clucked over him and his brother, continually admonishing Rupert to proper, gentlemanly behavior. At that moment she was reprimanding him for pinching the serving wench.

If she only knew. While they were supposed to be educating themselves in Heidelberg under the finest teachers in the Holy Roman Empire, Rupert had spent more time carousing than studying. And as Rupert misbehaved, Wilhelm had continued sending out spies in search of Moncore.

His younger sister, Osanna, smiled at him from across the table. Wilhelm smiled back and winked. She'd grown up in the two years he had been away. He missed the freckle-faced maiden who used to trail behind him, begging him to teach her to hunt or fish or shoot arrows.

His father sat at the head of the trestle table, on Wilhelm's left. He put down his knife and wiped his hands on the cloth across his lap. Then he took a drink from his goblet and turned to Wilhelm.

"So, son, you are still scouring the country for Moncore." He peered at him from beneath bushy eyebrows. "You'll get him."

Wilhelm remembered how his father had awed—and intimidated—him as a child. His greatest desire was to make his father proud of him. "Thank you, Father."

His brows lowered in a scowl. "You must."

"Yes, Father."

"Your responsibility is to your people and to your betrothed. You must not let them down."

Did his father say these things because he doubted him? He had worked hard to become mighty in strength and swordplay, believing that would please his father. But there was still one thing he had not been able to accomplish; one thing that would exalt him in the eyes of his father, as well as the entire region.

"Wilhelm." His father nudged him with his elbow, pointing toward the far end of the table. A man dressed in leather hunting clothes stood near the door of the Great Hall. He nodded at Wilhelm, tucked his chin to his chest, and backed out of the room.

"Pray excuse me." Wilhelm stood and stepped over the bench where he sat with his family and the guests who had come to welcome him home. He strode from the room.

"Lord Hamlin." The courier stood in a shadowed corner of the corridor outside. He handed a folded parchment to Wilhelm then bowed and slipped out the door.

Wilhelm glanced at the wax seal, confirmed it was from his spies, then ripped open the missive.

Lord Hamlin, we have reason to believe Moncore is in our region. Be on your guard.

Wilhelm crumpled the note in his fist. "Glory to God."

After Wilhelm's six years of failing to locate the evil conjurer, the fiend had come to him.

If he were able to capture Moncore, he could tell his future father-in-law, the Duke of Marienberg, to bring his daughter out of hiding. Wilhelm's betrothed would finally be safe.

But Moncore had eluded him before. The fact that one man had continued threatening Lady Salomea's safety, despite Wilhelm's best efforts, was a frustration like he'd never known, a splinter he couldn't gouge out no matter how hard he tried.

With long strides, Wilhelm headed back into the Great Hall. He'd

find Georg and Christoff and discuss where to hunt for Moncore. They
would ride out in less than an hour.

❧

Morning sunlight winked through the narrow window as Rose moved
about the southwest tower. The only sounds were the blows of the
blacksmith's hammer ringing from the castle courtyard. She straightened jars of herbs, checked to see which of them needed to be re-
plenished, and began sweeping up the old straw from the stone floor.
Once finished, she would sprinkle new rushes and dried lilac over the
chamber floors.

Rose so wanted to impress her mistress, but had failed miserably.
Frau Geruscha never turned ashen at the sight of blood, never shrank
from the bad smells, never grew squeamish when sewing up a wound.
O God, make me like Frau Geruscha.

Because one day she would be expected to take over her mistress's
healing work, Rose grew increasingly more desperate to be a good
healer. If she returned home a failure, her mother would torment her
until she accepted one of her suitors—a desperate widower with nine
children, an old man with no teeth, anyone with a little money.

A commotion in the courtyard cut her musings short. She put her
broom away in case the noise was the result of someone in need, coming to the healer for help.

As the shouts drew closer, her stomach knotted. Frau Geruscha
was away and might not be back for several hours. *Please, let them not
be coming to see Frau Geruscha.* She stood in the middle of the room
and held her breath as she stared at the door, waiting.

"Frau Geruscha!" a masculine voice boomed. Someone pounded
on the door.

Rose rushed to unlatch the door. Three men stood at the thresh-
old. The middle one's arms were draped over the shoulders of the
other two. His head hung down so that she couldn't see his face. Sweat
dripped from the dark hair clinging to his brow.

She recognized the men on either side as the two knights who
yesterday had traveled alongside Lord Hamlin and Lord Rupert. That
meant the one in the middle was—

Lord Hamlin lifted his head, his face pale. His eyes riveted her
with a look of pain.

The Healer's Apprentice

Melanie Dickerson

Two Hearts. One Hope.

Rose has been appointed as a healer's apprentice at Hagenheim Castle, a rare opportunity for a woodcutter's daughter like her. While she often feels uneasy at the sight of blood, Rose is determined to prove herself capable. Failure will mean returning home to marry the aging bachelor her mother has chosen for her—a bloated, disgusting merchant who makes Rose feel ill.

When Lord Hamlin, the future duke, is injured, it is Rose who must tend to him. As she works to heal his wound, she begins to understand emotions she's never felt before and wonders if he feels the same. But falling in love is forbidden, as Lord Hamlin is betrothed to a mysterious young woman in hiding. As Rose's life spins toward confusion, she must take the first steps on a journey to discover her own destiny.

Softcover: 978-0-310-72143-7

Talk It Up!

Want free books?
First looks at the best new fiction?
Awesome exclusive merchandise?

We want to hear from you!

Give us your opinions on titles, covers, and stories.
Join the Z Street Team.

Visit zstreetteam.zondervan.com/joinnow
to sign up today!

Also—Friend us on Facebook!

www.facebook.com/goodteenreads

- Video Trailers
- Connect with your favorite authors
- Sneak peeks at new releases
- Giveaways
- Fun discussions
- And much more!

ZONDERVAN®
.com